I0547543

HIGH STRANGENESS

BY

ERIC BICKERNICKS
with JAN BRADY

01

Ken

I shouted over to Noodles, "A crashed saucer is an oxymoron!" I gripped the steering wheel of my Ford Taurus, raised my index finger and continued, "That's just another example of stupid extraterrestrial syndrome."

"Stupid extraterrestrial syndrome?" he said.

"Yeah. They're so smart they figured out how to get here, but were too stupid to avoid crashing into our planet."

Noodles slumped into his seat. "But something can always go wrong, right?"

"Not if you've avoided every little particle in outer space between here and your home planet. Do you know what happens if you're going at the speed of light and you hit something the size of a pebble? You're toast! They're *that* smart."

Noodles thought for a moment. "What if they took a wormhole?"

"Great!" I threw my hands up in the air and slammed them

down on the steering wheel. "Now you're saying they've learned how to bend space…but not how to avoid huge chunks of dirt?" I did an alien-as-surfer-dude impression: "Hey Zork, what's that? A planet? WHOA!!" I made the classic car crash sound.

"Pffffffffff…."

"Then why do so many people say they've seen a crashed UFO?"

I gritted my teeth and exhaled deeply. "Because they're delusional." I kept trying to drive my argument home every time he brought up crashed saucers. He seems to get it only some of the time. We sat in silence as I focused on the road. Noodles is my friend Terry that I've known since childhood. We met at Quashnet Elementary School in Mashpee here on Cape Cod. We called him Noodles because he was this incredibly skinny kid, and the name stuck. I just wish he closed his mouth more often when he wasn't speaking. A bud is a bud; unfortunately you can't pick your friends' attributes.

Cape Cod is a sixty-mile-long peninsula that extends out of Massachusetts into the Atlantic ocean. Back in 1914 the Army Corps of Engineers lopped it off from the mainland with the construction of the Cape Cod Canal. I wasn't sure if the engineers were trying to make it easier for boats to navigate up the coast, or to isolate its residents from the rest of the continent. As in any island nation, you either live "on Cape" or "off Cape". There are three bridges that allow us to escape our little "paradise". In the summer, why would anyone sweat their asses off inland when they can come here? It's around this time of year, right after Memorial Day weekend, when things get crowded that everyone starts to go mental.

Noodles and I were driving down Route 6, which is the main highway that goes down the middle of the Cape. We passed exit 9, or the start of "Suicide Alley". It's the spot where the divided highway merges into a two-lane, crash-test-dummy delight of oncoming high-speed vehicles. Plenty of drunk, distracted or suicidal people have drifted over the line and taken somebody else out with them. I've told myself, if I ever see anyone drift over the line, I'm putting my car into the ditch. Even if I'm going sixty miles an hour—I don't care.

Noodles was zoning out while he stared through his window. "I heard people see ghosts walking around out here."

"What? Dead drivers looking for their cars in the after life?"

"I passed a weird-looking guy a couple of months ago who was just standing there at the side of the road with his thumb out. I was gonna give him a ride, but by the time I managed to turn the car around, he was gone."

I sighed. "A ghost looking for a ride?"

"He was pretty weird-looking."

"Dude, most hitchhikers are pretty weird-looking. How's this for an explanation: he got picked up before you came back?"

"I didn't see any cars pass me."

"Or how about: he went into the bushes to take a leak?" I shook my head. "There aren't any ghosts. People who say they've seen one are just looking for things to support their religious views."

We passed a car with a flat tire on the side of the road. Beside it was a guy pulling a jack out of the trunk. Noodles turned to scrutinize him as we went past. The guy wasn't transparent, so it wasn't a ghost having a bad day. He went back to watching the oncoming traffic. "Where are we going, Kenny?"

He's been calling me Kenny since we were kids. He knows I like to be called Ken, but how the hell am I supposed to stop him? "We're going to Namskaket Marsh," I said. "I found a good field of phragmites to make our crop circle in." Noodles nodded his head slightly and continued to monitor the roadway.

There's two things you should know. First, phragmites are a tall, reedy grass that you find in New England wetland areas.

They're considered an invasive species and are the closest thing to a wheat field that you'll find here on the Cape.

Second, crop circles are total bullshit. They drive me crazy; they're just another example of stupid alien syndrome. If you had to set your spaceship down on this planet, wouldn't an Amazonian rainforest or the Grand Canyon be more interesting than a wheat field? Did they need some flour for their trip home? Of course this all started when some nitwit made a circle in somebody's crops and claimed a flying saucer made it. It's not that hard to flatten wheat using a board.

The problem I have is when these "aliens" decided to start making intricate patterns as art projects and people still believe they are extraterrestrial in origin. There's plenty of footage of people showing how they made these things, yet the myth won't go away. So I decided to do something about it. Noodles and I were going to make our own crop circle. Since there is no wheat growing on the Cape, a field of reeds would have to do. We were gonna film the whole process; that way when people went nuts over a crop circle appearing on Cape Cod, we could show that they're idiots for believing such a thing. It's hard enough to get people to take the idea of extraterrestrial life seriously; I wanted to at least root out all the obvious bullshit.

I found the perfect place, just off Route 6A, in Namskaket Marsh behind the greenhouses of Hanson Farm. Google Maps shows that near the farm there's an access road that goes out to the marsh. We got to the farm just as it was starting to get dark and noticed lights were on inside. We went down the dirt road about half a mile and pulled over. Noodles got out of the car first, turned on a big LED flashlight and shined it up into the trees. Stark, skinny shadows whipped through the branches.

I snapped at him, "Dude! Turn that thing off!"

He smiled. "It's my Fenix LED flashlight...two thousand lumens."

"You can't use that, someone's gonna see us!" He nodded his head and turned it off. I opened the trunk of my car and got our equipment: an industrial-length measuring tape spool and a board with a rope looped through holes on each end.

He studied it for a moment. "What's this?"

"This is what pushes the reeds down." To illustrate, I stepped on the board and held the rope taut. "You lift your foot up like this to push down on the reeds. You keep stepping forward to flatten everything in front of you." I did a few quick steps as an example. "You're gonna be the anchor and hold the measuring tape." I showed him my sheet of graph paper. "This is what we're making—an alien head."

"That'll be cool! Everyone will think the aliens drew a portrait of themselves."

"That's the whole idea."

"Where do you want me?"

I pointed to a couple of black dots on the paper. "You're gonna stay at these anchor spots and hold one end of the measuring tape while I hold the other end and walk in a big arc. You got my infrared camera?"

"It's on the back seat." He climbed into my car while I grabbed my rubber boots from the trunk. I knew it was going to be mucky out there. He appeared a moment later holding a pair of wooden Bigfoot feet and asked, "What are these?"

I finished putting on my boots and stood up. "That's another hoax I'm working on. Anybody can create fake Bigfoot tracks; I want to show how easy it is. Those are just crude plywood tests, I need to make real ones out of flexible silicon."

Noodles studied my handiwork. "Ah cool! Can I wear these?"

"No, we don't want to confuse the folklore. Leave 'em here." Noodles dropped them next to my back tire. That would have to be an off-Cape expedition, some other time. Could there be a huge primate living in the forests of North America? Or better yet, Massachusetts? Perhaps so, but like UFOs, there is way too much false data that needs to be filtered out before we can objectively study it.

It was getting darker and the stars were just starting to come out. I closed the trunk of my car and showed Noodles a map of our area. "We're standing here," I said. "Once we make it through that tree line, there's about ten acres of reeds out there." I unfolded my graph paper plan and illuminated it with the phone screen. "We'll do the almond shaped eyes first, then do the outer, oval shaped head last."

Noodles took the phone from me. "How big are we gonna make this?"

"I want to go for at least a hundred yards wide."

"Cool," he laughed.

I didn't realize how dark it would be out there. The moment I stepped off the dirt road into the marsh, my right foot sank into several inches of water. As I felt it flowing over the top of my boot I thought, *Wonderful…now my foot's gonna be soaked for the rest of the night.*

While I struggled with my foot, Noodles said, "Oh shit, I forgot the camera."

"Great," I said as I dismissed him with a wave of my hand, "Go get it." Noodles scampered back through the bushes to the car. I sat down on a rock, pulled my boot off and emptied out a trickle of water. At the farm, more lights were coming on. To my left was Cape Cod Bay; I could just make out the lights of Provincetown on the horizon. I sat there and listened to the sounds of crickets and a few random spring peepers. I was beginning to enjoy my moment of solitude when I was startled by a bite on my neck. I smacked it as my whole body tightened up.

Fucking mosquitos.

I heard a voice behind me in the dark, "Kenny? Where are you?"

"Over here!" I called out. Noodles came out of the darkness

and I went over to him. I pointed out into the marsh, "We need to go about two hundred yards in that direction." I noted our starting point on the phone and we set out, pushing through a section of reeds.

He asked me, "How's anyone gonna find this?"

I pointed over my shoulder and kept walking, "Barnstable Airport is in that direction. Some pilot is gonna see this for sure." After a few more mosquito bites, we managed to get to our starting spot. I illuminated my graph paper plan and showed Noodles, "OK, you're gonna stand here and hold the measuring tape. I'll walk in that direction; when you see I've gone fifty yards, tell me to stop. That will be the bottom of the left eye." He studied my plan and nodded. I trudged through the reeds, pulling the tape measure behind me. I was making a decent amount of racket, sloshing through pools of water and snapping the dried reeds. I walked for maybe five minutes before I realized I hadn't heard anything from Noodles. I stopped and listened. Nothing. I called out softly, "Noodles!" I waited a beat. Still nothing. At that point I just yelled, "NOODLES!"

I heard his voice faintly in the distance, "I said stop!"

I thought, *Christ, this isn't going to work.* I let go of the tape measure and walked back towards him. "Dude, I can't hear you."

"But you said not to make too much noise."

I let out a deep breath and thought about it. "OK, where's your phone? Let's stay connected the whole time."

I dialed his number and he answered in a slow drawl, as if someone else was calling him, "Hello?"

"Dude," I said impatiently, "I'm right here in front of you."

"Sorry;" he said, "force of habit."

"OK, let's try this again." I followed the tape back to my original spot. "OK, how about here?" I said into my phone.

Noodles said "Yeah, that's fifty yards."

"OK, I'm gonna stomp down an arc in both directions from

here. You keep the tape measure tight."

"Got it."

"You rolling the camera?"

There was a pause while I heard him trying to get a shot. "I can't see anything, you're too far away."

I thought, *Shit. He's right. I'll have to film myself making my own tracks, and hopefully we'll get some additional footage when everything is done.* I told Noodles, "OK, let me do this section first, and when we switch places, I'll grab the camera from you."

"When we're done, can we go to Cobie's to eat?" Cobie's is a fried seafood joint in Brewster that's been around forever.

"Yeah yeah, fine," I said. "Let's get this done." We worked for another hour, creating two almond-shaped areas of flattened reeds. It was a pain in the ass. I'm sure flattening wheat is much easier than flattening phragmites. You really have to use your full body weight on the board to push the stuff down. I eventually got the hang of it, stomping down small sections at a time before moving forward. I had to cradle the phone on my shoulder to hear updates on my position from Noodles. I stopped occasionally to film my handiwork.

The final thing we needed to do was surround the eyes with an oval shaped alien head. Once I got Noodles anchored in the final spot, I began forming the wide arc that would be the top of the alien's head. I grinned as I thought about my big reveal: *Suckers! Why the hell would extraterrestrials form an alien head in the middle of a marsh in Brewster? Look…here's the footage of me making them!* I pushed forward with a renewed burst of energy, mashing down reeds as fast as my foot would go. The force I had to exert on the board suddenly disappeared and I found myself standing in an area of already flattened reeds. *What the hell is this doing here?*

I whispered into the phone, "Did we just screw up?" I tugged at the tape measure to make sure it wasn't slack, "I thought I had another six hundred feet or so to go."

"No, you should still be on the forehead," Noodles replied.

I was standing in the middle of a curved path, a little wider than my own stomping board. *Did some cranberry harvesting machine come through here?* I knew I didn't make it. I reluctantly went up this new path. After walking a few yards, I heard the sound of cracking reeds—the same kind of sound I had been making. As I moved closer, I could make out the outline of another figure. I crept up to it and went, "Hey!"

The person froze. It was completely quiet out there. I could feel my heart pounding in my chest. They slowly turned around to get a look at me. The body was humanoid but the face looked like a robot. This freaky figure asked me, "Are you a cop?"

I held up my phone and shined some light in its direction. It was a guy wearing a camouflage outfit with a pair of night vision goggles on his head. I quickly regained my composure and said, "No. What are you doing here?"

He took off his goggles. "What does it look like I'm doing?" He was dragging a rope attached to a board similar to mine. He spotted the same piece of equipment in my hands and demanded, "What are *you* doing out here?"

"I'm doing the same thing you're doing," I said. "And you just screwed up my design."

"*Your* design? I've been out here for three hours working on a mandelbrot set. What have you been working on?"

I hesitantly said, "An alien head." A mandelbrot set are those patterns that have infinite detail as you keep zooming on on them. I wasn't going to admit to this prick that his pattern had way more detail than mine.

"Oh that's so fucking lame." He spoke into a walkie talkie, "Stanley, get over here!"

I thought, *"Oh shit, he's got a partner too. It's gonna be two against one."* I quickly yelled into my phone, "Noodles! Come here! Hurry up!"

Noodles replied, "What's going on?"

I back-pedaled a couple of steps away from the guy. "I need your help! C'mere now!"

"Where are you?" he said.

I frantically scanned the horizon for him. I couldn't see shit, so I yelled into my phone, "Turn on your flashlight! Quickly!"

"You said not to do that."

"Fuck that! Let me see where you are!" An intense light darted around the field about seventy-five yards to my left. I yelled into my phone, "Point it to your right!" Two thousand lumens of light hit me right in the face. I squinted and said, "Right here! Walk this way!"

The guy in camo shouted, "Turn that fucking thing off!" I could now clearly see what he looked like. He was maybe in his forties, tall with blonde hair and a long face.

Behind me I heard someone else yell, "Ow!" Somebody— Stanley, I assumed—pulled off his night vision goggles and squint-ed. He had just been hit with two thousand lumens of light. He looked to be in his late thirties, had dark hair was and shorter than the blonde guy.

The blonde guy yelled at me, "Hey! Tell your friend to turn that shit off!"

I was getting pissed. He had ruined what I was trying to do, so I got sarcastic with him, "Oh! Oh! Mandelbrot set! Why don't we see your Mandelbrot set?"

"We can still salvage it!" he said as he walked towards Noodles' light source. "Now turn that off!"

I didn't bother speaking into the phone, I just screamed, "Noodles, look out, he's coming after you!"

I heard faintly in the distance, "Who is?"

I screamed again, "Never mind! RUN NOODLES!"

The blonde guy sprinted down the path towards Noodles' light source and I took off behind him. The beam of light whipped back and forth across the marsh as Noodles went into a full sprint. He let out an occasional yelp as he fled. I was sure he was shitting his pants, imagining he was being pursued by the Cloverfield monster. When the blonde guy got to within twenty yards of him I yelled, "NOODLES, HE'S RIGHT BEHIND YOU!"

He screamed like a little girl and yelled, "You take it!". The flashlight spiraled end over end in a big arc towards me.

I picked it up and thought, *Why didn't he just shut the light off?*

The camo guy was now heading in my direction, so I took off back the way I came. While running, I tried to find the power button on the flashlight. I felt something with my thumb and pressed that. The light began to blink off and on. *Wonderful,* I thought, *I can now get rescued by the Coast Guard.*

I continued sprinting forward, the strobe light giving the marsh a surreal appearance. As I ran past Stanley, he was just standing there with his arms by his sides with a passive expression on his face. I gripped the flashlight with both of my hands and began to twist it. After a couple of turns it came apart and I felt the batteries bounce off my thigh. I stopped running; it was dark again.

I caught my breath and looked back towards the farm lights. I could hear the faint sound of somebody pushing through the reeds out in the middle of the marsh. Hopefully it was Noodles, heading back to the car. I screwed the empty flash light back together and stuck it under my armpit. I pulled out my phone and oriented my position on the GPS map. I saw that I needed to go towards a dark clump of trees on the horizon. That's where the car was. It then occurred to me, *"Fuck, where's my camera?"* It was someplace out there, in the middle of the marsh. I'd never find it.

Noodles was already waiting for me by the car. He flinched as I stumbled out of the darkness and whispered, "Kenny, is that you?"

I groaned and said, "Yeah." I hit the button on my car remote.

The dome light blinked on as my car woke up. I pressed another button and popped my trunk.

Noodles looked distraught. "What was that chasing me?"

I slowly walked to the back of my car. "There were some other dudes doing the same thing we were doing." The trunk light illuminated where we were standing. Noodles had on my plywood Bigfoot feet which were now covered in mud. "Dude, why are you wearing those?"

"When I saw how mucky it was, I went back and got them."

"You've been wearing them the whole time?"

"Yeah, I only had sneakers on. These worked great."

I was too exhausted to yell at him. "You gotta be kidding me."

"What?" He stood there and looked at me like a kid who didn't know he'd done anything wrong.

I was not a happy camper. All the planning I did to try to pull this off was now wasted. So much for exposing how easy it is to make fake crop circles. My legs were completely soaked and they were throbbing from all the running. I leaned against my car in silence for a minute, beaten.

Noodles peeped up, "Can we go to Cobie's now?"

"Fine," I sighed as I slammed the trunk shut. "Let's go to Cobie's."

02

Melissa

"Stupid twat!" I yelled. Some asshole in a blue Corolla had forced her way into line at the CVS drive-through on Main Street. Because my anxiety had been increasing lately I asked my doctor for a refill of clonazepam. I don't like depending on it, but sometimes the lamotrigine isn't enough. After making sure I had a therapy session scheduled (as if there's anything new to discuss), she sent the prescription in. I spent the next ten minutes drumming my fingers on the steering wheel and complaining out loud as the line inched forward. Finally, it was my turn, and before leaving the parking lot, I opened the bottle and washed down one little yellow pill with my iced latte.

Getting to work wasn't too bad that time of year, in early June. The insanity that is Memorial Day weekend had just passed and full-blown summer hadn't yet arrived. There's a precise correlation between my overall anxiety level and the start of tourist season, when zombie hoards of mainlanders begin swarming over the bridges. Even after years of dealing with it, I still dread the approach of summer.

I made it to the parking lot outside the Orleans bureau office of The Cape Cod News, where I worked. It's in a weathered old home-turned-office-building built around the end of the 19th century. I had to climb the creaky outside stairs to get to our office on the second floor. Norm, the bureau chief, was already sitting at his computer, sipping a coffee, focused on his screen.

I passed him in silence and dropped my bag onto the floor beside my desk. We had an agreement—no morning pleasantries, no smiles or cheerful "good mornings" until we'd both had our coffee. The only sound in the office was the hum of computers.

The bureau office consists of four rooms—the one we were in, a break room, a bathroom and Norm's office. Since it was mostly just Norm and me, he set up his computer in the main room which had three desks, some chairs and a few filing cabinets. Our job was to cover the news on the lower Cape and send it back to the main office in Hyannis.

Norm spoke first, "We're getting an intern." I recognized that tone of voice and looked up.

"An intern? Why the hell would they send someone out here to intern?"

"I'd guess they were full in Hyannis. Or maybe they're trying to punish us."

I shook my head. What was an intern supposed to learn out here? I did my internship at the Boston Globe, a place that felt like the center of everything. When I graduated from Wellesley College, an office building on the Cape was the last place I saw myself in. As a stepping stone to something bigger, sure, but the Globe—or anyone else—hadn't called. In my defense, there are more aspiring journalists than there are good jobs.

"She starts Wednesday," Norm said.

"They give us two days' notice—how generous. Who is it?"

I looked over at him. Tall and lanky with eccentric fashion choices and youthful blue eyes, his dry humor was probably the main reason I'd decided to work here. Like me, he was over-educated for the job, but unlike me he'd never left the Cape so he knew practically everyone. He liked to pretend otherwise, but he really did care about the community.

"Her name is Mildred and she has a degree in English Lit from Smith College. I met her on Friday. She's one of those earnestly healthy types, you know—no refined sugars, Birkenstocks…"

"…denim sack dress and organic cotton socks?" I finished.

"Speaking of socks…" He lowered his voice, "…the hair on her legs is longer than my beard."

"Well, clutch my imaginary pearls! Hairy legs and Smith College—can this be possible?"

"Swear to god!" He held up two fingers, like a Boy Scout. "I thought she was wearing argyle socks!" The phone rang and he answered it.

In college I read Joan Didion, Hunter S. Thompson, Ambrose Bierce, and thought, *One day I'd write like that.* Instead…well, here's a few of the stories I've written in the past month or so:

—"We're Gonna Need a Bigger Boat" (about the increase in great white sharks in the area)

—"Where the Grass is Greener" (upcoming recreational marijuana sales)

—"Backroads and Byways" (favorite on-Cape destinations of local residents)

Thoughtful, elegantly written prose—that dream seemed as dead as a Truro beach in winter. I stared at my computer; the screensaver—the dripping green code lines from The Matrix—kicked in. I moved the mouse to end it and opened the mail server. I saw the usual batch of spam, stuff from some mailing lists I subscribed to and something from my brother. He lives by himself out near the beach in Truro. The header read "YOU WON'T

BELIEVE WHAT I SAW!" I was about to open it when Norm walked up and handed me a piece of paper.

"Seriously?" I said, after reading it. "A sea monster washed up in Brewster? What mind-altering substance was he on?" Norm's expression didn't change. "Nothing better happened over the weekend?"

Norm rubbed his beard. "Cheer up! You get to leave the office and go to the beach. The eyewitnesses are there now."

A sea monster…ok, fine. I looked at my inbox again, hoping to find something more compelling, but the only legitimate item was a notification of upcoming local Independence Day events. No reprieve. I grabbed a camera, put it in my bag and made a lot of noise leaving. On my way out the door, Norm yelled "Bring back some doughnuts!"

About half an hour later (mileage becomes irrelevant during the summer here, it's all about the traffic back-ups) I pulled into the parking lot of Crosby Landing Beach. I got out of the car and saw a small group of people several yards from shore and surmised they were gawking at the "sea monster". The beach is part of a large tidal flat. At low tide, the water recedes an unbelievable distance from shore, exposing mud flats and sand bars—and things that get stranded on sandbars. As I walked towards the people, I could see a large, grayish thing lying in the mud.

As I approached with camera and bag, one of the people spotted me and pointed. He whacked the guy standing beside him and yelled, "Holy shit! It's Fox twenty-five news!" Everyone turned to look. "Lenny, I told you Fox news would wanna cover this!"

"Hello; I'm Melissa Howard from the Cape Cod News," I said, feeling like I'd let everyone down.

Undeterred, he stuck out a grubby hand and, when he saw my hesitation, he wiped it on his stained tank top. "Sorry, I've been choppin' up bait! I'm Ralph and this here is my buddy Lenny. We was gettin' ready to go out fishin' and Lenny here heard over the radio how some monstrous thing had washed up on the beach so we had to come see. I mean, look at this fuckin' thing!"

I picked up the camera and moved closer. It was about the size of a truck tire, grey in color, and the one eye I could see had the opacity of death. Even the experts can't agree on what causes these strandings, although in this case, it probably got caught in the shallows when the tide receded. I sighed and turned to my audience. "It's a sunfish."

Everyone started talking at once. "I told you so!" a woman said. "A sunfish?" someone repeated.

Ralph said "Nah! That ain't no sunfish. Those things are tiny."

"It's an ocean sunfish. Not very common in these waters but they have been found before and—"

A voice behind me interrupted, "The ocean sunfish or common mola (*Mola mola*) is the heaviest known bony fish in the world. Adults typically weigh between 247 and 1,000 kilograms. The species is native to tropical and temperate waters around the globe. It resembles a fish head with a tail, and its main body is flattened laterally." I turned to see a slightly overweight thirty-something guy in a Nintendo t-shirt. He looked up from his iPhone as if expecting applause. "Wikipedia," he added.

"All righty!" I replied, turning back to the fish. "Would everyone mind stepping back so I can get a good photo?"

I snapped a couple from different angles.

"Hey! How 'bout one with me and Lenny here—you know, for scale?"

"You guys found the fish?" I asked.

"Yes m'am!" Lenny replied, speaking up for the first time. He wore a blue t-shirt that had *Wicked Tuna* stamped over a patriotic fish and around his neck was a gold religious medallion that said *St. Andrew Pray for Us* .

"Ok—go ahead and stand there." I pointed in back of the fish. They jostled each other, almost stepping on a fin, before deciding to go for the bromance pose, arms around each other's necks.

"Lenny here thought it was fuckin' turtle!" He rubbed his friend's head.

"Well, you said it was a baby whale."

"Dude!"

"Did anyone call fish and wildlife, the police, anyone?" I asked.

"We did," said the guy with the iPhone.

"Great. Ok, then; thanks for your help." As I headed towards the car, I mentally chanted "*The press needs the public, the press needs the public.*"

"Don't you want our names?" Ralph called after me.

"Ralph and Lenny, right?"

"Leonard Sheehan and Raphael Morris—from Revee-ah."

That stopped me. "Raphael?"

"Yeah, you know—like the painter." He shrugged. "My mother was Eye-talian."

I was about ten minutes from the office when my phone rang. The caller ID showed it to be Norm. "Hey, how's the monster chasing?"

"Haha," I said. "Dead sunfish. And two bros from Revee-ah."

"Well don't head back just yet. I have another one for you."

"Let me guess, someone spotted a mermaid sunning with the seals on Monomoy Island?"

"Even better. We have multiple reports of a UFO sighting in Truro last night."

I hit my brakes hard to avoid slamming into the back of a boat on a trailer. The boat's name, "In Decent Seas", filled my windshield. "Are you serious?"

"It just popped up on their police website."

I pulled over into a parking lot filled with inflatable pool chairs and boogie boards, called up the Truro police website on my iPad and went to their dispatch log page. Listed amongst the traffic stops for that day were:

> Time: 02:05
> Unidentified flying object observed
> Location: North Pamet - Officer Anderson
> Time: 02:16
> Unidentified flying object observed
> Location: Pamet Marsh - Officer Wright

I always talked to the police to get the facts straight on townie stories, so I knew Officer Anderson. I spoke to him the previous weekend about the big scuffle in the Wellfleet Beachcomber's parking lot. His number was already on my phone. I hit dial and waited for someone to answer.

A male voice picked up and said, "Yeah?"

"Hey! This is Mel from The Cape Cod News. Is this officer Anderson?"

"Hey Melissa--how's Norm holding up?"

"He's doing fine. I have a couple of questions for you."

"Shoot."

"I saw the UFO report from last night. Can you tell me what you saw?"

He laughed. "I thought someone would be calling about that. What I saw was a group of lights on the horizon moving towards Gull Pond."

"When did you first see it?"

"Around two a.m. I heard the report over the radio, and since I wasn't too far away, I decided to check it out. When I first saw it, it just looked like a row of white lights. I assumed it was a plane of some sort, but when I got closer, I didn't see any wings or tail. It was moving very slowly on the horizon—slower than a plane would."

"How long did the sighting last?"

"I watched for about two minutes before it headed out towards the ocean. You really want to speak to Officer Wright. He got a good view of it. You want his number?"

I entered it into my phone, said, "OK; thanks!" and ended the call.

I dialed Officer Wright's number. It rang twice, then a somber voice said, "Hello."

"Hello, this is Melissa Howard from the Cape Cod News. Officer Anderson gave me your number. Can I ask you some questions about the UFO you saw last night?"

There was a long pause. "Hello?" I said.

"Have you spoken to anyone else about this?" he asked.

"Just Officer Anderson."

"What did he say?"

"He described an object with lights and suggested I call you as you got a better look at it."

I heard him exhale like he'd been holding his breath. "OK...." He paused again. "I'm not on duty right now. You know Arnold's?"

"Yes."

"I can meet you there."

"I'm in my car now. I can be there in five or ten minutes." I hung up.

Arnold's is a roadside seafood joint on Route 6 in Eastham. They have good clam rolls but everything is ridiculously pricey. I pulled into the parking lot, my tires crunching over the crushed seashell driveway.

I parked my car and headed for the entrance. I saw Officer Wright sitting outside by himself at a picnic table; he was out of uniform so it took a few seconds to register that it was him. The last time I saw him he was on duty and I was asking him about a fatal accident near this part of Route 6. He was holding a cup of coffee and had a box of fried scallops in front of him.

I sat down at his table; he glanced at me and mumbled, "Hey

Melissa," then went back to studying his coffee cup.

I took out my notebook, put it on the table and said, "I understand you saw something last night?"

He leaned backwards, then shook his head and looked down. I thought for a moment he was done talking. He kept turning the coffee cup around in his hands. "Somebody called in saying they'd seen something the size of a two-story house floating in the sky out by Ballston Beach."

"When did you get the call?"

"Just a little before 2 a.m. When I heard that, the first thing I asked dispatch was: is the caller DUI? She said he was serious. Since I was in the vicinity, I turned onto North Pamet Road. When I got close to Pamet Hollow, I saw a row of lights approaching me, just over the trees. I assumed it was an aircraft, maybe a plane in distress that was coming in too low. I asked dispatch to contact Otis to see if they had anything in the air. As it got closer, I could see that it wasn't an aircraft—at least not any kind I'm familiar with and I grew up in the Air Force."

Otis is the informal name for the Joint Base Cape Cod. Until the mid-seventies, it was known as Otis Air Force Base. Now the biggest tenants are the Coast Guard and the Air National Guard. There are still some military aircraft coming and going, but it's not what it used to be when the Air Force had F-15s out there.

"What did these lights look like?" I asked him.

He took another sip of coffee and put his cup down. "There were two rows of bright white lights along each side, in the shape of a V." He paused and looked up at me. "The object was silent. I couldn't estimate its height, but it was large—bigger than a 747. Much bigger."

I nodded as I quickly scribbled some notes, "How long did you see it?"

"I never took my eyes off of it. I got back on the radio and told dispatch I had the object in sight. She wasn't too happy with me—she said when she called the base they laughed at her. And they told her they had nothing at all in the air that night. I told her I was looking right at and described it to her." He smiled quickly, shook his head. "Yeah. She gave me the Twilight Zone music."

He pulled a prescription bottle out of his pocket and shook an oblong white pill into the palm of his hand. I recognized it as Xanax. He saw me looking at it. "Ulcers," he said, shrugging. I understood; ulcers were more respectable than anxiety, especially for a police officer.

He washed the pill down with a big gulp of coffee. "I've heard these kinds of reports—of UFOs—but I've always been skeptical." He shook his head. "You never really know what it's like until you see it for yourself."

"When did you lose sight of the object?"

"It did a slight turn and headed towards Hanging Valley. It wasn't going that fast, so I was able to follow it as far as the beach parking lot before it headed out over the ocean."

"So what do you think you saw?"

"There are no commercial aircraft flying over the area; we're not in their flight paths. And out at the military base, the only things left are Coast Guard helicopters and a few small search and rescue planes." He paused for a moment then stared out beyond the parking lot. "I don't know what else I can tell you. I don't know what I saw."

I thanked Officer Wright for his time. As I was walking back to my car I got a text message from my brother.

Brian: I saw a UFO!!

03

Astro

I was just sitting there in our backyard, squinting my eyes, panting slightly and enjoying the sunshine on my fur. I felt a drop of saliva leave my tongue. I quickly licked my chops, did a swipe over my nose, shook myself off then sat back down. I went back to my slow steady panting. It was a nice day, I felt really content, but I wasn't sure what to do with myself. I threw myself down and scratched at my collar, giving it a complete turn. Something was biting me, probably a flea or something. I sat still for a moment.

Any more nibbles? Nope. I think I'm all set.

Eventually I wandered over towards my drinking bowl, and that's when I spotted it.

Turkey poop.

It was just lying there in the grass, how could I have missed it! Let me tell you, if you want something to roll around in, turkey poop is the way to go. It has this wonderful intense odor that will let anyone know you're coming. I wasted no time flipping over and dropping onto my back into my little trophy of poop. I flailed my legs into the air and let the stuff settle right in. I could feel the wetness soak past my fur and spread out over my skin. I instantly snapped back to my feet. I thought I heard something. Was it a bird? I quickly scanned the yard.

Nothing.

I sat back down and relaxed. I bent over and examined my balls. A quick lick put them back in order. I could feel the next wave of boredom come over me as my eyes began to close. I needed to do something interesting.

Why not explore the neighborhood?

I trotted behind our tool shed and studied the hole I had been digging under the chain link fence. When I tried to go under it, the edge of the wire pressed deeply into my back.

Damn it, not quite.

I got a cloud of dust going by scraping out some more dirt with my front paws and kicking it behind me with my rear legs. I tried going under one more time, pushing harder with my rear legs.

I made it.

Oh boy! This is gonna be great!

I never really had the chance to explore our neighbor's property by myself. I've always been connected to my best friend. I could finally cover some serious ground without dragging him behind me. I froze once I got to the middle of our neighbor's yard. A faint odor caught my attention. It was something dead or rotten.

What the heck is it?

I had to discover its source. I cut through our neighbors yard and trotted down our street, past all the familiar houses. I must have gone about a mile when I came to a little bridge crossing a stream. I carefully picked my way down the side, through some fallen branches, to the water. My feet got wet while I licked up mouthfuls of water, then continued towards the source.

Wow, whatever that thing is…it really reeks!

Each step I took, the smell got stronger. I picked my way around a large rock and spotted something on the edge of the stream just ahead of me. It looked kind of like one of those bones my friend sometimes brings me. I picked it up in my mouth and was filled with this wonderful taste.

I've bitten into some pretty ripe dead squirrels, but this is really something!

I sat down next to the stream and let the flavor dribble down my throat. I had to drop it after a few seconds before it got too intense.

I'm keeping this. There's no way I'm going to leave it out here for somebody else to find.

I could probably chew on the thing for days. It needed to come home with me. I had to widen the hole under the fence so I could squeeze myself back under. Once through, I dropped my prize in the middle of the yard and gave it a couple more licks.

This is wonderful!

I laid down and held it between my paws. This would take some serious gnawing. I sat up. I heard the sound of our car entering the driveway!

He's back! My best friend is back!

I did a quick spin in place then sprinted towards the back door. I can't tell you how excited I get when I know he's finally come back. The door swung open. I ran up to him and flung my paws onto his chest.

HE'S BACK!

04

Alien

01010111 01101000 01111001 00100000 01100100 01101111
01100101 01110011 00100000 01100001 01101110 00100000
01000101 01100001 01110010 01110100 01101000 01101100
01101001 01101110 01100111 00100000 01101100 01101001
01100011 01101011 00100000 01101001 01110100 11100010
10000000 10011001 01110011 00100000 01100010 01100001
01101100 01101100 01110011 00111111 00001101 00001010
01000010 01100101 01100011 01100001 01110101 01110011
01100101 00100000 01101001 01110100 00100000 01100011
01100001 01101110 00101110 00001101 00001010 00001101
00001010 01000001 00100000 01101000 01110101 01101101
01100001 01101110 00100000 01100010 01100101 01101001
01101110 01100111 00100000 01110111 01100001 01101100
01101011 01110011 00100000 01101001 01101110 01110100
01101111 00100000 01100001 00100000 01100010 01100001
01110010 00100000 01100001 01101110 01100100 00100000
01110011 01100101 01100101 01110011 00100000 01100001

01101110 00100000 01000101 01100001 01110010 01110100
01101000 01101100 01101001 01101110 01100111 00100000
01101100 01111001 01101001 01101110 01100111 00100000
01101001 01101110 00100000 01110100 01101000 01100101
00100000 01100011 01101111 01110010 01101110 01100101
01110010 00100000 01101100 01101001 01100011 01101011
01101001 01101110 01100111 00100000 01101000 01101001
01110011 00100000 01100010 01100001 01101100 01101100
01110011 00101110 00001101 00001010 01001000 01100101
00100000 01110100 01110101 01110010 01101110 01110011
00100000 01110100 01101111 00100000 01110100 01101000
01100101 00100000 01100010 01100001 01110010 01110100
01100101 01101110 01100100 01100101 01110010 00100000
01100001 01101110 01100100 00100000 01110011 01100001
01111001 01110011 00101100 00100000 00100010 01000010
01101111 01111001 00101100 00100000 01001001 00100000
01110111 01101001 01110011 01101000 00100000 01001001
00100000 01100011 01101111 01110101 01101100 01100100
00100000 01100100 01101111 00100000 01110100 01101000
01100001 01110100 00101110 00100010 00001101 00001010
01010100 01101000 01100101 00100000 01000010 01100001
01110010 01110100 01100101 01101110 01100100 01100101
01110010 00100000 01110010 01100101 01110000 01101100
01101001 01100101 01110011 00101100 00100000 00100010
01011001 01101111 01110101 00100111 01100100 00100000
01100010 01100101 01110100 01110100 01100101 01110010
00100000 01110100 01110010 01111001 00100000 01110000
01100101 01110100 01110100 01101001 01101110 01100111
00100000 01101000 01101001 01101101 00100000 01100110
01101001 01110010 01110011 01110100 00101110 00100010

05

I had to put both my hands on my golden retriever's back to push him off of me and yelled, "Astro! Get down!" I felt a stripe of moisture in the middle of my palm, then the the stench hit me.

Turkey shit.

"Astro - get out of here!" I frantically pushed him back out the door. He ran down the stairs and spun around in the middle of the yard, still happy to see me. I closed the back door with my elbow then stood there for a second with my fingers wide open. I didn't dare touch anything.

Noodles leaned against my kitchen island and winced, "Holy shit, your dog smells like shit."

I stuck my hands under some running water in my sink. I said, "That fucking dog has to roll around in this stuff every time he finds it." I soaped my hands and scrubbed. "I don't have time to give him a bath." I tore off a paper towel from the roll hanging under the cabinet and walked towards my living room as I dried my hands. "You gotta see the latest render tests," I said. He followed me into the next room. I sat down at my computer. On the wall behind it was a poster of a UFO that said I WANT TO BELIEVE, just like the one in Mulder's office on the TV show X-Files. I made a living doing freelance graphics and video editing for all sorts of corporate clients, but this was my own little project. I shook the mouse and the screen came back to life. I loaded up the final test movie and smacked the space bar to start it. I stood back next to Noodles and watched.

The video showed Noodles out on a boat in the ocean, cheering as he was reeling in a fishing pole. The camera panned down to a fish being pulled out of the water, then up to Noodle's face as he steadied the twitching fish. His expression changed suddenly as he looked off camera and shouted, "DO YOU SEE THAT?"

The camera whipped over to a silver, disk-shaped UFO silently gliding over the water, a couple hundred feet in the air. The camera followed the UFO for a good fifteen seconds seconds as it headed out towards the horizon, then panned back to Noodles still holding his fish. He let out a big dramatic "WHOA!" towards the camera, then the shot ended.

"I think I overdid the whoa at the end," he said.

"You were fine," I said. "The radiosity render settings doesn't quite look right on the craft though. I gotta tweak the logarithmic exposure control some more."

Anyone can fake a night time UFO—it's just a point of light in the sky. Faking a UFO in daylight is much harder. First, you gotta get the perspective right on your 3D model so it will fit your scene. Then you have to track everything in your original footage so it will line up with the "UFO". A week ago we shot the footage of Noodles in his boat pretending to spot a UFO.

"I think it's gonna work," he said.

I studied the last frame of the movie. "It's getting there." The plan was to toss the video up on YouTube, see who fell for it, then reveal how gullible they were. With all the editing software out there, people really shouldn't believe everything they see. If we're going to seriously study UFOs, we need to raise our standards of what constitutes proof. I wanted to show just how easy it is to fake a realistic-looking UFO.

Noodles said, "What if it works *too* good? What if no one believes you when you say that it's fake?"

I rewound our thirty second movie and played it back with a single mouse swipe; the whole thing zipped forward in half a second. You can hear the word "fake" spoken in a high pitched voice. I swiped the playback head a couple more times. The same chipmunk voice repeated: Fake. Fake. Fake.

"I digitally stretched me saying that over the entire length of the video," I said. I played the video at normal speed; Noodles listened intently. The voice was gone. "When my voice is slowed down that much, it's just this rumbling sound in the background. Only if someone plays the entire video super-quick will you hear it."

"And then they'll know it's fake?"

"We just have to show the world how it's done—when we're ready."

The Skype alert sounded, notifying me that I had a video call coming in. It was Zeke from CCUFOG, the leader of the Cape Cod UFO Group. Zeke is a wingnut who believes anything emitting light in the night sky is extraterrestrial in origin. He would be the first person I sent my fake footage to. I hit the "confirm call" button and answered, "Yo dude, what's up?"

Zeke's face appeared on my monitor. "Did you see the report in the Cape Cod Times today?" He sounded all torqued up.

"No."

"There was a UFO over Truro! You gotta do the show to-night!"

Zeke managed to get a license to run an LPFM 100-watt

radio station setup in his garage in Hyannis. It's a low powered signal that can broadcast out to a radius of about 6 miles. He gets to spout his conspiracy theories to anyone listening between exits 5 and 7 on route 6. I'm the guy he calls when he wants to have a skeptic argue with him on his stupid show. The only real chances of anyone hearing his shows are after he dumps them into his podcast. I snatched up a piece of yellow salt water taffy that was sitting on my desk and unwrapped it. I leaned back in my chair and said, "Lemme guess, some nitwit reported Venus again?"

"No man, it was this huge V-shaped craft! A cop followed it for a mile!"

I stopped fiddling with my candy. Noodles sat down next to me and we watched the monitor together. Zeke had our attention. I asked, "What do you mean by huge?"

"The cop said it was easily three hundred feet across. He was right under it."

Damn.

Typically these reports are just about a single dot of light that's moving oddly in the distance, but shit, that sounded close. It also helps if a police offer reports it, since they're better-trained witnesses than your typical crackpots. I asked, "Were there any more witnesses?"

"I think so." Zeke typed something off-screen then quickly said, "Look, I gotta get this up on my blog. You coming tonight?"

I nodded, "Sure. What the hell."

He said, "OK, see you here at nine," then abruptly ended the call.

I looked over to Noodles. We both didn't know what to make of it. Noodles leaned back in his chair and looked at me, "That sounds cool."

"Yeah, maybe he's got something interesting for once."

Noodles and I got to Zeke's garage studio right at nine o'clock.

"Studio" is rather a strong word for Zeke's setup—a plastic folding table sitting on a patch of green outdoor carpet. In a corner, sitting on some plastic milk crates, the station's amplifier gave off a subtle hum. Gardening tools hung on the walls and a rusty tool chest stood off one side. He had a land line phone sitting in the middle of the table so he could take outside calls.

Zeke was in his forties and kind of tall and thin. His flunky Eddie was already there, sitting at the end of the table with a pair of headphones on. He gave me a nod as he took a sip from his can of Narragansett beer. Eddie was a little younger and shorter than Zeke, had darker hair and was more out of shape. He looked like he hadn't shaved in a few days.

Zeke was fiddling with some knobs on his audio mixing board when he saw us walk in. He frantically pointed to the microphones on the card table and said, "Take a seat! We're gonna be on the air in thirty seconds!" Noodles and I sat down and put our headphones on. Zeke pulled his chair up to the table and hit the start button on a CD player. Cheesy "outer space" music—a theremin played through tons of reverb—started. He snuggled up to his microphone. "Welcome to another episode of Anomaly, the show where we examine all aspects of the paranormal—UFOs, cryptozoology and the unexplained. I'm your host, Ezekiel Brandon—your Zeeker of Truth."

I kept a groan to myself. I rolled my eyes so much I think I tore my optic nerve.

Zeke continued, "As always, we have my co-host, Eddie Butler, field researcher."

Eddie leaned into his mic and raised his beer, "Here! here!"

"So give us a call anytime and join the conversation. Tonight we have back with us Ken Wakeman and…" Zeke had to think for a moment, "Noodles…?"

Noodles leaned into his mic, "It's just Noodles."

"OK, Noodles it is." Zeke turned to me, "So Ken, what do

you call yourself?"

"Rational."

"No no. You have an intense interest in UFO's?"

"Well yeah, I've been studying them for as long as you Zeke, I just don't get all emotional about it."

"I bet you would get emotional if you met an extraterrestrial, right?"

"That's precisely why they wouldn't want to talk to us. Primitive cultures go mental when they see something they don't understand."

Eddie said, "What about ancient aliens visiting us?"

Wonderful, I thought. Now I was going to have to argue why Erich von Daniken's view that humanoid squiggles on cave walls were just a modern interpretation of extraterrestrials. He wrote a bunch of books about this in the 1970s. More dumb aliens hanging out with even dumber civilizations. I said, "Look, I'm sure extraterrestrials exist. Who said they had to say hello and shake our hands? That's my answer to the Fermi paradox."

Zeke said, "I don't think the Fermi paradox exists. They're already here."

With the Fermi paradox, the earth should have been already visited by extraterrestrials, given the age of the universe plus the Drake equation. Which leaves the question of why they haven't contacted us, or at least left a sign? I said, "I guess your aliens, Zeke, are the primitive ones? They have to physically touch us to get a good idea what we're about? Why can't they observe us from the orbit of Neptune? Or hell, even the Oort cloud? I mean their powers of observation are much more advanced than ours, right?"

"Then how do you explain all the abductions?"

"Delusional people and dumb aliens? You guys aren't giving the extraterrestrials much credit for being advanced."

Zeke leaned into his mic, "Call us now, what do you think? Are aliens that dumb?"

I collapsed in my chair; the guy wasn't listening to me. I leaned into my mic and said, "The people, Zeke—delusional people!" I restrained myself from adding, "—like yourself."

Zeke continued, "Call in and tell us, are there extraterrestrials out there?"

"I'll tell you what's *not* out there, Zeke—your listeners!"

Zeke looked like he'd just bit into a lemon. It was my job to tell him things he didn't want to hear. "What do you mean? We get callers all the time."

I had come prepared this time. Usually Zeke gets his mom to call in from the kitchen and ask some lame question. I knew nobody listened to this stupid show and I had to call him out on it. I leaned into the mic and said, "OK, to anyone who is now listening…" I held up a twenty dollar bill and an envelope which I then scraped against the microphone. "This is a stamped envelope. I have a twenty dollar bill in my other hand. If anyone calls in and just tells me their address, I'll write it on this envelope and mail them a twenty dollar bill. It's free money."

Zeke ignored me, turned towards Eddie and said, "So you have an interesting report this week. What can you tell us about it, Eddie?"

Eddie set his beer down and cracked open his laptop. He read off the screen from the Cape Cod News website. "A V-shaped UFO flew over Truro last Tuesday. There were multiple reports. An Officer Wright reported that it flew directly over him and said it was as large as a 747."

"It says the craft was totally silent. The officer said that he followed it for over a mile, then it flew out over the water."

I had to admit, that did sound kind of interesting. Cops are professional witnesses; they typically don't get hysterical if they see something weird. I planned on doing more research on this later.

Zeke said, "What the officer saw sounds a lot like the Phoenix lights sighting."

"Hold on," I said. "There were *two* sightings associated with that back in 1997. A huge V-shaped thing flew slow and low over Phoenix Arizona at night that legitimately freaked out a bunch of people. And then there was a bunch of morons who got worked up over watching some military flares dropped from an aircraft descend behind some mountains."

"The flare hypothesis was never proven," said Zeke.

"Yes it was," I said between gritted teeth. I felt my neck tighten up as I moved away from the mic and I exhaled. Zeke always did this to me; I knew I would regret doing his show. I went back to the mic and spoke methodically, as if it would help, "They overlaid the nighttime footage of those so-called UFOs with daylight footage and it clearly showed where the light disappeared - behind some mountains."

"They never substantiated the sightings with any military maneuvers," he said.

I slammed my palms onto the table in frustration. "Yes they did! Look…" I had to pause for a second to gain my composure. "The point is the first V-shaped sighting is the interesting one. Why…" I had to stop myself. This wasn't getting anywhere.

I pulled out a five dollar bill from my wallet and held it up. "OK, I have an additional $5. Noodles? You want in on this?"

Noodles leaned forward and went for his wallet. "OK, I've got $10."

I grabbed Noodles' money and waved the cash above my head. "OK, this is thirty-five dollars! I've got a stamped envelope. For the love of God, will somebody please call in and tell us you're listening?"

I dramatically fell back in my chair and looked over at Zeke and Eddie. They sat there in silence for a moment. Eddie finally spoke up, "We understand that a Loch Ness monster was spotted on a beach in Chatham this week."

Nobody called the entire the night.

06

"It was right there; I saw it right there!" Brian shouted as he shook his finger at the horizon. My brother Brian lives out near Lecount Hollow Beach in Wellfleet. I wasn't crazy about driving out there at night, but he insisted he had to show me where he saw his UFO. He thrust his arms above his head as if a building were going to fall on him, then opened his fingers wide. "It went right over my head! It was huge!"

I glanced up at the night sky. There's very little light pollution out there so I could see the Milky Way, a faint mottled band across the sky. I tried to imagine his UFO. I said, "So what did it look like again?"

He paced back and forth in his front yard, passing in and out of the pool of light from the lantern on his porch. "I came out here to have a smoke; then I saw it." Every time he finished a thought, he would bite his thumbnail, then turn around and go back the way he came. I'd seen him agitated before, but this time I was a bit concerned he might lose it completely. "It was a V-shape! Two rows of lights that formed a V! I mean you should've seen the thing!" He wandered out of the light and continued pacing in the dark as he spoke, "Why did they come here? Can you believe it? Why were they looking for me?"

My "baby brother" Brian, who is seven years younger than me, has an anxiety disorder. He likes living out here because it makes him feel safer, away from whatever perceived threat that's out to get him. We can thank our parents for giving us lousy genetics, but he seems to have gotten the worst of it, at least in terms of how well he handles it. I am much more objective about what's going on inside my head and I know the stupidity of stopping your meds when you feel better. From the look of him, he was off his again. "Come here!" I said. "What are you doing out there in the dark?" I tried to reassure him, "They're not looking for you."

"How can you say that Melissa? I don't want them to see me."

"But they're gone." I glanced up into the sky, just to be sure. I immediately felt slightly foolish.

I knew it was futile trying to argue with him when he was this paranoid. He came back into the light, pointed to the sky and said, "Melissa, they were right here! You believe me when I say I saw them, right?"

"Yeah, yeah…of course. A couple of policemen also reported something."

He bit his fingernail again and nodded his head. It fit in with what Officer Wright told me; something did fly through here. The question was—what? My first thought wouldn't be flying saucers. He headed towards his front door, "Ok, let's go inside."

It was a tiny place, a cottage that was meant to be used during the summer months only, but he lived here year round. I went inside and I got further confirmation of his mental state. He's not the stereotypical hoarder, with piles of trash everywhere; I didn't need a shovel to move around. He kept all his stuff filed away in cardboard boxes, each with a contents list attached to the side. His entire living room was surrounded by boxes, stacked four to five high, almost up to the ceiling. It looked like he was living inside a storage locker.

He followed a path between columns of boxes to his kitchen, "You want something to eat? I have chocolate covered Twinkies."

I looked around for a place to sit that wasn't completely covered in boxes or magazines. "Sure," I said. At either end of his sofa were two boxes that double as end tables; on top of each was a lamp. Behind them a wall of cartons looked ready to buckle forward. The bottom ones struggled to support the weight. I tested its stability with a little push to make sure nothing fell on me. I didn't want my last meal to be a Twinkie.

I reluctantly sat down in a clear spot on the couch and called out towards the kitchen, "Listen, why don't you rent a storage locker? Think of all the space you'd have." A crinkling sound from the kitchen stopped and there was a moment of silence. "I don't want to," he said. The crinkling resumed.

"They're not that expensive."

He came back holding a plate of two unwrapped Twinkies and placed it on the table in front of me. With his foot, he slid a box up to the table, sat down and bit the end off of one of the them. "I don't trust the guys who run those places," he said with his mouth full. "They've got keys to everything. Besides, I want my stuff where I can get it when I need it."

I picked up the other Twinkie; it was covered in chocolate, like a Hostess Cupcake. I bit into it, "These are really good! What are they called?"

"Chocodiles. Not every place carries them."

As I ate, I studied the columns of boxes that surrounded me. Out loud, I read the neatly printed manifest on a box to my left. "*Contents - two 300-watt computer power supplies (broken). One, computer case with 486 motherboard, Twelve nine pin serial cables and a catchers mitt.* "Why do you need this stuff? What are you going to do with it?"

He stared at the far wall as he slowly chewed, "You never know," he said. "I might need a part."

"Look, I'll help you move it. We can use my car."

He sprang up and said, "I need some milk," then darted back into the kitchen.

I knew I wouldn't get anywhere with him. Every time I tried to speak to him about improving his life, he did the same thing—refused to talk about it. I knew he wouldn't leave the kitchen until he thought I'd forgotten about it. I pulled out my phone and checked my email. There was a message from someone I didn't know, Ken Wakeman.

> From: Ken Wakeman <kwakeman3@gmail.com>
> Title: Recent Truro UFO Report
>
> Hello Melissa!
>
> I saw your recent report on the Truro UFO sighting in The Cape Cod News. I'm an independent researcher of UFO phenomenon, living on the Cape. Do you have any more information on the sighting that you can disclose? Also: I loved your report called "The Grass is Always Greener" on the marijuana sales. In the future I'll know where to find some "hooch" on Cape Cod.

He loved my report—yeah, right. An independent UFO researcher? Well, maybe I could find out something that might help Brian. Something was out there, something outside of the ordinary. I replied:

> From: Melissa Howard <0callmemel0@gmail.com>
> Title: re: Recent Truro UFO Report
>
> Ken - "Hooch" should do really well on the Cape. There's not much to tell on the report, but feel free to come down to the office any-

time after 3 pm on Friday. I'll give you what I have.

Brian stopped what he was doing and said, "You know the Barnstable County Fair is happening this week?"

I laughed and said, "You still want to go on the Zipper?" The Barnstable County Fair is the biggest thing that happens on the Cape in July. It's a classic fair with rides, animals and games. Our parents took us there when we were kids. When Brian was ten he insisted on going on the Zipper ride, an evil looking piece of machinery that throws the riders in all directions. He puked his guts out while he was on it and they had to stop the ride. We teased him about it well into adulthood.

"Can you go with me?"

That is one of his things: he hates going out in public and will only go places if someone he trusts goes with him. Most of the time that's me and that's OK, but something as chaotic as a fair presents an extra challenge. There was a good chance we'd get there and he'd freak out after fifteen minutes. I could picture the whole thing. On the other hand, I like to encourage anything that resembles "normal" life and gets him out of that cottage. I said, "Let me see what my schedule looks like."

"How about Saturday then?"

"I said I would need to check my schedule."

Brian looked at me, grinned and said, "We could get fried dough. And I bet they even have fried Oreos!"

Sneaky bastard; he knew I loved those things. Whoever invented them was evil. An Oreo is dunked in batter, dropped into a fryolator and out comes a lethal nugget of yumminess. You can only get them at carnivals and fairs. I said, "You realize Saturday is the busiest day, right? There'll be people all over the place."

"So?"

"So I have to check my schedule." I lied; we were going. I just didn't want to make it easy for him.

07

The whole trick to making a good curry is getting the right ratio of turmeric, coriander and cumin into your sauce. Don't even bother with that crap from a jar, you've got to make it yourself. Like I've always ranted to my friends, if you want some decent Indian food on the Cape, you have to make it yourself. I mean how many clam rolls can a person eat? (Apparently a lot around these parts.)

The rice cooker light came on, notifying me that my basmati rice was done. Astro swiped at my leg with his paw. He wanted a taste of whatever I was making. It's just the two of us in this house, so he gets a piece of everything. He learned a long time ago that I'm a sucker for a begging dog. I flicked a piece of pre-cooked diced chicken off the cutting board towards the floor. He easily snatched it up with his tongue.

I had just dumped the chicken into the sauce when Noodles let himself through my back door. Astro ran up to him and put his front paws onto his chest. "Astro!" he said as he gave the dog a vigorous rub behind his head.

I stirred the sauce and said, "Hey—good timing!"

Noodles sniffed the air and squinted, "What's that?"

"I told ya, we're having curried chicken. Haven't you had Indian food before?"

He looked around with a concerned look on his face. "Do you smell that?"

"What? The cumin? It's an important ingredient."

"No, something smells rank."

"You gotta be kidding me—you've never had Indian food before?"

"No dude, I've had plenty of Indian food. Something smells off. I noticed it when I came in."

I leaned over my simmering pot and sucked in a chestful of aroma then exhaled deeply. I was getting annoyed by my friend's remarks. "It smells great, what are you talking about?"

Noodles and his nose wandered around my house, firing off a short sniff every few feet. Astro playfully followed behind him, thinking he would be getting more attention. Noodles stopped in the middle of my living room and frowned. "It smells like ass over here."

I slammed my spoon down on the countertop. "Seriously? Did Astro just take a dump?" Although I had given Astro a little bit of the curry sauce, I didn't think it would come out the back end that fast. I knelt down on the carpet and scanned for the despicable discharge. Astro got down next to me in a play bow. He didn't realize he was ten seconds away from a severe scolding. I spotted a weird lump of something under my sofa. I reached for it and was enveloped in its sphere of stench. My first thought was, *How did Astro get a pile of turds under my sofa?* It looked solid enough and I was able to grab it. It was brown, hard and looked like the end of a cow's femur. I had to hold my breath as I held it up to show

Noodles. Astro got excited as if I was going to play fetch with it.

Noodles backed away from me. "What the fuck, dude?"

I held it out at arm's length as I strode towards the kitchen door, kicked it open and chucked the thing into the middle of my back yard. Astro scampered down the steps after it. I quickly closed the door and took a deep breath. I shouted "Jeeeesus Christ!" as I wiped my eyes, "That thing was vile!"

"What the hell was it?"

"It looked like the end of a bone of some sort. The animal must've died recently."

Through the kitchen window, we watched Astro play with the thing in the back yard. He eventually laid down with it between his paws and started gnawing at it.

"If the dog wants to chew on that thing all night, he can stay outside." I said.

Noodles approached the stove. "Is this stuff ready?"

"Yeah, grab a plate." I went over to the sink and washed my hands. "There's rice in the cooker."

While Noodles loaded up on rice, I pulled two Coronas out of my fridge and handed him one, "Here, they're not Flying Horse, but close enough," I said.

"What's a flying horse?" he asked.

"Indian beer."

We sat at the kitchen island, chowing down on dinner. Noodles swallowed a mouthful of food then said, "So whatta ya think of: 'Your windows are the eyes of your home'?"

"Making up proverbs now, are we?"

"I was gonna use that at work." Noodles worked as the event marketer for a shitty little company that sells replacement windows and doors to homeowners. I supposed it was better than delivering pizzas, which is what he used to do. He glanced around my living room quizzically. "You know, windows may account for more than thirty percent of your home's heating loss."

I didn't look up from my plate. "My windows are fine," I said, my mouth full.

Noodles studied each window. "Do you know what the R-value of yours are?"

Annoyed, I shot back, "Will you knock it off with your marketing shit? Nobody gives a crap about windows."

Noodles became fixated on the window on the other side of my living room for a moment then asked, "Is that Astro?"

"Where?"

"I thought I saw Astro in your front yard."

"Astro is out back," I said. I got up, opened the back door and scanned my yard. He wasn't there. Noodles and I turned around and went to the front door. I opened the door and there he was, sniffing a light pole next to the street. I thought, *What the hell's he doing out front?* I shouted, "Astro! Come here!" He joyfully bounded up to me and sat down, giving me a look of complete innocence. I petted him on his head and asked, "How did you get out here?"

A voice yelled from the porch next to mine. "Keep that damn dog on your property!" I called him Drunk Scott, my asshole neighbor who was a raging alcoholic. With his white hair and stooped shoulders, he seemed perpetually old and permanently cantankerous. Civility between us ended long ago.

I said, "I didn't let him out, you old coot."

"I don't want to see that dog shitting on my lawn!" Drunk Scott bellowed.

"He didn't shit on your lawn."

"That damn dog has been running around the neighborhood for the past week."

"What are you talking about? He's been in my back yard since I moved here. There's a six foot fence around it!"

Drunk Scott flailed his arms in the air. "He pissed on my mailbox yesterday."

"You were probably hammered and saw another dog piss on your mailbox. He didn't do shit to your property. He's fenced in."

He picked up a little bag of something from behind a flower pot on his porch. He shook it at me while he screamed, "I have the shit! I have the shit!" as if it were a vital piece of evidence to some murder trial. "I had to clean it up two days ago. He's been up and down the street!"

"It's not *my* dog's turd, you drunk fossil! Do I have to genetically test a bag of dog feces to convince you?" I pointed towards my back yard and stressed again, "My yard is fenced in!"

"That was *your* dog I saw!"

I realized I wasn't getting anywhere with him. I calmly said, "Look, I'm taking him back now."

He yelled out, "I don't want to see that dog out here again," and slammed his front door.

I muttered "fuck me" to myself. There was no way I was going to convince the old mummy that he saw another dog. I led Astro through the side gate and let him go. He bounded to the middle of the yard, spun around and looked at me. Wagging his tail, he thought I was going to play with him.

Noodles said, "How do you think he got out then?"

"I dunno. The gate was shut." Noodles and I walked along the inside perimeter of the yard, studying the fence as Astro followed us.

"Do you think he could've jumped it?" he said.

"I doubt it." We stopped at my tool shed and I pushed at a clump of weeds with my foot. I muttered, "Oh shit." Astro had dug a hole under the fence. The weeds blocked the view from the house; you had to stand right where we were to see it. Astro admired his handiwork, wagging his tail beside me. Noodles and I exchanged looks of embarrassment. I guess the old coot was right. We found a couple of concrete paving stones and wedged them under the fence. I grabbed a shovel and filled the rest of the hole in. I certainly wasn't going to apologize to Drunk Scott. He could keep his prized bag of dog shit.

08

"What are you doing?" Norm asked, pouring coffee into his cup.

"Cleaning my desk. You know how I am about clutter."

"Maybe if you gave your little friends a new home…" he waved his cup in the direction of my action figures, spilling coffee onto the floor. "Shit." He put the cup down, grabbed a handful of paper towels from the counter and bent over to wipe the spill.

That's when the new intern walked in—Norm's butt in the air and me holding a Game of Thrones Jon Snow action figure. She stood for a moment, taking in the scene. This was the first time I'd seen her and Norm's description was largely accurate. My eyes went to her legs before I could stop myself, but they were covered. She wore loose Indian-style pants and a t-shirt that said "Just say no to GMO".

"Hi—you must be Mel…or do you prefer Melissa? People are always calling me Milly, but I prefer Mildred—although I didn't always feel that way." She stepped forward, hand held out. I shook it and said, "Mel is good."

"Mildred Pierce," she said, pushing her hair behind her ears. I must've given her a blank look because she continued, "You know—the movie. My mother was a big Joan Crawford fan."

Norm startled both of us by shouting "No more wire hangers!" in his best Joan Crawford voice. He grinned and pointed at the white paper box in Mildred's hand. "You brought us doughnuts?" he asked hopefully.

"Oh, yes. I mean, no—not doughnuts." She opened the box. Inside I could see half a dozen round objects studded with what looked like raisins. "They're whole grain carrot muffins. They use applesauce instead of sugar and dried cranberries instead of raisins. I would've gotten the ones with walnuts, but I didn't know if either of you had allergies."

"Thanks, " I said, standing up. I felt compelled to take one and raised my eyebrows at Norm who stared silently at the muffins as if they were live ordinance. The muffin had heft and I resisted the sudden urge to see if it would put a dent in the wall. Norm hesitantly removed one for himself. I knew he'd drop it in the trash, untasted. "I think I'll warm it up," I said, heading for the break room.

"You can have that desk," Norm said, pointing to the corner. That's not the fastest computer, but it works."

Warmed up, the muffin was barely edible. When I returned from the workroom, Norm was showing something on the computer to Mildred. I was about to open a file when a voice said, "Is there a Melissa here?"

I stood up and faced the intruder—a thirty-something guy with brown hair and blue eyes. I said, "I'm Melissa, can I help you with something?"

"My name is Ken, I'm here to get some more info on the UFO report?"

"Oh yeah—that's right," I said. I spun my chair around and motioned him towards my computer. I completely forgot that he had emailed me two days ago. I pulled another chair over and motioned for him to sit. He sat down and moved his chair closer to mine. I resisted the urge to move back—I have a thing about people encroaching on my personal space. Ken was holding a manila folder. I cleared a space on my desk next to him. "Do you want some coffee?" I asked, "Or a muffin perhaps?"

Ken carefully placed his finger on Jon Snow's head. "What do you think of Jon Snow going out with Ygritte in real life?"

I smiled and said, "I was kind of hoping he'd hook up with Daenerys. Of course, they still might—on the show, that is."

He continued to study the little action figure. "Aren't they related?"

"The characters? Yeah; she's his aunt." I shrugged. "Of course, there's a lot of speculation about what might or might not happen."

Ken smiled and settled into his chair. "You follow that stuff online?"

"Mostly through Facebook groups."

"Like what?" he asked.

"Everything Game of Thrones is a good one. And there's Alt Shift X on YouTube. He has some great theories."

"Have you read the books?"

"Yeah...the story's good, of course, but I was always kind of put off by the 'Ye olde" stuff."

Ken nodded in agreement and continued, "OK, I've got a joke for you: Why doesn't George RR Martin use Twitter?"

"Why?"

"He already killed 140 characters."

I smiled; I'd heard that one before. "So what were we supposed to be talking about?"

"The Truro UFO report."

"Well, I looked back through my notes and there's really not much else I can tell you. Like I said, I put everything in the report. The officer spotted the UFO over Pamet Hollow, followed it for a while, then lost it."

"Where did he lose track of it?"

"At the end of Long Nook Road, going out over the ocean towards Hanging Valley."

Ken thought for a second then said, "There's a parking lot out there, and a path that goes down to the beach."

"Yeah, I used to go to the beach there. I almost broke my neck going down that cliff."

He laughed, "That was our high school drinking spot. The cops wouldn't chase us down there. We would just wave at them from the beach."

"Speaking of drinking," I said, "the Wellfleet Beachcomber is just south of there."

"I've been there a million times! Remember Smitty the bartender?"

A brief image of Smitty flashed in my mind: curly brown ponytail, scruffy goatee, tattoos. He mixed me many a Sea Breeze, my drink of choice at the time. "What did he always say? If you're drinking to forget…"

Ken continued, "…please pay in advance!"

We both laughed. Ken asked, "Did you ever see The Incredible Casuals there?"

"More than once; best way to spend a Sunday afternoon if you were sick of the beach."

"And wanted to start your drinking early." He pulled out a book that had been hiding behind his manilla folder. "I noticed this sighting was in the same area as the Budd Hopkins sighting.

"Yeah; I've heard of him."

"Did you know he was also an expressionist painter? He had a Truro studio and he used to go swimming at Ballston Beach. I have this copy of his book, called Art, Life and UFOs: A Memoir." He handed it to me and I flipped though it while he spoke. "He experienced a UFO sighting back in August of 1964. He was driving through Truro on Route 6 when he saw a lens-shaped object in the sky." Ken handed me a piece of paper. "This is the sketch he drew of his sighting." The sketch showed a road, labeled Route 6, heading towards Provincetown. Little arrows indicated wind direction and where the UFO was in relation to the dunes and water. Ken continued, "He watched it for a while as it moved in front of and behind some clouds until it eventually moved out over the ocean."

I looked at the sketch. "Budd's UFO looks like it's in the distance. The one here was, apparently, right over Truro. The officers I spoke with said it was huge and V-shaped."

"It affected him so much that he started researching other UFO sightings. New York Times called him 'the father of the alien-abduction movement'."

"Did he ever say he was abducted?"

"No," Ken said. "He just studied people who claimed they were."

"It sounds like he was the Fox Mulder of the sixties."

"So you're into the X-Files too?"

"You do realize there was an episode of the X-Files set on Cape Cod?"

"Was it the spontaneous combustion guy episode?"

"That's the one," I said. "though, of course, it was filmed in Vancouver."

Ken said, "Right, Vancouver…Cape Cod, who the hell's gonna know?"

I laughed. Mildred appeared beside us and said, "Excuse me, Melissa?"

I corrected her, "Mel."

"Sorry…Mel, sorry to interrupt," she said in a slightly singsongy voice. "Is there a water dispenser here of some sort?"

"No, but there's a couple of Cokes in the fridge if you're thirsty."

Mildred frowned. "Do you know if we're going to get one?"

"A water cooler—here? You'd have to ask Norm, but they won't even send us a decent printer so I doubt they'll pay for a water cooler."

"OK thanks," she replied, and backed away from my desk. Ken and I watched her wander over to Norm at his computer. He stopped typing and looked up at her, his expression blank. "Hi! Sorry to bother you," she said. "Can I ask you something?" Norm just looked at her. "Do you think we can get a water dispenser here?"

His eyes went quickly to me. "There's a sink in the break room."

"Will we be getting a bottled water dispenser at some point?"

Norm shrugged, "I doubt it, but anything's possible."

"Oh I hope so!" she said, "I have negative reactions to fluoride. It's important that I have access to, at the very least, bottled water."

He looked over at me for a second, then hesitantly said to her, "Okay...?"

"Do you know what really works best? A reverse osmosis system." Mildred was oblivious to the 'what the fuck' look on Norm's face. She continued, "It's the best method of removing contaminants from your drinking water. I usually bring my own, but I forgot it today, so I thought I would ask." She gave him a quick smile and went back to her desk.

Ken leaned closer and whispered, "Negative reactions from fluoride?"

I muttered to Ken, "I get negative reactions from millennial entitlement."

"What was that quote from Dr. Strangelove? Fluoridation is part of a Communist conspiracy...?"

I continued "…to sap and impurify all of our precious bodily fluids!"

We laughed together. Ken and I spoke for another twenty minutes, comparing places on the Cape that we've explored and movies that we liked. I eventually had to shoo him out of the office because I had some deadlines to hit.

09

"Excuse me!" The voice came from a guy sitting under a blue tent. "Would you like to learn about the cost benefits of solar?" I had made it a point not to make any eye contact with him as I walked past. I thought I was far enough away so I could pretend that I didn't hear him, but it didn't work. "Huh? No, that's all right," I said.

"You do realize that for every kilowatt of solar power installed, it's like removing two cars from the road?"

I accelerated my pace. I didn't give a shit about solar; nor did I give a shit about remodeling my bathroom, fixing a wet basement or replacing broken concrete. I called the giant metal industrial building I was in "the most un-fun place at the Barnstable County Fair." A county fair is known for its rides, animals, food and fun. This structure was for the poor souls condemned to hock industrial services to the few explorers who either wandered in by mistake or were taking a shortcut to the port-a-potties. I promised Noodles I would visit him at his booth, but when I saw him, he was speaking with a potential customer. Eventually the customer disappeared and I was able to approach Noodles. "Yo dude, 'sup?" I said.

He smiled, fiddling with a pile of brochures on the table behind him. "Hey! I'm doing pretty good today; I think I got three referrals."

I scanned his posters of assorted windows. There was also a tiny demo window. I imagined they were used on energy-efficient dog houses. I asked him, "Who you selling to? Contractors?"

"No, no—homeowners. We do the whole installation."

On the floor beside the table was a inflatable green alien. I picked it up, "Is this yours?"

"Oh yeah, I won that at the hoop shots game."

"Cool. How many tries did it take?"

He pulled out a box of flyers from under the table and started flipping through them. I could tell he was trying to ignore me by pretending to be busy.

I asked him again, "How much did you blow on this?" He fiddled some more; I waited him out.

Quietly, he said, "It cost me thirty bucks."

"Thirty bucks?" I hooted. "You gotta be kidding me! I bet you could get one on eBay for nothing."

"I wanted to impress the girl who works with the pure-bred chickens. She said she liked the movie Close Encounters, so I wanted surprise her."

"So why didn't you give it to her?"

Noodles frowned. "She wasn't there when I went back."

I squeezed his inflated alien. "Did you get her name?"

"No."

"Dude, you gotta at least start there." Noodles was notorious for failing to initiate connections with women. I tried getting dates for him; that shy-guy thing he had going would only get him so far. I put the alien down and said, "OK, so you got yourself an expensive pool toy. I'm gonna take a walk around. You want me to get you anything?"

"I'm good," he said.

It was just starting to get dark and lights were on all over the fairgrounds. I had already gone through the animal displays and had my fill of goats, prized hogs and horses. I followed the smell of grilled meat, onion rings and cotton candy past tents displaying luggage, jewelry and sun catchers.

I walked up to the dunk-the-clown booth. Some jamoke was desperately whipping baseballs at the target that, when hit, would silence his painted tormentor. "Check out the guy with the Red Sox hat," the clown yelled in a nasal voice, "Red Sox suck!"

I noticed a Yankees emblem on the front of the tank. I watched the guy pay for a couple of rounds of baseballs with no success. It made me wonder if the carnies had put an ad on the New York Craigslist? *Wanted: fat obnoxious Yankee fan willing to torment Cape Codders.* It occurred to me that I could easily throw my arm out at a dunk-the-conspiracy-theorist tank, lured in with such taunts as: "Hey pal! The World Trade Center came down with explosives!"

The aroma of grilled sausages pulled me over to a guy shoveling a mound of peppers and onions onto a grill. I experienced a Pavlovian response as I watched everything sizzle on the greasy surface. I ordered a sausage with onions and paid the guy. With my dinner in hand, I needed something to drink. A beer would make a great complement. I saw a penned-off area labeled "Beer Garden". Beside it stood a giant Bud Light banner. I would've labeled it "Industrial Booze Farm" if that's all they were offering for beverages. I stood there holding my meal, squinting at the serving table, trying to see if they served anything that could remotely be considered a craft beer.

To my right, a female voice called out "Ken!" I scanned the tables packed with beer drinkers, then spotted Melissa waving at me. She wasn't alone; some guy was sitting beside her. I walked over, planted myself in the one remaining chair and scooted it up to the table.

She said, "I thought that was you! Ken, meet my brother Brian."

My right hand was covered with sausage and onion grease. I clumsily switched the sausage to my other hand, saw that it was hopeless to offer him a clean hand to shake, and said, "Sorry."

Brian waved me off.

Melissa smiled. "So what are you doing here at the fair?"

I was excited to see her again but I tried to be nonchalant about it. I thought we had a real connection going when we spoke at the newspaper. At the time, I was dying to ask her for a phone number, but it didn't feel right doing it in front of everybody at her office. I had decided I would come up with a bullshit excuse to email her again and finagle my way back there, but fate dealt me a lucky break. I took a bite from my sausage, swallowed, and tried not to spit on her. "A buddy of mine works at one of the exhibits."

She looked up and said, "Oh, which one?"

"The depressing one. He sells replacement windows inside the big warehouse building over there."

"I haven't been over there yet," she said.

I shook my head, "You don't want to. This food court is more interesting than what he's doing. So what are you guys gonna do tonight?"

Brain said, "We need to get some fried dough."

"Oh that stuff is great!" I said, "I love the deep fried veggies—what are they called?"

"Tempura," Melissa said.

"Right!" I took another bite of my sausage then asked Brian, "So what do you do for a living?"

He hesitated, then said, "I do stuff."

"Brian works from home," Melissa said. "Did you know he

actually saw the Truro UFO?"

"Really? You didn't mention that in your report."

"Brian is kind of private; he didn't want the publicity."

"That's understandable," I said to Brian. "I've been studying UFOs for a while now. That's how I tracked down your sister.'

Melissa said to her brother, "Ken also likes the X-Files."

Brian said, "I liked the Lone Gunmen show better."

The Lone Gunmen show was a spin off of the X-Files where they took three of the more kooky characters and gave them their own show. It only lasted one season. I said, "I never really got into it. Maybe they should've done an episode on faking the moon landing. That would've been funny."

"But the moon landing *was* faked," Brian said, dead serious.

My mind immediately flashed to the footage of Buzz Aldrin punching that guy who called him a liar and insisted the landing was faked. I abhor violence, but boy, that was the most patriotic punch I'd ever seen. I looked at Melissa and smiled. She looked at me and raised her eyebrows. I could tell she'd had this argument with him before. Trying not to sneer, I said to Brian, "Sooooo... the entire Apollo 11 mission was faked?"

"There weren't any stars in the photos," he said calmly. "The flag was flapping when they planted it; there's no air on the moon. The government set the whole thing up in a studio somewhere so Stanley Kubrick could film it."

"So what did we see leaving the ground? Are you saying the Atlas rockets were fake?"

"No, they were real. They just never left Earth's orbit."

I pressed him further, "Well, then what about the Apollo 10 mission? The one where we only went around the moon and back? We faked that one too?"

"Yeah."

"What about the Gemini missions—were they faked too? When did all this start?"

"No, they were real," he said.

"OK, so you're saying that leaving Earth's orbit kicked NASA's ass? That we couldn't figure out how to fire a rocket at just the right time to leave Earth's orbit and put us on a trajectory towards the moon? The math was too hard?"

Brian didn't say anything. He just sat there quietly, chewing on the lip of his empty plastic beer cup.

Melissa gave her brother a reassuring squeeze on his arm and said, "Brian has his own ideas about certain things."

I knew I better drop the topic before it looked like I was attacking her brother. I wasn't sure how protective she was of him; to me he sounded like a complete idiot. "So what are they offering for beer around here?" I asked. "Anything crafty?"

"Nope," Melissa said, "unless you want to call Sam Adams Summer crafty."

"You guys want another round? I'm buying."

Melissa picked up her half-filled plastic cup. "I think we're all set. I've already tried pouring some liquid courage into my brother so he would go on some of the rides with me."

Brain turned away from us and murmured, "I don't like going on the rides."

Melissa said, "He's had some bad experiences in the past."

Brian began to rock back and forth slightly. "I'm not going on the rides."

"I'll go on the rides with you!" I said to Melissa. "Which ones do you want to do?'

She laughed, "Nothing scary. I just want to say I went on something, for old time's sake."

We all left the beer garden, entered the midway area and found the ticket booth. Melissa started to pull out her wallet when I stepped in front of her and said, "I'm buying, since I couldn't pay for any of the beer."

Melissa stepped back and swept her arm towards the window

like she was a game show model. "Knock yourself out."

Pleased with myself, I bought twenty dollars worth of tickets. This was starting to feel like a date.

Melissa looked towards the Ferris wheel. "How about we start off easy?" She turned to Brian and asked, "Are you sure you don't want to go up with us? How scary is a Ferris wheel?"

He shook his head as he looked up to the top of the wheel. "I'm gonna play some skee-ball," he said, and wandered off down the midway.

We waited ten minutes at the ramp for the previous riders to get off. A carny wearing a dirty orange t-shirt and a "Make America Great Again" hat opened the gate and we climbed into our gondola. He was chewing on something and looked completely bored as he engaged the lever to start the ride.

Melissa seemed to be checking out the stability of our gondola as she spoke, "I think I saw that guy on America's Most Wanted."

"You're not regretting getting on this ride, are you?"

"No, I'm just checking for any missing lug nuts. I'd hate to think that guy was the one who assembled this."

"I like to think they use the competent ones to assemble the rides."

She settled down and gazed off into the distance. "I'll take your word for it." It was a slightly cool, overcast night. A breeze hit us as we crested the top of the ride.I experienced that slight sense of euphoria as the subtle G-forces followed us down towards the ground. Melissa leaned back, closed her eyes and smiled. "I remember doing this as a kid."

I said, "Where did you grow up? On the Cape?"

"My father was in the Air Force; we were stationed at Otis twice."

"I went to Mashpee High School, then ended up at U-Mass."

Each time we rose, you could see John's Pond, and beyond that the lights of the military base. I pointed this out to her as we crested another revolution, "Do you think that's the runway lights?"

She was looking the other way, towards Falmouth. "That's weird," she said.

I turned around but we were descending and our view was blocked by a row of trailers. "What?"

"Look that way," she said and pointed towards Falmouth. We did another revolution and I could see the horizon again. There was a pattern of lights, hovering off in the distance, about a quarter of a mile up off the ground. "What do you think it is?" she asked.

"I dunno. Something trying to land at Otis?"

We descended again and looked at each other, confused. I stood up and held onto the center pole, hoping to get a better look as we went around for another pass. There it was again, this time bigger. "Holy shit," I said, "it's moving towards us!" I frantically patted my pockets, trying to find my cell phone, I needed to get a photo of this. The next time around we could clearly see two rows of lights. I was frantically mashing the power button on my phone, trying to get my cell phone to power up. I called out, "Are you getting it?"

She already had her phone stabilized on the railing in front of her. "Yeah," she replied, focused on her screen.

It was frustrating as hell. As the Ferris wheel went around, we lost sight of it and had to wait for the wheel to lift us back up again. As we reached the top again we could see the object was v-shaped and heading right towards us. As we descended, I frantically pointed to the sky and screamed to the people below us, "DO YOU GUYS SEE THAT?" A few people looked up.

The Ferris wheel went around again and this time the thing looked huge. By now it must have been over Route 151. You could clearly see two rows of lights about fifty feet apart that formed a right angle in the shape of a V. I'd say there were about twenty of those lights along the object's edge.

As we got to the bottom, I could hear gasps and shouts as people watched the thing flying above their heads. I kept repeating to myself, "HOLY FUCKING SHIT! HOLY FUCKING SHIT!" At that point we could clearly see it even from the bottom of the ride. I was trying to hold my phone steady and shouted to Melissa, "IT'S A REAL LIVE FUCKING UFO!"

"Yes it is," she said, unruffled.

It was directly above us. At the top of the Ferris wheel, we were as close as anyone could get to the thing. I had to pan my phone's camera around just to get the whole thing in frame. If I'd had a rock to throw, I would've thrown it—just to prove it was real. In the crowd below us, people were screaming. I tried yelling at the carny, "STOP THE RIDE! STOP THE RIDE!" and pointed towards the top. He didn't notice me and just watched the UFO float above the fairgrounds.

Now I really hated him.

With each revolution of the Ferris wheel, the object grew smaller as it receded away from us. The noise from the crowd continued; hundreds of people had seen it pass directly overhead. There was no way anyone could deny that something that size flew directly over us. I was still hyperventilating when I looked over at Melissa, "Can you believe it? Can you *believe* it?"

Melissa checked her phone and calmly said, "I believe it."

We were let off the ride into a swarm of blathering people. It looked like they were all losing their minds. Some were crying; some were running towards the parking lot. One woman was on her knees, praying. I saw a guy come out from under the spinning Starship 3000 UFO ride and peer up at the sky. I wondered, *Does he think it's safer under there?*

Panting like crazy, Brian ran up to us, pointed to the sky and shouted, "That's what I saw! That's what I saw!" The poor guy looked shell-shocked, like a death ray had killed everyone around him and he was the lone survivor. He spun around and sprinted off into the crowd.

I tried to get my bearings, calm down, and not get sucked into the emotion of the crowd. I looked over at Melissa and asked, "What do you think?"

She held up her phone and said, "I think I have tomorrow's story."

10

While I was standing out in my backyard, I saw this silver bowl-shaped object descend from the sky. It got bigger and bigger as it dropped straight down towards me. I ran back towards the house and watched it come down until it floated a few feet above the grass. It looked like my silver water bowl, but much, much larger. The fur on my back stood straight up as I watched this thing hover silently off the ground. I tried barking at it, but nothing would come out. I tried running away, but I couldn't move, something was holding me in place.

That's when I saw a weird head push through a flap on the side of the silver bowl. It looked something like a dog but it was grey in color with a vertical almond shaped nose that took up most of its face. It had tiny pointy ears at the top of its head but I couldn't make out any fur. I watched the thing pull itself through the flap and float away, as if it were a puppy being carried by a human. It had four skinny legs dangling below it with a lizard-like tail. It explored my yard for a few moments, sniffing at the air.

Then a metallic pole pushed its way through the flap, turned upright and just hung in mid air. Little metallic branches appeared to grow from its center. Once it was done transforming, it looked like our silver Christmas tree that Ken puts up every year. The creature floated over to it and raised one of its hind legs. A blue liquid squirted out from the creature and covered the base of the tree-thing. Drops of blue urine dripped from its base and fell onto the grass. Once the creature was done, the tree withdrew its branches and went back inside the craft.

Then the creature spotted me. It floated in my direction with its tail wagging. That was when the panic pants really started up. I was petrified. I didn't know what it was going to do to me. It floated right up to my face, I felt my fur being pulled towards its giant nostrils as it gave me long, drawn out sniffs.

Two more of these creatures floated out of the bowl and joined the first one, their snake-like tails wagging as they all sniffed all over my body. The first creature stuck out its snake-like tongue and licked me. I tried desperately to run or even move.

I was locked in place.

The others joined in, licking at my face with their pointy tongues. I had a hard time breathing, I couldn't control my emotions any longer. I wanted desperately to let out a howl.

That's when I woke up. I was still lying in my backyard, my fur felt hot from being out in the sun for so long. I waited for my heart to slow down before I stood up, gave myself a good shake and exhaled deeply.

That was a definitely a weird dream.

I went over to my silver water dish in the shade and lapped up some of its warm water. With water dripping from my jowls, I eyed the silver bowl suspiciously. Maybe if I dropped it over the fence, Ken would get a new plastic one. I wasn't sure what I was going to do with myself that day. I went over to the hole under the fence behind our shed. Someone had filled it in with a bunch of heavy blocks and now I couldn't get out. I tried scratching at them for a few minutes, but they didn't budge. There was no way I could pull them out with my teeth.

Bummer.

I sat there for a few moments, staring at the dilemma. I wanted to take a lap around the neighborhood and look for more of those delicious bones; instead I was stuck in my back yard for the rest of the day. I looked around to see if anything else was different.

Nope.

I sat there for a while, my fur soaking up the sun, my mind just a complete blank. Suddenly, out of nowhere, a thought appeared in my head. I wasn't sure what that meant or where it came from. I let it wander around inside my head a few times, repeating it to myself.

One plus one equals two. One plus one equals two.

A familiar smell distracted me from my thoughts. The wind had changed direction and I picked up a distinct odor coming from our neighbor's yard. It was another one of those bones, somewhere in the neighborhood! I had already buried one of them over by the shed, and another one by the lawn chair. The smell couldn't be coming from the ones I already had—they were deep underground. Then it hit me.

I have two bones!

One bone plus another bone equals two bones! It all made perfect sense—one plus one equals two! I stood up, my tail started wagging like crazy.

If I have one squeaky toy and got one more squeaky toy, I would have two squeaky toys!

This was mind-blowing. I think I just learned how to count! Another bone was out there beyond the fence, calling me to go get it.

Wait a minute, what would be the number if I got that other bone?

I froze while I attempted to work it out in my mind.

If I got another bone, then added it to the two I already had, that would be…three bones! This new concept was completely nuts. I paced around the back yard, desperate to get at that third bone. Leaning up against the shed was a tall board, higher than the fence itself. An idea occurred to me.

What if it fell onto the fence? I bet I could use it to climb over!

I stood up on my hind legs and scratched at it with my front paws, like I do when I want to go out. The board slid over a bit. On my second try it slid away from the side of the shed and hit the fence with a crash, forming a narrow ramp.

Why didn't I think of this before? I could've gotten out of the yard a long time ago, and I wouldn't have needed to do all that damn digging.

I slowly placed my front paws on the board and put some weight on it. It felt safe. I was able to carefully walk up the ramp, clear the top of the fence and jump down. I sprinted through my neighborhood towards the smell of that third bone. Freedom had never been so easy.

11

"Oh-my-god, the thing is huge!" Laurie said, transfixed by the footage on my iPhone in her hand. I watched it over her shoulder as she sat behind her desk in her office. Laurie Rudd was the managing editor at the Cape Cod News. She'd been around for a while, knew what she was doing and was able to deal with all the shit the company and public threw at her. I both admired her and wondered why she was still there. Norm and I were only occasionally asked to come to the main office, which is nestled between a bank and a pizza joint on Main Street in Hyannis. Every time I went there I appreciated the fact that we were insulated from all the corporate crap by being stationed out in our satellite office.

I spoke to Laurie the previous night about what happened at the fairgrounds. It took a while to convince her that something substantial had panicked the crowd. She told me she wanted to see my footage and to come in early. I typically don't get up for anything at 6 a.m., but what happened last night was exceptional, so I dragged myself out of bed. The large Dunkin' Donuts cappuccino was the only thing keeping me vertical. "I thought you were talking about a little point of light the sky. How did you get such good footage?" she asked.

"I was on the Ferris wheel," I said.

I had a good steady shot of the V-shaped row of lights. In the video you could hear people screaming and, above the crowd noise, Ken could be heard repeating "Holy fucking shit, holy fucking shit!" Laurie sat motionless while the footage continued to play. The sounds of the crowd turned into complete pandemonium when the UFO filled the screen. Ken started up again, his voice clearly heard above the yelling, "Holy fucking shit, holy fucking shit!"

Laurie asked, "Who is that?"

"Someone I met doing my last story on the Truro UFO. We ran into each other at the fair."

People could be seen running for the exits as I panned my camera around, trying to get as much of the action as possible. She said, "Yeah, I saw your piece on the Truro UFO. I assumed the officer was on something; I wasn't going to run it."

"The cop was very distraught," I said. "After last night, I know why."

"What do you think this thing is?"

"I don't know. Military maybe? It was heading in the direction of the base."

The footage ended. Laurie looked up at me and said, "I know they don't fly anything exotic out of there since it's no longer an Air Force base, mostly Coast Guard helicopters."

Gregory Collins, the editor-in-chief, stepped into Laurie's office. "I just spoke with the police chief," he said. "He says he got flooded with calls about a UFO last night and the calls are still coming in this morning. He's concerned about a panic breaking out."

Laurie held up my iPhone. "We have footage of the thing right here. Mel was at the fair last night; she witnessed the whole thing."

She handed my phone to Greg and he glanced at me. I think he vaguely recognized me. Greg has been in the newspaper business his whole life. He was in his late fifties, won a Pulitzer Prize for beat reporting back in 1994 and had been letting his career run on cruise-control since then. I'd hardly spoken with him. He scrutinized the first minute of my footage. "Wow," he said, "I can see why people were upset. Do we know if the military had anything in the air last night?"

"I'm not sure," Laurie said. "I'll get Russell on it when he comes in."

My heart sank for a beat. Laurie was going to give this story to Russell fucking Holt, the brown-nosed prima donna who made me grit my teeth whenever our paths crossed. He's about my age—early thirties—prematurely balding brown hair that he tries to disguise with Hair Illusion. I don't think he's ever had a missing button or a single wrinkle in his shirts. Several of us had to listen to him pontificate about his accomplishments during our last company team-building picnic. At one point they had to call an ambulance for him when a hot hamburger patty slid off the bun and into his lap. Second-degree burns my ass. Apart from a reddened crotch, he was fine and enjoyed every bit of the attention. Russell was the assigned reporter for the Barnstable area, but he wasn't at the fair. He didn't see what I saw.

Greg continued watching my footage. "Wow. It looks like a lot of people saw this thing. When did you shoot this footage?"

"About 9:30," I said.

"Did it make any kind of sound?"

"Nothing."

He shook his head, mesmerized by what he saw, "We're going to be dealing with a shitstorm of questions."

I said, "There was a similar UFO seen over Truro last week.

My brother said this one looked exactly like what he saw."

"You didn't mention that in your report," Laurie said.

"I couldn't use him as a source," I said. "He has privacy issues."

Russell Holt appeared at the door. "We're already getting phone calls about the UFO over the Barnstable County fair," he said. "I've started speaking to some of the witnesses to get a description."

Greg handed my phone to Russell and said, "We have some footage."

Russell seemed mesmerized by the images on the screen. He watched for a few seconds with his mouth agape then asked, "Who shot this?"

"I did," I said.

"If this checks out," Greg said, "it will probably end up on the front page."

Russell said, "I'll get started on it. How many words are we shooting for?"

We? Is he planning to interview a fellow reporter? I was about to say something when Laurie spoke up, "I was thinking of having Melissa do this story; she already did a report on a similar UFO sighting last week. She was a witness herself; she got the footage."

I watched Greg's reaction, then glanced over at Russell. Our eyes met and he frowned at me. He knew this story could be pretty big and that I would be getting the candy he so desperately wanted. I thought, *It's mine, you little shit.*

Greg nodded and said, "OK, that works." He pulled my phone from Russell's hands and gave it back to me. "You'll have no problem signing the release for your footage, right?"

I nodded.

"Put a copy on our servers and tell Bill that we're going to need a still from this," he said as he headed for the door.

"Holy fucking shit! Holy fucking shit!" emanated from my from phone.

Greg paused and said, "And tell Bill to edit that for content."

"Russell, give Melissa your contact info at the base," Laurie said. "We'll obviously be needing a statement from them. Melissa, if you need anything from me, let me know. We'll want this out first thing."

Russell stood there for a moment; I could see him struggling to maintain his professional veneer. Leaving me to follow him, he turned his back on me and headed towards his desk. I had never been to Russell's corner of the newsroom, but I'd have known it was his space in an instant. There wasn't a speck of dust in sight and everything was aligned flush to the edge of the desk. His ten-year plaque gleamed alongside his Youth Merit Award from the Rotary Club and—his special prize that he never ceased bragging about—the Robert Arnold Community Journalism award for his piece on Wind Turbine Syndrome. He even had a framed photo of himself receiving the award from the old fossil who originated the award.

Russell sat down at his computer, launched Outlook and scrolled through a list of names. "The public affairs officer you want to contact is Daniel Patterson," he said.

"Ok," I said. "Can you email his info?"

"It's right there," he replied, pointing at the screen.

Of course, that would be asking too much. I pulled out my phone, leaned closer to the screen (I saw him inch his chair back) and created a new contact entry.

"You did the *Grass is Greener* story, about recreational marijuana sales?" Russell asked.

"Yeah," I replied.

"You buried the lead."

"What are you talking about?"

"We didn't learn of the potential site locations until the very end of the story."

"The story was about the legalization of recreational marijuana," I said, "not where they might be selling it. And the places listed were only proposed sites—nothing definite."

"People want to know if a dispensary will be in their town."

"Tell you what, when I find that out, the first ounce is on me."

"I don't smoke that stuff!" he said, straightening the monitor.

I scanned the office for a place to park myself and make some phone calls, away from Russell's desk. "Maybe you should," I mumbled. There was a break room in the back. As I headed towards it, I said over my shoulder, "Thanks ever so much for your assistance." I hoped he heard the sarcasm in my voice, but I doubted it.

I sat down and called the number Russell gave me. A voice answered, "This is Officer Patterson."

"Hi, this is Melissa Howard from the Cape Cod News. A UFO was sighted over Barnstable County Fair last night and…"

He cut me off, "Yes, I've been flooded with calls about that since last night. Whatever you saw, it was not one of our aircraft. We had nothing in the air that night."

"I saw the thing myself; it was huge."

"I can't comment on what you saw."

"I'm not the only one who saw it or captured it on camera."

"I don't have any comment," Officer Patterson said.

I asked, "Did the tower see anything?"

"They reported nothing unusual—just the standard traffic coming in and out of Barnstable Airport."

"How could they miss it? It was probably the size of a commercial airliner."

"According to the FAA, there was nothing in the air over Barnstable last night that shouldn't have been there. They would've known about anything because pilots have to submit a flight plan and get the necessary clearances."

I asked, "Will anyone be releasing a formal statement?"

"There's nothing to say."

I thanked Daniel for his time and hung up. I could see the military stonewalling some wingnut who got worked up over seeing Venus following his car, but this was something completely different. How do you tell hundreds of people with cameras that they didn't see anything? I found the supply closet and grabbed a pad of yellow legal paper. I had a a lot more phone calls to make.

12

Ken: Interested in a drink? Noodles is with me.

Mel: Noodles? You at the Tiki Harbor having Chinese food?

Ken: No, my bud Noodles. I'm at the Tap City Grille.

Mel: I could use a drink after today. Sure. I'm right down the street from there.

I finished texting and put away my phone. Noodles and I were sitting at a little table next to the bar. Everything was made out of dark wood, giving it a cozy "ye olde" look. Imagine the British Beer Company chain of restaurants, but without the Britannia crap on the walls. I took a sip of my beer and glanced up at the television on the wall. The 5 o'clock news was on. Melissa and I were going to come here after last night's sighting, have a drink and calm down a little, but her brother was desperate to get home. He was pretty worked up after the sighting and was afraid the UFO might come back. I wanted to establish some kind of rapport with Melissa and get to know her better. It's almost like we became war buddies after our UFO sighting. We lived through a traumatic event together and have become kindred spirits of sorts.

I could overhear two jamokes sitting at the bar. For the last twenty minutes they had been giving a dissertation on what they witnessed at the fairgrounds. I think the taller one with the Red Sox baseball cap was called Lenny and his pal was Ralph. He shouted, "It was fuckin' unbelievable! The fuckin' thing flew right ovah us!"

A woman sitting at the bar asked, "How large was it?"

His friend Ralph said, "You could fit the thing inside Fenway Pahk!"

Lenny threw his arms out wide and said, "No, no, biggah!"

Ralph lifted his shot glass and earnestly said, "I thought they were gonna start shootin' death rays at us," then knocked back another drink.

Lenny nodded vigorously. "Yeah, like in War of the Worlds."

"Yah, we couldn't fuckin' believe it," Ralph said. "First we saw a Loch Ness monstah on the beach, now aliens!"

Lenny leaned forward. "We had a reportah speakin' to us and everything."

Ralph said, "We ain't seen nothin' like this in Reveah."

"Yah!" Lenny said with a big smile, "Cape Cod is wicked pissah!"

I looked at Noodles and he smiled back. The pair were a riot. I asked him, "So what did you see of the UFO?"

"I didn't see it fly directly overhead because I was inside the building," Noodles said. "I heard all the noise outside and saw it leaving the fairground. Your video of it was pretty amazing."

"I set up a YouTube channel called capecodufo and uploaded it there," I said. "I got over 9,000 views since last night. I grabbed the same domain name and set up a Twitter account. Melissa's footage came out a little better though."

"Was she the reporter chick you met?"

"Yup, she's coming by right now."

Noodles sipped his beer then asked, "Is she cute?"

"Definitely."

Noodles went back to watching the news. My phone rang. It was Zeke from the Cape Cod UFO Group. I answered "Hey."

"I saw your footage on YouTube," Zeke said, "Holy fucking shit is right!"

"How did you find it?" I asked.

"How can you not find it? It's going viral."

"I just uploaded it last night. I was going to send you the link."

"What was it like watching it fly overhead?" he asked.

"Scary as hell," I said. "I was probably the closest person to it. I was riding the Ferris wheel when it came over."

"I'll bet you it was the same UFO that flew over Phoenix."

I had to correct him. "That one had a single row of lights, this one had two rows of lights, all the way around it."

"Yeah," he said excitedly, "but they were both V-shaped and huge! It's gotta be from the same extraterrestrials."

"Who said anything about extraterrestrials?" I was still trying to be the objective one about this. It certainly looked like a full blown UFO had flown directly over me, but I couldn't rule out some secret military aircraft. What was it doing over Cape Cod? I didn't know. I couldn't let myself automatically jump to aliens, even though my mind was certainly going in that direction.

Zeke sounded all torqued up, "People are going nuts over this thing. You need to go on the air with me."

"C'mon Zeke," I said, "nobody listens to your show. I proved it."

"No no no," he said. "We're doing a guest appearance on WCOD. It's 50,000 freakin' watts - everyone on the Cape will be listening to it!"

Well how do you like that? I thought. Zeke pulled some connections somewhere and managed to get himself planted in front of a real, live audience. I wanted to discuss what I saw with other people—not just with him and his flunky sidekick. "Alright, I'm in," I said.

"Show up at the station at 5 o'clock tomorrow."

"Right."

"Listen," Zeke said. "I gotta go. Just be there, OK?"

I said "OK", then hung up. WCOD is one of the bigger stations on the Cape. I'm impressed that Zeke managed to get himself attached to a legitimate place like that, but what happened last night wasn't something typical.

I spotted Melissa at the door and waved her over to us.

"Christ, it's been insane today," she said. "I spoke to every hysterical person in town, as well as the military and every police station from here to the bridge. I need a drink."

I motioned to Noodles with my glass and said, "Mel, this is my friend Noodles."

They shook hands. Noodles said, "Mel?"

She said, "As in Melissa. Noodles?"

Noodles replied "As in skinny as…"

Melissa said, "Nice to meet you," then sat down. She spun around towards the bar and studied the beer list. "What do they have on tap?"

"Everything," I said.

"What are you guys having?"

"Noodles and I ordered the Yeti Imperial Stout, just because we liked the name."

"Screw it," she said. "I'm going with a Kentucky Bourbon Ale at 8 percent ABV. You guys want anything?"

We both shook our heads. She got up and pushed her way to the bar.

Noodles looked at me with a raised eye brow and smiled.

"Told ya she was cute," I said.

Melissa came back after a couple minutes and sat down with her beer. She took a sip and said, "You wouldn't believe what I'm finding out. We've already had one person in Mashpee claim they were abducted. Another guy who worked at the fair claimed one of his cows got a big gash from the UFO."

"How the hell did it have time to do a cattle mutilation?" I said. "It just casually flew over."

"I'd guess his cow had some sort of injury and he wanted someone or something to blame," she said.

I asked her, "Did you talk to the anyone at Otis?"

"They completely deny that anything was flying over Barnstable County."

"It was flying north," I said. "It should've gone right over the airfield."

"Nothing." Melissa took another sip of her beer. "The weird part is nobody else saw it in the surrounding towns. No one saw it fly over Route 6. None of the cops in Sandwich, Barnstable or Bourne reported seeing anything unusual."

"That's weird," I said. "Everyone at the fair definitely saw it."

Noodles said, "It could've just gone straight up at some point."

"I suppose," she said. "But if it wanted to be seen, it definitely chose the right spot."

On the TV above the bar a graphic of a V-shaped UFO appeared and the news anchor said, "Panic has been spreading over Cape Cod after a large unidentified flying object flew over the Barnstable County fair last night. Our reporter Jill Steinman has the story."

Jill was standing at the entrance of the Barnstable County fairgrounds. Behind her, a crowd of people were waiting in line to get in. She spoke to the camera, "Hysteria has been sweeping Cape Cod after a large V-shaped UFO allegedly flew over the Barnstable County fair last night, frightening the attendees."

They showed a shot of a woman standing in front of a kiddie ride, holding a stuffed animal in her arms. She said, "It was very upsetting. I couldn't believe what we were seeing."

We next saw a shot of a guy standing in front of a ring toss game. He said, "I didn't know what I was watching. It looked like it approached us very closely."

After that, Ralph and Lenny—the same two guys at the bar—were standing in the middle of the midway, a crowd of people were flowing past them. Ralph pointed to the sky behind him and said, "Yah, it flew in from ovah theah and it went right ovah ah heads."

Lenny said, "I couldn't friggin' believe it! The thing was friggin' HUGE!"

Ralph said, "Yah, it was like Close Encountahs!"

The bar area erupted in cheers. Everyone raised their glasses in a toast to Ralph and Lenny as they shouted in unison, "FOX NEWS!" and then pumped their fists into the air.

The next scene was of a reporter standing somewhere on Main Street in Hyannis. The title below him was "Russell Holt, Cape Cod Times" He said, "We have been getting reports of sightings from people all day. In addition to the stories in the paper, people can get the latest updates on our website where we have actual footage of the sighting. What your viewers might not know is that there was another report earlier this week of a similar UFO sighting over Truro."

The interviewer said off-camera, "What you are going to watch may be upsetting to some viewers." Melissa's footage came on the screen, clearly showing the UFO from our spot on the Ferris wheel. I could hear my voice shouting the whole time. Every one of my "fucks" were censored with a loud beep. Russell's face reappeared onscreen as the interviewer asked him another question.

Melissa practically spit out her beer and yelled towards the screen, "That shithead! He didn't bother telling me they wanted an interview?"

"Who?" I said.

Melissa pointed at the screen, "That rat-faced reporter. I was on the road the whole damn day, doing my job. They wanted to use my footage and needed a statement. He could've called me, the little shit!"

A shot of a man in an Air Force uniform standing in front of a jet appeared next. His title read, Lt. Colonel Daniel Patterson, DPA Officer, 102nd Intelligence Wing." He said, "There were no military vehicles in the air at that vicinity last night. We can't comment on what people thought they saw."

The reporter asked him off camera, "Was the object seen on radar?"

Patterson kept a stone-face and said, "Nothing was recorded for that area. There were no scheduled flights coming in or out of the joint base at that time."

"Was it a UFO?"

Office Patterson shook his head, "We had nothing in the air."

"Have you seen the footage of this thing?"

Officer Patterson started to walk away from the camera, "I can't comment on that. Thank you."

The reporter shouted, "What do you think it was?"

Officer Patterson shook his head as he walked away and repeated, "Thank you."

The county commissioner appeared next. He was standing in front of an office building with a row of people behind him. His title read, "Joseph Spooner, Barnstable County Commissioner". He had a smirk on his face the whole time he was speaking. "We've been collecting reports from the people who said they saw the aircraft. The situation is being looked into. There's nothing to worry about."

The reporter asked, "Many people have gotten upset over what they saw. Are you worried that a panic might break out?"

The Commissioner laughed and crossed his arms. "There's

nothing to panic about. It was just a couple of lights up in the sky. That's all, people."

Another reporter asked, "What about reports of people abducted?"

The commissioner rolled his eyes. "We don't have any confirmation that such a thing happened. As far as we know, no one was harmed during this…event." He faced away from the camera and addressed the crowd, "Police in all surrounding towns have been alerted. If there are any further developments, we'll notify the public."

The anchor at the desk came back on. Beside him a stock photo of a crop circle in a wheat field appeared. He said, "In what may be a related story, crop circles were recently discovered in a field of reeds at Namskaket Marsh in Brewster. This seems to have coincided with the wave of UFO reports that have appeared over Cape Cod. The owner of nearby Hanson Farms, Michael Hanson, made the discovery.

A shot of Michael Hanson standing in front of a greenhouse appeared. The reporter asked him off-camera, "When did this happen?"

"This was about two weeks ago," Michael said, pointing behind him. "It was near closing time when I saw lights moving over the field back there. I didn't know what to make of it. Then I heard these weird jabbering sounds. Like some kind of strange creatures were talking amongst themselves. The lights began to move much more quickly, then the sounds turned these awful high pitched screams. It scared the bejesus out of me. That's when I went back inside."

The reporter said, "What did you find the next day?"

" That's when I found all these weird extraterrestrial designs," he said. "I don't know what to make of them."

They showed aerial footage of our work. You could clearly see the half-finished alien head Noodles and I had started, intersected by an intricate spiral pattern.

God, that looks like crap.

After all that planning and effort, that whole adventure had turned into a complete abortion. I sank down in my chair and moaned.

Melissa looked at me and said, "What?"

Noodles sat there with a-shit eating grin on his face.

I didn't have the heart to tell Melissa that Noodles and I had traipsed through a marsh just to pull a prank on everyone. Who knows what she would have thought of us. I was trying to make points with her and come across as somebody rational. I looked down at the empty glass in front of me and said, "This is all too much; I need another beer."

13

"So, let's see where we left off last time." Dr. Winston turned to her computer and read out loud: "Your brother seemed more reclusive than before; you were feeling good about your job and… there's been no change in your meds." She looked at me.

"Sounds about right," I replied.

She swiveled her chair around to face me. "So how've you been?"

"Pretty good, on the whole. Work's been a bit busier than usual, but that's fine—not too much to handle."

"That's good. What's made it busier than usual?"

"Well, apparently aliens are interested in vacationing on the Cape."

She raised an eyebrow.

I smiled.

In order to see a shrink, who prescribed my meds, I was obligated to see a therapist. I had to drive to her office in West

Yarmouth about once a month. It was a pain in the ass at times, but it had to be done. I'd been her client for almost five years and she knew all about my family history of anxiety, depression and general craziness. The last real "crisis" I'd had happened five years ago when I lost my job at the bookstore. (Not my fault, that time; they went out of business—unsurprisingly.) We both knew that if I stayed on my meds and didn't experience too much stress, my life would proceed more or less smoothly (as much as one could expect, that is).

Dr. Winston said, "The county fair UFO? I saw it on the news."

"I was there," I said.

"You saw it?"

I nodded. "If you watched the video—that was my footage."

"That was remarkable."

"People were freaking out, running around, screaming—it was crazy. Brian came with me, but when the excitement happened I was trapped on the Ferris wheel."

Her eyebrow went up.

"I was fine, but I had no idea where Brian was. He went off to get fried dough while Ken and I went on the Ferris wheel."

"Who's Ken?"

"A guy I met at the paper; he's doing some kind of research on UFO sightings. Anyway, he was helping me look for Brian, who wasn't answering his phone. Eventually we found him, cowering in a port-a-potty. He was a mess—convinced the UFO had followed him from Truro until I calmed him down. If he starts talking about being abducted, it might be time for an intervention."

She sat up and leaned forward slightly. "If that happens, call 911. Don't try to deal with it yourself."

"I really don't think it would come to that—as long as he stays away from weed. That just makes his paranoia worse." I paused, shaking my head. "Abductions—what the hell is going on with people who believe that?"

"Well, one theory is that UFOs, or—more specifically—being forcibly taken into one, is a kind of protective metaphor for a traumatic event. Something happened to the person—the reality of which they can't face. They then create the more acceptable—an odd term I admit—reality of alien abduction. Some theorize it's a combination of sleep paralysis and suggestibility."

"Or maybe they just don't get over the bridge often enough."

"Well..." she said, trying not to smile.

I've always thought that a large portion of year-round Cape Codders are certifiable. What sane person would want to live here year round? I guess it takes one to know one.

"Does any of it bother you?" she asked.

"Only if the aliens show up on my doorstep unannounced. You know how I am." I don't like surprises, especially if they take the form of uninvited visitors, no matter who it is.

I finished up my session with Dr. Winston, set up my next appointment with the receptionist and headed over to the Cape Cod Times main office. I left my favorite coffee mug there (I blame Russell) and wanted to grab it while I was still in the area.

With less than a mile to go, I was sitting in traffic on Main Street, a few blocks from my destination. Main Street is lined with eateries and boutique shops that attract tourists like seagulls to fish guts. I found myself stopped in front of The Pincushion and my hand involuntarily went to my nose. Years ago, a friend and I decided—probably under the influence of illicit substances—to get pierced. She wanted her navel pierced and I wanted another hole in my nose. Her piercing got horribly infected and she ended up in the ER, and her family blamed the whole thing on me, the "bad influence".

A couple shops down I saw a woman in a TOS Star Trek uniform holding a hand-painted sign with a drawing of a V-shaped UFO. She had written below it, "BEAM ME UP". I couldn't tell if she was being ironic. And why the original series? Did ET decide to hit the galactic highway before The Next Generation debuted? I'd hate to think their vision of humanity was limited to brawling redshirts and scantily-clad females.

It's bad enough we get invaded by off-Cape "aliens" every summer, but now, apparently—according to some—we had to deal with the real thing. If the souvenir trade on Rt. 28 was paying attention, they'd be stupid to not take advantage of the situation. I could picture it: polyresin ETs in flip-flops and sunglasses, standing on a clamshell, shot glasses engraved with bug-eyed alien heads. . . They could shelve them next to all the great white shark tchotchkes.

I finally found a parking spot and ran inside the office. I found Laurie Rudd speaking to Russell Holt at his desk. When she saw me she said, "Your UFO footage crashed our server."

"We should've put it on YouTube," Russell said.

"I don't know why Bill didn't do that in the first place," Laurie said. Turning back to Russell, she said, "See if you can talk to the Falmouth PD or someone from the fair to find out exactly what's going on." To me she said, "Apparently there's some Wampanoag camping out at the fairgrounds, refusing to leave—something about a sky god or—"

Russell cleared his throat, "They're probably referring to the Thunderbird, the mythological—"

I cut him off. "When were UFOs a part of their culture?"

"I don't know," Laurie said. She looked at a notepad in her hand. "There were reports of a drum circle and someone burning 'smudge sticks'." She looked at Russell. "The fair organizers have been having a hell of a time getting their equipment out of there. See what you can find out"

Russell did his best Jimmy Olsen impression. "Will do, boss!" *Brown-nosed twonk.*

As Laurie was leaving, she turned to Russell and said, "Oh

yeah, before you work on any stringer offers, you'll focus on the tasks at hand, correct?"

"Of course!" he said, standing up. "My job here always comes first!"

"What stringer offers?" I blurted out before I could stop myself.

"The story has gone national. The Seattle Times asked me to write a story for them."

"Why the hell would Seattle care about some UFO sighting on Cape Cod?"

He arranged his face in what he thought was an offended look. "Some people like to be well-informed."

"The Boston news report—why did you do that?"

"Do what?" he asked.

"You knew I was on the road doing interviews. You could've called me."

He lifted his chin. "I'm the designated reporter for that area."

"Yeah, but I'm the one who actually saw the thing. I shot all that footage."

"It's now our footage; you signed the release."

"You know what I mean. You just can't resist any opportunity to get yourself on camera."

"I was just doing my job; you weren't available."

I had to leave before I slapped his stupid face. I found my mug in the break room and left. My next stop was Brian's house.

He had called earlier and asked if I could bring him some pan-fried dumplings and chicken fingers. Not exactly health food, but I figured anything was an improvement on the pizza he normally ate.

When I arrived, I dumped the take-out bag onto his kitchen table. There were about a dozen empty pizza boxes stacked up on top of his stove. I picked up the top one; it was empty. "How old are these?"

"Um, a couple of weeks," Brian said.

"You've been eating the same pizza for two weeks? No wonder you wanted something different."

Brian patted his pants pockets, looking for something, "Can you get me some groceries if I give you twenty dollars?"

"I can't; I'm on the way back to the office. Why don't you hop on your bike and go to the market?"

"I haven't left the house since we got back from the fair," he said.

"Why?"

He ignored me and ripped open the bag of food. He opened a container of dumplings, impaled one on a fork, took one bite, then sat down and began chewing. I could tell he was avoiding eye contact with me. I pressed him again, "Brian, why haven't you left the house this week?"

He stared at the half-eaten dumpling on his fork. "The UFO has been following me."

Uh-oh, I thought. *This will be hard to dismiss.* He was the only guy on the Cape who had seen the UFO twice. What was the old Joseph Heller quote? 'Just because you're paranoid doesn't mean they aren't after you.' From my brother's point of view it did look like they were following him. I tried to give him some reassurance. "Listen…no one is following you," I said. "Especially aliens."

"I saw the reports. People are being abducted."

I tried to calm the turmoil that was going on in my brother's head. "Brian," I heard myself say in our mother's voice, "no one is being abducted." He rocked back and forth a little as he continued to eat. "Look," I said, "It could've been a military aircraft we saw. Who says it has to been aliens?"

Brain shook his head. "I haven't seen any military aircraft like that."

Well, he had me there; I didn't have an answer for him. On the other hand, I didn't want to end up his caretaker and enabler.

I had plenty of things to do with my life besides bring him food and talk him down from a ledge every week. I stuffed a dumping into my mouth, made sure everything else was all right and headed back to the Orleans office.

I'd been working mostly at the Hyannis office this past week, covering the mania over the UFO story. It felt good to be back at our old squeaky-floored office. As I sat down at my desk, Norm appeared, holding something behind his back. "Nice to have you around."

"When corporate calls..."

He smiled. "Welcome back to the salt mine."

"I could use the rest," I said.

"I made you something." He showed me what he was hiding, a triangular tin foil hat.

"Ha ha, very funny, Norm."

"Put it on," he said.

I stuck it on my head and looked up at him. He laughed. "Great; thanks." I said. "My problem is I have too many thoughts trying to get *out* of my skull. My brother could use one though." I left it on my head as I booted up my computer.

Norm asked, "So what do you think you saw?"

"Beats me."

"Everyone has been talking about it this week," he said.

"I was directly under it and it seems I'm the only one not getting worked up."

"You don't think they're aliens?"

I looked at him. "I'm trying to remain objective about this."

"What if they look like the ones from War of the Worlds?"

"What?" I said, "The first movie or the Spielberg version?"

"The one with Tom Cruise."

"I liked the original better. That alien was so strange their first reaction was to hit it with a board. It had an RGB color pallet for eyes. *That* was an alien."

Norm smiled. "I'm hoping they'll be more like Men In Black."

Mildred approached Norm and handed him a sheet of paper. "Here are the names of the school committee members you wanted." She spotted the tin foil hat on my head and frowned. "We shouldn't be making fun of people with mental illness."

How did I know she was going to say that? I was determined to wear that stupid hat for the rest of the day.

She continued to frown at me.

Norm and I exchanged glances. "Well," he said with a grin, "I've got to go back to work." He left me there with her.

Mildred admonished me, "Some people are so ill they can't tell what's real and what isn't."

I'd had enough of her PC do-gooder crap. "I don't need anyone to lecture me about mental illness. Between my own head and the rest of family, we've got pretty much every diagnosis covered. And I've got the little brown bottles to prove it."

Mildred stared at me with her mouth open. Without a word, she turned and went back to her desk.

I launched Outlook on my PC and scanned the headers of my recent emails. Did I need any Viagra? Deleted. Selectmen in Orleans were proposing revisions to the July 4th parade and fireworks. I'd look at that later. There was something from David Brown of Carlisle Communications Inc, the big media conglomerate. I opened it.

David Brown
Editor-in-chief, Weekly World Gazette
Carlisle Communications, Inc
301 Elucidation Ave, Boca Raton, FL 33431

Hello Melissa,

I am David Brown, the editor-in-chief of the Weekly World Gazette. Perhaps you already know of us? We publish a weekly paper that covers sensational stories and entertaining facts. I've read some of

your pieces online and I like your style. We would like to commission you to write a report about the recent UFO sightings over
Cape Cod. I would love to speak to you about the requirements as
well as your fee. Please contact me via the phone number in the
footer below.

Of course I knew them; you couldn't miss the paper in the su-
permarket checkout line. Their headlines screamed of alien babies
and Bigfoot sightings. It was one of the most out-there tabloids
on the market. I had to smile when I read "sensational stories and
entertaining facts". Their "facts" were certainly entertaining. One
of their favorite obsessions was to feature "Mantis Man," an alien/
insect hybrid that tormented people while they slept. He was usually associated with UFO sightings. The image they used was a bad
Photoshop job of a praying mantis head stuck on a human body.
Normally I would never call the Gazette, but I was curious about
the fee. I was getting slightly behind in my car payments so I was
at least interested in what they offered. I had already written the
UFO story once, so how hard could it be? I dialed the number.

The phone rang for a bit before someone picked up and said
curtly, "David Brown."

"Hi, this is Melissa Howard from the Cape Cod News. You
sent me an email about a possible story commission?"

David's voice perked up. "Hello Melissa! I was hoping you
would call. How are you doing?"

Wonderful, I thought. *He wants to do small talk.* I'd throw some
snark at him right off the bat and see how he reacted. I pretended
to be excited and said, "I'm doing great! Did you guys ever find
Mantis Man?"

"Oh—Mantis Man!" David laughed. "He's our most popular
story! We're always on the lookout for him."

Does this guy believe his own bullshit?

David continued, "I've been reading some very interesting
reports about what's been happening on Cape Cod. We would like

to feature a story on the recent UFO sightings. Would you be up for it?"

"You mentioned a fee?"

"Of course. We pay $1,200 for 1200 words. Could you supply some photos?"

Damn, a dollar a word isn't too shabby. I could certainly use the money. David filled me in on what he was looking for: make it punchy, make it exciting, feel free to speculate on what's been happening and keep the alien aspect in the foreground. So much for my journalism ethics.

I asked him if he felt comfortable hiring someone who was actually wearing a tin-foil hat. He laughed and said they do it all the time. I don't think he got the joke. After I agreed to do it, he urged me to have it done by this weekend so he could hit his publishing deadline. After I hung up, I felt like I needed to take a shower. *Screw it; it's just money,* I thought. I tried to convince myself that none of this mattered and nobody cared what I wrote. There was only one problem: I had to admit my sins right away or I would never be able to live this down.

I got up to tell Norm.

14

The Agway commercial ended and Zeke's outer space theremin music started up again. I sank in my chair, knowing that they were going to use his stupid music as the show's bumper. I thought, *Christ this is gonna be a long night.* Noodles had a pair of headphones on and was sitting next to me in front of his own microphone. Zeke and his flunky Eddie were across from us on the other side of the studio table. Between us sat our host, Pistol Pete, WCOD's afternoon drive-time disc jokey. This place was a major change from Zeke's garage: professional microphones, a giant mixing board, triangular foam sound insulation on every wall.

We had already gone through the formalities of being introduced in our first segment before the break. Zeke had a look of intense concentration on his face, like his life had been leading up to this moment. I'm sure he was determined to show the world that he wasn't a crackpot after all, that his UFO conspiracies were finally starting to pan out. Eddie sucked on the straw in his

McDonald's cup. I could tell he already had a buzz rolling, I had seen him dump two nips of Southern Comfort into it out in the lobby. Noodles had a big grin on his face; he was just happy to be included. The music faded away as Pistol Pete leaned into his microphone and said, "Hey everyone, if you just joined us, I'm hosting some of Cape Cod's top UFO experts and hopefully we can get to the bottom of what's been going on recently."

Zeke said, "Hey Pete, thanks for having us on your show!"

Pistol Pete made a pair of guns out of his hands and pointed them at Zeke. "That's why we have the 'Zeker' of truth here!" Zeke and Eddie laughed, while I almost tore an optic nerve rolling my eyes. He turned to me and Noodles and said, "So both of you guys saw it?"

"Right," I said. "I was on the Ferris wheel the whole time, capturing it on my iPhone."

Noodles said, "I was working in the resource center. I caught it just after it went over."

"Holy effing ess, huh Ken?" Pete said with a grin.

I sighed and said, "I've calmed down since then. But, yeah, you would've said that if you were as close to a UFO as I was."

"Well holy effing ess is right, Ken. That was some incredible footage you shot."

Zeke said, "The UFO was a lot like the Phoenix lights from March 13, 1997."

"Yeah, that was a pretty awesome sighting," Eddie said next to him.

I said, "I agree, but let me point out there were two incidents on that day. A V-shaped object that flew from Nevada to Arizona, and a row of flares dropped from an A-10 Warthog that blinked out when they fell behind some mountains in the Phoenix area."

Zeke dismissed me with a wave of his hand and said, "That was never confirmed."

"Oh come on," I said, "when you matched up footage to

daytime everything lined up perfect. Look, the point is that a V-shaped object was seen by hundreds of people."

There have been other triangle-shaped UFOs," Zeke said. "The Highland Illinois UFO from January 5th, 2000 comes to mind. I think these could be the same craft."

I said, "The difference is our UFO had twenty lights, two rows of lights of ten along its outer edges. The others only had four or five in the middle of the craft."

Noodle said, "There were definitely more than five lights on what I saw."

"So where do you think they came from?" asked Pistol Pete.

"We don't know," I said. "But let me put it in perspective. Alpha Centauri is the closest star system with its three stars. Proxima Centauri is 4.2 light years away. We can only conceive of sending a spacecraft there."

"Project long shot," Zeke interjected. "A one hundred year trip going at 4.5% the speed of light."

"Forget about sending a frozen person," I said. "We just don't know how to do that."

Zeke raised his index finger confidently and said, "Yet."

"Fine. Yet," I said. "We don't even have an A.I. guidance system that could park a space craft into orbit once it got there."

Eddie said, "That's why we need HAL."

"The computer from the movie 2001?" Pistol Pete asked.

"Right," I said. "Point is, it's not likely they came from Alpha Centuri. Let's just say they came from a star that's only 10,000 light years away. That's crazy advanced. Let me throw this at ya - let's say they came from another galaxy. We're talking more than two million light years away. At that point your brain just melts trying to comprehend how to get there." I gave them a dramatic pause, glanced at everyone around the table then said, "But they did it."

Zeke said, "When you have civilizations that much older than ours, it makes sense that they can do these things."

"Right," I said. "But most people have a hard time imagining someone smarter than they are. Certainly Hollywood doesn't want its aliens winning in the end, that's a lousy story. We don't give them enough credit for being that smart."

Pistol Pete said, "Like what?"

"Crashed saucers," I said. "First off, they have to avoid hitting anything—even a tiny particle—between their planet and ours. Take a guess what happens if you're traveling at the speed of light and a tiny particle slams into your space craft. You'd be toast. So they managed to avoid everything from there to here…and yet they crashed into a planet? C'mon…give 'em some credit."

"But things fail all the time," Zeke said.

Zeke set himself up for my well rehearsed spiel. In a slightly condescending tone, I said, "The industrial age happened just over two hundred years ago. We only learned how to fly little over one hundred years ago. Of course *our* stuff breaks; we're still working on it. Where do you think we'll be after ten thousand years of guys in lab coats working on these problems? The extraterrestrials have already done it."

Noodles said, "Will all those extraterrestrials in lab coats ever cure adult acne?"

I tried to say something profound and he had to bust my balls. "No Noodles," I said as I shook my head. "They'll never do that."

Pistol Pete asked, "So how do you think they got here?"

"They most likely traveled through wormholes," Zeke said.

"OK fine", I snapped. "Let's say they can do that. They have the energy at their disposal to bend space. Forget about blasting energy out of a rocket and pushing yourself through space—they can *bend it*."

As if he was trying to blow our minds, Zeke slowly said, "Or they might be coming from another dimension."

"Where are you getting this information from Zeke?" I fired

back at him. "Transmissions from your-anus? That's all speculation."

"OK, so how do you think they found us?" Pistol Pete said.

"Obviously we're an interesting planet," I said. "Anyone who'd
seen our planet, going back millions of year, would've noticed that
we're covered in water and a nitrogen rich atmosphere. It's obvious
something is going on here. Everyone always brings up the radio
and tv transmissions. Who cares if we've been sending out radio
transmissions since the 1930s? I wouldn't be surprised if somebody
already came by and went 'Yup, lizards. The place is filled with
giant lizards. We need to come back later.'"

"They've been coming here since we started setting off nuclear devices," Zeke said. "They seemed very concerned about what
we're doing."

"Really Zeke?" I said. "They're surprised that we can finally
mimic the sun?"

"We now have the ability to destroy our entire planet," Zeke
said. "They don't want that sort of thing upsetting the balance of
the universe."

"How come they're not doing anything about supernovas?" I
said. "Worlds destroy themselves all the time."

Pistol Pete asked, "So what do you think they want?"

Zeke announced. "Our water."

"Oh c'mon Zeke!" I shouted. "There's water everywhere in
the universe. You're saying they can bend space, but haven't figure
out how to combine a hydrogen and oxygen atom together? We
know for a fact that Enceladus has water jets shooting out from
its surface. It's probably a frozen water world. They flew right past
it." I glared at Zeke for a moment. He wasn't looking at me, but I
doubted there was anything going through his mind at that point.
I was sure he thought he had everything figured out.

Noodles said with a grin, "I think they're coming to Cape Cod
for the clams."

"Wow," said Pistol Pete. "That's some pretty heavy stuff. Let's take some callers. This is Barbara from Yarmouthport."

A distraught female voice came through our headphones. "I'm really frightened about what's been happening recently. All this talk about aliens. My kids have been coming home from school extremely upset."

Pistol Pete said, "What does you think? Should anyone be concerned over this UFO sighting?"

"Hold on," I said, "nobody has seen any aliens at the Cape Cod Mall yet. We've just been talking about the possibility of extraterrestrial life out there."

"It's rare that anyone gets injured during a UFO encounter," Zeke said. "I don't think you have anything to worry about."

I thought, *Rare? What injuries?* I was sure he was thinking about those wacky abduction reports. I wasn't going to go there, I was still tuckered out from my previous rant.

"Thanks Barbara," Pistol Pete said. "Next we have Aaron from Falmouth. Go ahead Aaron."

There was a pause on the line and then some static. After a moment a menacing voice spoke slowly, "These beings are here because we've poisoned our environment and continue to destroy our mother Earth. They won't allow us to waste our prized resources."

I thought, *Hoo boy, here comes another "They're here because they care" adherent.* They really should've showed up at the turn of the century if they wanted to do the most good—like finishing us off. Maybe H.G. Wells actually knew something we didn't. I wasn't going to let Zeke run with this one.

"We should be taking better care of our environment," he said. "Or we really will need a higher intelligence to fix things."

Eddie said, "We need to fix things—or else…"

The caller continued, "They've been watching us wreck our ozone layer for decades."

Pistol Pete said, "So you think they are from a galactic Greenpeace?"

Zeke nodded, "That's not that far-fetched."

The caller continued in his monotone voice, "They told me, If we can't take care of our planet, they'll be taking it away from us."

Zeke asked, "How did they contact you?"

"They've been in contact with me telepathically for years," the caller said in his weird, flat voice. "Just last week they told me about a plastic garbage patch forming out in Cape Cod Bay."

"Like the one out in the middle of the Pacific ocean?" Eddie asked.

"Yes," the caller said. "This one is endangering our sea turtle population."

Zeke frowned and looked at Pistol Pete. Even Zeke couldn't run with this guy. I loved listening to these types of wingnuts improvise. Noodles cracked a smile and said, "I knew I should've picked up my water bottle when I was at Sandy Neck beach."

"They have established an underwater base in Buzzards Bay," the caller said.

"OK caller, thanks for that insight," Pistol Pete said as he hung up on him. "Next we have Tony from Osterville."

"Yeah, hi Pete," the caller said. "This whole UFO thing has given me the willies. I heard something about some guy getting abducted while he was sleeping."

"OK, hold on," I said. "Nobody is getting abducted. What you're talking about is night terrors, sleep paralysis. Google it. People are imagining more dumb aliens. First off, it's a hell of a coincidence that they breath the same ratio of nitrogen to oxygen that we do. So we can imagine Dr. McCoy diagnosing someone by waving a gadget over them but our aliens have to prod us with needles to see what's going on? It's just lack of imagination."

"Thousands of people have recalled their encounters through hypnosis," Zeke said. "It's a well known fact."

"Right," I said. "The aliens did something to them so they

wouldn't remember their encounter?"

Zeke nodded. "Yes."

"And we out-smarted the aliens through hypnosis," I said, getting slightly worked up. "They got the Hitler broadcasts, but never saw footage of Uri Gellar or the Amazing Randy? Again, these are some pretty dim extraterrestrials."

"Does that make you feel any better, caller?" Pistol Pete asked. We had to wait a second for a reply. "No," he said softly.

"They're not here to harm us. They're only observing," Zeke said confidently.

I shook my head. *Like that really helps, Zeke. Everyone can sleep better at night knowing they're only being watched.*

Pistol Pete said, "OK, next up is Robert from Mashpee. Go ahead Robert."

"Yeah, I saw the UFO too," the caller said.

"Oh really?" I asked. "Were you at the Barnstable Country Fair?"

"No, I was driving south on route 130 that night when it crossed over the road in front of me by Mashpee Pond. I banged a left at Cotuit Road and started following it."

Zeke perked up in his chair. "Oh really? Was it making any sound? How close do you think you were to it?"

The caller said, "I saw it out my driver's window. It looked like it was only about a hundred yards up in the air."

"How far did you follow it?" Zeke asked.

"Well," the caller said, then paused, "I followed it about a quarter of a mile, then it started to slow down until it was hovering over a cranberry bog. Then it landed."

I thought, *Wait a minute. I'm familiar with Mashpee Pond and Cotuit Road. It's all forest out there. The cranberry bog he's talking about is just an acre. The thing I saw was huge.*

Zeke was torqued up. "IT LANDED?" he cried. "Do you remember exactly where? We'd love to get some soil samples immediately."

"Yeah, and three aliens in dark space suits floated out in my direction. That's when my car died."

Eddie said, "That sounds a lot like the Pascagoula abduction."

The caller continued, "It looked like they were searching for something on the ground."

Zeke said, "There have been many reports of extraterrestrials leaving their vehicles to take soil samples."

"They were holding these triangular-shaped clear receptacles," the caller said.

Zeke leaned into his microphone, "Can you describe what they were holding in more detail?"

"Yeah, the things had long stems on them, something like a martini glass."

Zeke was transfixed. "What were they doing?"

"Well," the caller said, "they all scooped up some cranberries. Then one of them pulled out a bottle of Stoli 100. It looked like they were making Cosmos." The guy started snickering. "I think they were pretty shit-faced, because one of them spotted me and pulled down his space suit and revealed his alien ass cheeks to me." Laughing hysterically, the caller hung up.

Pistol Pete said sarcastically, "OK caller. Thanks."

Zeke frowned and said, "Listen, we've already got direct evidence that they landed. They recently formed crop circles at Namskaket Marsh."

"Yeah," Pistol Pete said. "I heard about those, Zeke. What's going on there?"

"There are hundreds of crop circles made every year," Zeke said. "Many of them have witnesses who were there at the time of their formation. That farmer saw what happened that night."

Uh oh, I thought. *My stupid prank has gotten way out of hand.* My point was to show how easy it is to fake them and that the whole crop circle thing is complete bullshit. But my camera was still sitting in the middle of the marsh. How was I supposed to prove that Noodles and I did it and that these guys were complete idiots? I said, "Oh come on, those can be faked. You take a board with a rope and start stomping. There's a million YouTube videos of people doing it."

Eddie said, "These designs were too intricate to fake."

I looked at Noodles, who shrugged and smiled.

Zeke said, "I went down there and investigated it myself. I found Bigfoot tracks; I made plaster casts of them. They were all over the place."

I thought, *Oh my God, this is getting worse by the minute. I told Noodles not to wear those stupid things.*

Zeke announced, "I have always maintained there is a connection to Bigfoot and UFOs."

I shouted, "OH COME ON!" Noodles starting laughing. I kicked him under the table.

"Ken, I have the plaster casts," Zeke said that stupid patronizing tone of his. "The farmer saw the whole thing."

I looked at Noodles. He practically had tears in his eyes trying to suppress a laugh. He was of no help.

Pistol Pete looked at me and asked, "Well Mr. Skeptic, what do you have for a snappy answer now?"

I was at a loss for words for once. I couldn't admit the truth. I just had to sit there and take it.

Fuck me.

15

There's nothing like an outbreak of hysteria to motivate the powers that be into action. The Barnstable Town Commissioner and the Assembly of Delegates held a press conference at the Superior Court Building to ease the public's mind over the whole UFO flap. It was my job to report on the day's events. The meeting was originally scheduled to be held in the Commissioner's conference room. The whole place was asses-to-elbows an hour before it was due to start; they had to relocate everyone outside to an impromptu podium between the granite columns on the front steps of the courthouse. The press conference was scheduled to begin with Roy Campbell, the public information officer who works for the Regional Emergency Planning Committee. I noticed on their website that his job description included "rumor monitoring and response". He would certainly make his pay grade that day.

I just squeaked in the deadline of my Weekly World Gazette article earlier in the week. With the help of a large iced caramel macchiato I burned up most of Saturday finishing the story. I took the last three reports I'd done for The Cape Cod News and combined them into a first-person perspective story (David's suggestion). I assumed he'd want a slightly hysterical tone, so I tossed in a few "I couldn't believe it!" and "Oh my God!" comments. He was happy that I included a few stills from my video. He also mentioned that he had final edit on the story. *What the hell?* I thought. He could do whatever he wanted with my piece of shit; I'd just shut up and take the money.

His final statement was, "If anything else happens, let me know." Once the check arrived, I intended to buy a big bottle of Bailey's Irish Cream. Alcohol and regrets just seem to go together.

As a crowd of people slowly formed around me, I planted myself on the front lawn next to the bronze statue of James Otis Jr. James Otis was the colonial lawyer who came up with the catchphrase, "Taxation without representation is tyranny". I looked up and studied Otis's upright finger jutting into the air, as if he was ready to let out an "Ah ha!" It occurred to me that there weren't too many modern-day sculptures being made of people in his profession. I wondered if he had known any good lawyer jokes.

Ken and Noodles eventually found me. I had mentioned to Ken that I would be there and he wanted to hear the "official" line on the UFO mania. I had yet to see Ken and Noodles separated; I already mentally referred to them as Shaggy and Scooby. Ken said eagerly, "Did you see this week's Game of Thrones?"

"Oh my God! Where to begin?" Few things brought out my inner fangirl like Game of Thrones. I'd watched it obsessively since its beginning, even all the actor interviews and behind-the-scenes stuff.

"Arya coming home!" Ken said.

"Drogon!" I exclaimed. "I like Jaime and Bronn, but when those Dothraki came screaming over the horizon...then Dany swooping in on Drogon--how badass was that!"

"I always liked Bronn, too," Ken said, "but when he fired that scorpion at Drogon--"

"I know! I was yelling "NOOOO!" We went on for a while, reliving, blow-by-blow, every highlight of the episode.

We calmed down only when Zeke and Eddie joined our group. Ken had ranted about them before, so it was interesting to finally match their faces to their names. Ken introduced me to Zeke, "This is Mel; she's from the Cape Cod News. We were on the Ferris wheel together when the UFO flew over the fairgrounds."

He shook my hand and gave me a cold stare. "So you're the UFO lady?" He nodded towards his buddy, "This is Eddie." Eddie just stood there as he tried to hide a beer can behind his leg. Zeke seemed agitated as he watched the people setting up at the podium. "This is just a goddamn dog-and-pony show!" he ranted. "They're not going to admit to anything!"

"Admit to what?" I asked.

"They'll try to cover anything up that's been revealed," Zeke said.

I glanced over at Ken who shrugged his shoulders and smiled.

"I'll see you later," Zeke said, then motioned to Eddie to follow him. They pushed their way towards the front of the crowd.

A squeal from the PA system got our attention. A man in a suit was tapping at the microphone on the podium. He asked the crowd, "Can you hear me?" A few people replied "yes". By then a couple hundred people filled the courthouse lawn. An enterprising ice cream truck driver had pulled into a parking spot on Main Street and the truck already had a line forming in front of it.

"Hello," the man at the podium said. "For those of you who don't know me, I'm Roy Campbell, the public information office-uh for the town of Bahnstable. We've been getting hundreds of UFO reports and phone calls from all ovuh the Cape. Some of you have been extremely upset ovuh what transpired at the fairgrounds.

We've brought together a few people who can address yoah concerns. Let me say this: there is nothing to worry about any longuh. We found the person responsible for the sighting." Murmuring rose out of the crowd as Roy Campbell looked towards the front door behind him, "Can we have Office-uh Morgan escort the accused out heah so we can all look at the guilty pahty? We caught him illegally fishing for quahogs on Sandy Neck."

A person wearing a silver space suit and a rubber alien mask was escorted out by a burly police officer. The "alien" stepped up to the podium carrying a quahog rake in its long rubber fingers. Roy said, "So you're the one abducting all those oysters?"

The alien raised the quahog rake like it was brandishing a scimitar. A few scattered laughs arose from the audience. He then removed the mask, revealing Joseph Spooner, the Barnstable County Commissioner. Several people laughed; some appeared uneasy.

Ken leaned into me and said, "You've got to be fucking kidding me! What does he think we saw—swamp gas?"

Spooner said, "We want to assure everyone there is nothing to worry about. There's been an investigation. The reports of abductions are simply not true. Everyone needs to calm down. There is nothing to worry about."

Someone called out from the crowd, "Will the military be looking into this?"

"I knew someone would ask that," he said "so I invited Lt. Colonel Daniel Patterson from Otis to speak to everyone here."

Spooner stepped away from the microphone and a man in military uniform approached the mic. "Hello, I'm Lt. Colonel Daniel Patterson, the DPA officer at the 102nd Intelligence Wing. Commissioner Spooner asked me to address your concerns directly. I've looked into this with the FAA and the North American Aerospace Defense Command. Nothing was scrambled, nothing was flying on the night in question."

Someone yelled out, "The thing was huge. How could you have missed it?"

"Nothing appeared on radar. There were no reports from the field or anywhere on base."

Another person asked, "Have you seen the footage?"

"Yes, I've seen the footage from that night. I can't comment on that other than to say it appeared to be an unidentified flying object."

Zeke raised his hand. "Has the military been in contact with any aliens?"

Patterson had a puzzled look on his face, "Aliens?"

Spooner leaned over into the mic, "Cuban boat aliens? You'll have to contact the Coast Guard." He stood there with a smug look on his face, like he'd come up with the ultimate zinger. Nobody laughed at his joke.

"No," Patterson added with a hint of sarcasm, "we haven't been contacted by any aliens."

Zeke said, "Why are you guys trying to cover this up?"

"There's nothing to cover up."

"Were you told by your superiors to deny this activity? How come you won't tell us?"

Patterson exhaled deeply. "Look," he said slowly, clearly annoyed at Zeke's line of questions, "if you insisted that there were leprechauns on the base, and I told you that leprechauns don't exist, but you deny it, what else could I possible say? How am I supposed to convince you that leprechauns don't exist?"

Zeke said, "Are you saying that UFOs don't exist?"

"I'm saying we don't have any more information to give you."

"Then why are you covering this up?"

Patterson buried his face in his left hand and took a moment to get his composure back. He looked out into he crowd and said, "Can I answer any more questions?"

A woman stepped up to the podium and said, "Do you have

any emergency evacuation plans for when the rapture comes?"

Patterson was at a loss for words. I recognized the woman; she was Abigail Bishop from the Church of Holy Doctrinal Unity, an ultra-conservative Christian group. They had their "headquarters" in a strip mall on route 132. I had spoken to her once when I was working on a story about what was then the only family planning clinic on Cape Cod. I needed a quote from someone who taunted the women entering the clinic and she obliged. I guess it was important to save all those unborn babies for the apocalypse.

Abigail held up a bible and announced, "Revelation 22:10 And he said to me, *Do not seal up the words of the prophecy of this book, for the time is near.*"

Patterson said, "Commissioner Spooner, I believe that would be a civil emergency, so it falls under your jurisdiction."

Spooner swapped places with Patterson at the mic and said, "The End of Times comes on Labor Day, when the tourists leave."

The rest of the meeting continued with Abigail giving us more bible quotes and Spooner handing out more platitudes. It looked like the excitement was over, so I put my camera and notebook back in my bag. I was about to say goodbye to the guys when I noticed a woman walking through the crowd. Even without the shiny silver unitard she would've stood out. Blonde hair, gorgeous face, curvy in a Scarlett Johansson way, the crowd literally parted as she wove her way through.

She stopped in front of us, smiled, and gave me a handout with the bold headlines "UFOs Over Cape Cod. Why are they here? Where have the come from? When will they land?" Looking at her in spandex and Adidas, I found myself wondering if some 10k run had finished at the courthouse. And, if so, how had she managed to keep her hair and makeup that perfect? Ken and Noodles continued to stare at her as she disappeared back into the crowd.

"Guys, put put your tongues back in your mouths," I said. I

handed the flyer to Ken.

Ken looked at the sheet of paper and read, "UFOs Over Cape Cod? When will they land?" Noodles stood next to him and studied it too. Ken continued, "The Fornacisians will be arriving shortly. Will you be there to join the galactic coition?"

"Galactic coition?" I said.

Ken smiled as he scanned the page and continued reading, "Blah blah blah, blah blah blah...If you have ever entertained the idea of amalgamating with a higher being beyond the Earth's confines, you will want to attend this meeting."

Noodles laughed. "I'm having a hard time amalgamating with any terrestrial beings. I didn't know I had other options."

Ken snickered, "You must've forgotten to add 'beyond our solar system' to your Tinder search parameters."

"I always swipe left when I spot anyone who looks like an extraterrestrial," I added.

Ken pointed to the bottom of the handout, "It says they're having a public meeting tomorrow in lecture hall B at Cape Cod Community College.

"Well," I said, "if I was looking for impressionable young adults, 4Cs is where I'd go."

About a year ago, the main office asked Norm if he'd be interested in giving a lecture at the college about newspaper management. He had told me, somewhat bitterly, "They only asked me because everyone in the main office turned it down." I pointed out that he was, officially, an alumnus, which set him off. I had to listen to him rant about "small town mentalities" and how the college was where "fake professors go when they can't get real college jobs".

"These guys sound like a riot," Ken said. "You want to go?"

"Sorry; I'm not interested in having coitus with any Fornacisians," I said. "Besides, I've got a ton of work to do."

16

Sticking your head out of a car window is like having your life sped up. I always enjoyed the wind blowing my ears back, watching people zip past, but it was frustrating that I never got the chance to lick any of them. Just the phrase "car ride" makes me go crazy.

On a recent trip, Ken took me to a room filled with other dogs and their humans. It was fun exchanging sniffs and making new friends. There were a couple of cats there too, but I never really cared for them. They never seemed to want to participate in any of the fun and their owners didn't seem to be too enthused either. The only downside to that trip was when they placed me on a metal table and a guy with a long coat stabbed me in the butt with something. He seemed nice enough earlier. What did I ever do to that guy?

Returning home, I smelled our neighborhood long before I spotted our driveway. Ken opened the door and I jumped out and pee'd in my usual spot on the front lawn. He immediately shouted at me about something. I don't know why he always does that. Doesn't he realize that is my usual spot? He headed towards the gate to the left of our house and asked me to follow him. He opened it and I dashed through to our backyard and found my rubber pork chop. I grabbed it, squeaked it a few times and tried to get him to play with me. I watched him close the gate and go back out to the front of the house. My tail slowly stopped wagging and I let the pork chop drop from my mouth.

I guess the fun is over.

I now had the back yard all to myself. I sniffed along the per-mitter of the fence, scratched at a dirt spot next to the shed, then sat down. I felt content to be back home, even though my back end was still sore from what I went through today.

Typically after dinner, I liked to gnaw on a couple of bones that I had collected from around the neighborhood. I wanted to take them into the house, but Ken insisted on throwing them back out into the yard. He never seemed to understand the craving I had for those things. Most humans have a lousy sense of taste, so I didn't hold it against him. It had become my obsession to collect those bones. I had stashed away exactly twenty-five of them in our yard. Instead of burying them randomly, I amused myself by de-positing them equally distant from one another in a grid pattern— that way I could easily find them all. I reflected on the actual number of bones I had: twenty-five. It occurred to me that this number could be divided by five, which, when multiplied by itself, got me back to twenty-five. I called this type of number a *box base*. I imagined drawing lines between all the bones and forming trian-gles. It occurred to me that the box base of the side opposite the square corner is equal to the sum of the box bases of the other two sides. I think this is called 'geometry'. I didn't know why it never occurred to me up until now. I was having fun coming up with all sorts of concepts like these. After all, a dog can only lick its balls for so long. . .

I was just about to nod off when I noticed a powerful odor coming from the front of our house. It smelled like a giant version of one of my bones. I trotted towards the fence and sniffed around. It seemed to coming from down the street to my right. It definitely needed investigating, but how could I get out? I looked over towards the shed. Somebody had removed the board I used to get over the fence; I couldn't get out that way. How could I get through the gate? It was the way that Ken used, so why couldn't I do the same? I noticed a little moving part at the top of the gate. Ken always did something with it before he opened the gate. I went to the gate, lifted myself up with my front paws and gave the thing a lick.

It moved.

I studied this apparatus for a moment. It made a rattling sound when I gave it a few more licks.

If it moves, I should be able to push it with my nose.

I gave it a little shove and it flipped upright! When I sat back down, the gate slowly swung open towards me.

So that's how those things work!

As I let myself through the gate, I spotted our next door neighbor waving his fist and yelling something at me. I reminded myself not to play fetch with that guy, even though his front yard was a fabulous place to take a poop. I trotted out to the street, and hoped that Ken would still be there, happy to see me.

Nope. Nothing.

The car was in the same place; I guessed he was inside the house. I looked down the street towards the enticing smell. I had been exploring the neighborhood pretty throughly the past few weeks on my bone collecting excursions and I knew there were some good hunting spots out in that direction.

I trotted for about ten minutes through some woods towards the alluring smell. I ended up at a dead end street where a car was parked. It was a boxy-shaped thing with its side door open. A man wearing a shirt covered in flower patterns was leaning through the side door, doing something. As I approached, the smell of bones became overwhelming. I sat down behind the man and watched him playing with them. I was able to count how many he had— twenty-two.

This new skill of mine has sure come in handy.

The man in the flowered shirt saw me standing there watching him. He said something that sounded like a warm greeting and patted my head. He kept asking me something, but I couldn't understand what he wanted. I kind of recognized the word "fella" and the last word sounded a lot like "come". My tail started wagging, he seemed friendly enough.

I could like this guy; we have the same interests.

Looking at all those bones he had piled up inside his car made my mouth water. I'd love to take a car ride with him and add them to my collection. He kept looking at something he was holding, then glancing out into the woods. I followed his eyes out to where he was looking. There was probably another bone out there beyond the trees, but I was much more interested in what he had collected. He said something about "staying" as he headed off into the woods. I watched him go off on his journey, his footsteps getting fainter as he disappeared through some trees.

Can you believe that? He left all these bones for me!

I guessed he didn't want them. I counted the pile one more time, definitely twenty-two bones. It was going to take me a while to carry all of them back home, one at a time. I decided to go for it. It would take less time than exploring my neighborhood looking for more of them.

From the top of the pile I grabbed one that was the size of a soft ball and began to trot off towards home with it in my mouth. I stopped after three steps.

Wait a minute, if I come back for another one, they might not be here. If the car is gone, they'll all be gone. I'll miss out on a huge stash of these things.

I went back to the car door and sat down. I needed to think this thing through. I had to drop the one in my mouth because its flavor was getting too intense. When I let it go, it rolled to the edge the road and went under a guardrail. I noticed a little stream that went alongside the road beyond it.

Interesting. What if I dropped all of them into the water?

It occurred to me that the man in the flowered shirt wouldn't find them down there; the water would mask the smell and there was plenty of tall grass to hide them behind. I could come back later and carry them home one at at time.

I liked this idea. I quickly grabbed another bone from his car, crawled under the guardrail and dropped it into the water. A frog distracted me as it jumped into the water with a splash. Normally I'd go crashing through the water in search of it, but I had to let it go; I had work to do. It took me a couple of minutes to shuttle the remaining bones from the car into my temporary hiding place. I took the last bone in my mouth and confidently sprinted towards home. I would have enough of them to chew on for years.

17

Noodles and I pulled into one of the parking lots surrounding Cape Cod Community College. We wanted to see the UFO cult for ourselves and learn what "amalgamating with a higher being beyond Earth's confines" was all about. It was apparent that the recent UFO sighting had brought all sorts of non-tourist crazies to Cape Cod. I unplugged my phone from the USB charger and glanced at my back seat to see if I needed to spread a beach towel on anything worth stealing.

Noodles asked me, "What did you major in?"

"I majored in recreational services in college," I said. "My focus was on the pool tables and video games they had in the student activities room. I completely didn't apply myself in college." We got out of my car and I unfolded the flyer the woman had given us, I wanted to make sure we had the right building. The parking lot continued all the way around a batch of centrally located brick buildings. I thought, *We could be on the wrong side.* "We need to find the Atrium inside the Lorusso technology building, can you Google a map or something?" As Noodles was fiddling with his phone, I spotted a woman wearing a silver triathlon suit on the other side of the parking lot. When we got closer I could see she was the same one who gave us the flyer at the town meeting. From the trunk of her car, she was trying to pile a bunch of diet Coke bottles onto a stack of pizza boxes. We walked over to her and I showed her the flyer. "Hey," I said, "I think you gave this to us. Do you need help carrying anything?"

"Oh hi!" she said with a smile. "Are you here to see Klick?"

"Who?"

"Our Copacetic Coition Ambassador!" One of the liter bottles she was balancing started to topple over. Noodles grabbed it just in time before it hit the ground. "Thank you!" she said. "I could really use the help. My name is Jennifer!"

"Noodles," he said as he filled his arms with Coke bottles.

"Noodles?" Jennifer said, "That's really nice. Noodles are one of my favorite things to eat!"

Noodles flashed me a shit-eating grin. I thought, *wouldn't we all love to be eaten by this woman.* "Yeah," I said as I tried to keep a straight face, "we're interested in joining the galactic coition."

Jennifer dumped another bag on top of the pizza boxes and closed the trunk. "Oh great! I'll take you there—follow me!" She spun around with a swish of her ponytail. This woman was the epitome of bright-eyed innocence; there was no way she would've picked up on my snark. Noodles and I practically had to sprint to keep up with her as she dashed towards a building. "What's your name?" she asked me over her shoulder.

"Ken."

"I had a Ken doll!" She grinned and said, "You wouldn't believe what I made Barbie do to him."

Jennifer led us to the atrium. It had a wall of windows, several long tables and a monitor on a stand. A screensaver was showing space-porn images of planets, galaxies and Saturn's rings. Noodles followed Jennifer over to a group of women who had on the same outfit. He dumped the soda bottles onto a table and was quickly introduced to them all by Jennifer. I drifted off towards the windows and fell back to a wing-man position. I left Noodles to bask in the cloud of estrogen.

I was interested in seeing the kind of people who would come to a meeting like this. Way in the back were a bunch of bros wearing baseball hats and t-shirts. They were whispering and laughing to themselves as they watched the attractive girls hovering around Noodles. I'm sure their only exposure to extraterrestrials was what they had seen in the Star Wars movies. There were an assortment of uncomfortable-looking geek types randomly scattered around the tables, plus a goth-looking couple who had their noses firmly planted in their phones.

One woman with frizzy hair sat with her eyes closed, a pair of earbuds hanging off her. Every few minutes, her eyes would open for just a slit, she would draw in a breath, then go back to her catatonic state. I couldn't tell if she was listening to some sort of meditation tape or was just uncomfortable having strangers near her. Standing behind the monitor were three young men with their arms crossed. They all wore extremely tight bicycle shorts the same color as the women's leotards. They leaned casually on the wall, not caring that their junk was clearly outlined by their uniforms.

I watched the image on the monitor slowly dissolve from a solar eclipse to the Orion Nebula. Noodles was still being helpful, arranging pizza boxes and dealing out paper plates. From behind the men's room door next to me, I heard a toilet flush, followed by the sound of water running and paper towels being ripped from a dispenser. After a pause, the occupant made a noise like he was mimicking an engine of some sort.

"Vvvvvvvvvvvvvvvvvvvvvvvvvvvv"

I expected him to complete the utterance by going "vroom!" I slid a little closer. Next I heard what sounded like an angry squirrel.

"CHIT! CHIT! CHIT! CHIT!"

He had my complete attention.

"Sssssssssssssssssssssssssssssssss"

He must've held it for at least fifteen seconds. What was he trying to imitate: a snake? A running faucet? I inched even closer, my head was practically on the door itself.

It flung open and my spine snapped backwards in a startle response. My heart rate took off in a sprint. A bald man in his early sixties, wearing black silk pajamas, strode out into the atrium. He raised his arms and shouted, "Who wants to be indoctrinated?" There was complete silence as all eyes went to the bald-headed stranger. "I'm kidding!" he shouted. "Let's have some fun!"

A round of laughter came from all his followers. They all jumped to attention as he approached the laptop connected to the monitor, then broke into a round of polite golf claps. Noodles looked uncomfortable, finding himself suddenly standing alone at the front of the room. I took a seat near the back and motioned Noodles over.

"Holy crap, Jennifer is gorgeous!" he said.

"I thought Leeloo from the Fifth Element was your type," I said.

"That works too."

The old guy wearing the Hugh Hefner outfit shook away the screen saver with the mouse and launched Powerpoint. A Celtic-looking symbol appeared on the screen. It resembled the outline of a penis, superimposed on a circle. I think I doodled similar designs as a twelve year old, only mine weren't as well designed.

He took a step forward and waited for everyone to settle. "Hello everyone!" he said as he stretched out his arms in a tel-evangelical embrace. "What I'm about to tell you today will sound unbelievable. Crazy, even. But I'd have to be crazy to not tell you

what I've learned. I will be asking you to start an incredible journey that could take you beyond infinity! But you must be willing
to take that first step—your first step to euphoria!"

Noodles whispered, "Did he just quote Buzz Lightyear?"

I said, "If we make it through this, do we get a coupon for a
free Venusian timeshare unit?"

The next slide came up with the header: *Who Am I?*, followed
by a bullet point: *Klick*.

"My name is Klick," he said. "I must acknowledge my father.
He is not a human father. He is a Fornacisian called Tick. I know
what you're thinking—does he sound like James Earl Jones and
wear a black helmet? No….he was very different."

A photo of a farmhouse appeared on the screen.

"I grew up with my mother on a farm in Winkle, Ohio. My
stepfather went on long business trips and left my mother and I
for weeks at at time."

The next image was an illustration of a silver UFO with stairs
coming out of its bottom. You could tell it was a UFO from the
fifties because all spaceships used stairs back then.

"One day, in June of 1955, a spaceship landed in our back
yard. A Fornacisian, my father, descended from the spaceship
and told my mother where he had come from. My father was an
extremely attractive individual and he seduced my mother."

The next image was an alien who looked very much like a
cross between James Dean and Elvis. The Mojo Nixon song "Elvis
Is Everywhere" immediately came to mind.

Klick continued, "I was born of that union. Over the years,
the Fornacisians returned on a regular basis to see how I was doing. But as I got older, I saw them less and less. I know that sounds
incredible. If you are an intelligent person, you must be thinking: extraordinary claims require extraordinary proof. I have that
proof." He gestured towards the screen like a magician and said, "I
shot this footage when I was twelve years old."

He showed some grainy 8mm film footage of what looked like a UFO floating over a field. It was obviously a little spinning silver model dangling by a string in front of the camera. Beside me, I heard Noodles snicker. I groaned and whispered to him, "Oh come on! It looks like a pie plate! Ed Wood did a better job than that."

The next slide appeared: *Who are the Fornacisians?*

"The Fornacisians are from the star Alpha Fornacis," Klick said, "the brightest star in the constellation Fornax, which is 46.4 light years away. They are an advanced civilization who strive to live in a perfect state of euphoria. They are all pansexual and gender-fluid."

Another slide: *When did they get here?*

"They were our mitochondrial Eves, visiting us 152 thousand years ago and mating with our African ancestors. They have been coming back over the centuries. We are all descendants of Fornacisians."

A series of stock photos of Greek, Roman and other statues appeared.

"Eros, Aphrodite, Freyr, Saint Anne, Haumea—we called them fertility gods. They were all Fornacisians," Klick said.

The fourth slide: *Why are they here?*

"They needed cultivars to maintain their genetic code and increase heterosis, which is the improved or increased function of any biological quality in a hybrid offspring."

The next slides showed different examples of animals mating. The first was of a huge bull mounting a cow, its penis clearly extended. The cows then dissolved into a pair of humans humping. I wasn't sure if these were supposed to illustrate hybridization, or if Fornacisians were actually into bestiality.

"They will be arriving shortly to unite with us," he said.

The fifth slide: *Who are they looking for?*

Klick's voice turned somber. "Their morphology is highly developed and they're looking for specific phenotypic traits.

One: The humans must have highly symmetrical features. Two: They must be intelligent. Three: They must be healthy people, fit enough to survive copulation with a Fornacisian. Let me tell you, when I say 'out of this world orgasms', I'm not just talking about the Oort cloud."

I thought, *Oort cloud? Did they discover Carl Sagan's porn stash on the Voyager disc?*

The final slide: *Are YOU ready?*

"If you meet their strict criteria, you will be taken aboard their spaceship and travel to other worlds to experience the sensual interplay of some of the most alluring extraterrestrials from across our galaxy." Klick paused dramatically to let his words sink in. "I know this sounds crazy, but what if I'm right? What if you're going to miss out on the most amazing journey of your life?"

Everyone sat there in silence, dumbfounded.

"Thank you for coming," he said. He made a broad sweeping gesture towards the table of food. "Please continue to enjoy what we have to offer. And I would love to answer any questions you may have."

I studied the offerings: a bag of Doritos, diet Coke, a box of Twinkies and Papa Gino's pizza. I guess Fornacisians didn't sweat the empty calories, or perhaps junk food was considered human bait?

A bro from the back raised his hand and yelled, "Yeah, I got a question. What time does the psych van come to take you away?" The bros laughed, cracking themselves up as they filed out the back door. Klick was probably the funniest thing they'd seen since truck nuts.

I was ready to follow them out when Noodles said, "I want to say good bye to Jennifer."

"Seriously, dude?"

"C'mon, let's have a slice of pizza."

I followed Noodles to the snack table. Jennifer handed him a slice of pizza and said, "Klick was instrumental in helping me find my path to euphoria."

Noodles nodded his head as he bit into the pizza.

Jennifer gushed, "The Fornacisian spaceship sounds wonderful."

"We saw the UFO at the fair," he said.

Jennifer's eyes widened. "You guys saw the spaceship?"

"I was probably the closest one to it," I said.

"Oh my God! Did they try to contact you?"

"I wouldn't know," I said, "I was too busy trying not to shit myself."

"Klick!" Jennifer called over to him. "These guys were at the sighting!"

Klick came over to us, accompanied by two of his female subjects, one under each arm. "Oh really?" he said. "You guys must be very special. The Fornacisians only show themselves to people they trust."

"Well, me and a hundred other dart, ball and hoop throwers on the midway," I said.

"They were scanning the crowds looking for those special people," Klick said. "You were invited; that's what led you here to us."

I thought, *Oh come on, now he's just lifting plot points from Close Encounters Of The Third Kind.* I was there to make fun of those people. "So, interesting footage of that UFO you shot," I sneered. "Was it from a blueberry or apple pie?"

Klick smiled at me. "The fruits of my labor certainly have paid off."

Great, I thought, *he completely missed my pie plate joke.* "No," I said, "that footage was pretty sketchy as far as UFOs go."

"I apologize for the quality. We didn't have high def back then."

In my mind I heard Scotty saying, "We've fired two snark torpedoes but they haven't gone through his shields, Captain!" The guy wasn't getting it.

"You both should come by and join us at our base of operations some time," he said. "You would have an incredible experience."

Never in a million years, I thought. The whole thing had a major Heaven's Gate vibe. I did not want to end up under a purple tarp, wearing Nikes.

18

"Can we get an entire box of pastel de nata this time?" Brian asked me, as he stared out the car window. The Portuguese Bakery in Provincetown was one of our mandatory stops.

"Not sure if they'll keep that long, but sure," I said. Pastel de nata are egg custards in a puff pastry shell. They're so good when they're warm; just the thought of them made my mouth water. Norm called last night and said people were freaking out about a v-shaped UFO over P-town. Terry, one of my brother's few friends, lived in Provincetown and said he had seen it. I knew if I bribed my brother with a food reward, I could get him to go with me to Terry's apartment. The idea of seeing an old friend wasn't enough to get him out of that cottage.

A day earlier I gave David Brown a call at the Weekly World Gazette and told him about the new Provincetown sightings. He had his checkbook out in an instant. I told myself I would never do this sort of thing again, but after totaling up my car payments,

I changed my mind. So I now had two stories to write, which would give Norm another opportunity to tease me.

Provincetown is the last stop on Cape Cod. It's about a half-hour's drive from Brian's cottage. The Mayflower first landed there and spent the winter in its sheltered cove before ending up in what is now Plymouth. Over the centuries, Provincetown had morphed from a fishing and whaling outpost to an artist colony to an LB-GTQ vacation spot. You can still spot John Waters and his buddies walking around there if you're lucky.

We left my car at Duarte's. Trying to find parking is challenging during the season. We got there early enough in the day to find a spot, although I had to hand over $15 for the privilege. Terry lived one street over in a grey shingled house, so it would be an easy walk. Brian lifted the brass knocker and let it fall twice against the door. Terry answered, his face covered in pancake foundation, a stocking over his head and one eye fringed with false eyelashes. "C'mon in," he said. "I have to finish my other eye." We stood in the middle of his cramped living room as he disappeared into his bedroom.

Brian called out, "Why do you have makeup on so early?"

"Can you believe it?" Terry said, "We have a corporate client that wanted a matinee. Normally I'd be asleep right now." There was a pause; we heard water running and teeth-brushing. "I'd offer you coffee, but I drank it all!"

Terry worked at the the Crown & Anchor, an entertainment complex on Commercial Street. If you want watch a man dressed as Cher belt out a version of "If I Could Turn Back Time", that's the place to go.

"Mel wanted to ask you some questions about the UFO," Brian said.

"I didn't see it," Terry said from his bedroom. "I just missed it."

I whispered to my brother, "I thought you said he saw it?"

Brian shrugged at me then said, "I thought you said you saw it?"

Terry came back in, pulling a red sequined dress over his head. "I was inside at the club. I heard all the commotion in the street and saw some lights disappearing behind Pilgrim Monument. I didn't know what the big deal was."

"We're trying to figure out if it's the same one we saw at the fairgrounds," I said.

"And it flew over my house," Brian added.

"Oh sweetie," Terry said as he shook his head, "you've been spotting flying saucers for years. You've got to get a grip."

I said, "A lot of people have seen it; Brian's not the only one."

Terry turned around said, "Can one of you guys zip me up?" Brian stepped forward and tugged at the zipper. "I'm going to be upset if this attracts even more crazies to this place. It's bad enough dealing with the regular tourists."

"Do you know anyone who I saw it?" I asked.

"All I know is it came up Commercial street," Terry said. "Someone must've had a better look at it than I did."

I said to Brian, "Well, I'm going to take a walk, are you fine staying here?"

Brian nodded his head. "You're going past the Portuguese bakery, right? Can you get the pastels?"

I assured Brian he'd get his pastries, left him in Terry's apartment and set off down the street. Commercial Street is considered "quaint" by some, and it can be, off-season, but from May to October it's another story. During the season—especially weekends—there are herds of tourists shuffling down a narrow street, eating ice cream, wandering vacantly into art galleries and tchotchke shops and gawking at the locals. The street wouldn't be as bad if they made it pedestrian-only, but it's not really possible in such cramped quarters. Whenever a nitwit inches their vehicle down the street, everyone is forced to squeeze onto the sidewalk, which in some spots is blocked by benches, steps or racks of merchandise.

I stood under a row of rainbow flags and got my bearings while a stream of people flowed around me. A Channel 5 news van was parked across the street. A cameraman was setting up his shot in front of a female reporter holding a mic. I passed a second news van as it pulled into the parking lot. It looked like I was at the bottom of the media totem pole today. I needed to find somebody who wasn't a tourist and worked in that area. Shop Therapy, P-town's "World Famous Alternative Lifestyle Emporium", was to my right. It's a hippie paraphernalia, novelties store and sex shop rolled into one. The front of the two-story building is covered with colorful cartoons of animals and robots. Above the doorway is a row of cartoon aliens. I took it as an sign that this was the place to go.

The first thing I spotted was a display of HUF brand socks with marijuana leaves printed on them. Clothing and accessories downstairs were; bongs and dildos upstairs. A guy with a huge spider tattoo on his arm sat reading a book behind the knife case. I asked him, "Did you see yesterday's UFO sighting?"

Without looking up, he replied, "Bongs are upstairs."

"Hold on—I'm a reporter," I said. "I'm looking to interview anyone who saw it."

"I wasn't here yesterday."

A pair of voices behind me said, "We saw the UFO!" I turned to see two fifty-something men wearing identical rainbow scarf ties; they each had an arm around the other one's waist. "Did you say you were a reporter?" the taller one asked me. He had sunglasses on his forehead and his shorter friend had on plaid shorts.

"Yeah," I said, "Cape Cod News." I pulled out my note pad. "Can I ask you guys a couple of questions?"

They both nodded and said, "Sure."

"Where did you first see it?"

Plaid Shorts said, "We were hanging out by the meat rack

when it flew right over us."

The "meat rack" refers to the park benches in front of the town hall. Back in the seventies it was a notorious cruising and pick-up spot. The town even removed the benches at one point to discourage "undesirables". Most tourists who sit there during the daylight hours are oblivious to whatever "immoral" activities might occur after dark.

Sunglasses said, "A beam of light came down and froze us all in place."

Plaid Shorts said, "It then lifted the whole group of us right up into the spaceship." He grinned and then said, "And then the examinations started."

The other one snickered, "I got probed!"

"No, they probed me first!"

They were cracking each other up. I stopped writing.

Mr. Sunglasses said, "They took out this thing I called the alienator and that's when it really got intense."

The other one recoiled in mock horror. "Oh my God!" he said, "I was terrified! What were you yelling?"

Sunglasses: "We just got our asses kicked, pal!"

Both of them screamed hysterically.

"Thank you, Private Hudson," I said, to let them know *OK, I get it.*

Their snickering faded away as they wandered out of the store.

Wonderful. I thought. *How many times will I have to listen to that today?*

I heard a voice behind me yell "Mel!"

Coming down the stairs was Noodles wearing, of all things, a pair of silver spandex bicycle shorts. With him was the woman who gave me the UFO flyer at the courthouse. She wore the same silver unitard I'd seen her in before.

"Hey, Noodles."

"Hey!" Noodles said, "Fancy meeting you here. Have you met

Jennifer?"

"Hi," I said, "We met quickly at the town hall. You gave me a flyer."

"Oh nice! Have you met Klick yet?" she said.

"Klick?"

Noodles jumped in, "He's the dude who's waiting for the UFO."

"Ken mentioned that you guys went to see him," I said.

"He's giving a seminar right now at the Dungeon nightclub," Jennifer said. "Would you like to meet him?"

Ken had given me the complete rundown of his meeting with the UFO cult at the college. He said this Klick was "completely nuts"; that he spoke about fornicating with Fornacisians and about their genetic hybridization of alien species. All I could think about was the line from The Green Mile, *"I think this boy's cheese slid off his cracker."* I said, "I'm looking for witnesses who saw yesterday's UFO."

"Oh, everybody there saw it!" Jennifer exclaimed. "Klick is giving answers to everything. We all drove up here last night when we first heard about it."

I exhaled and had to think for a moment. Should I torment myself further by walking down Commercial Street, asking strangers if they saw a spaceship, or listen to a lecture from a UFO cult leader? After all the UFO craziness, I told myself I'd never again grumble about covering another boring selectmen's meeting. "All right," I said "Let's see what you've got."

"OK great!" Jennifer said. "Follow us!"

I followed them down Commercial Street, Jennifer's ponytail bobbing with every step. Someone already had inflatable alien dolls for sale out on the sidewalk. I thought, *That was fast.*

We ended up at the Dungeon, the notorious B&D nightclub. I looked around and saw a couple of sturdy ceiling hooks that looked well beyond the design specs for hanging pendant light fixtures. The walls were covered with paper maché stone blocks, like something you would see on a movie set of Frankenstein's laboratory. An image flashed through my mind of Gene Wilder being strangled by the monster as Marty Feldman shouted out "Give him a sedagive!".

A group of fifty or so people were sitting in chairs and on the benches that ran along the outer wall. A bald guy wearing a silk robe stood next to a computer monitor giving a presentation. A graphic displayed the URL: hoodasnew.org. Behind him stood three men wearing the same silver bicycle shorts Noodles had on. My eyes went straight to their bulges. *So this is how a guy feels when he sees a woman in a tight top.*

I guessed that the bald guy was their leader Klick. He continued, "One of our causes is the fighting the barbaric practice of male circumcision, what we call male genital debasement or MGD. I founded the organization with the the goal of assisting all MGD victims who want their foreskin rebuilt. Most men with a degraded penis don't realize what they're missing - who here has been circumcised?" Several hands went up. "The Fornacisians are never circumcised. They were appalled when this practice started a few millennia ago. We want to bring back all experiences of pleasure that aren't filtered through the beliefs of ancient sociality." He paused for a moment to let his words sink in. A few people were nodding their heads. "Thank you for coming. Please continue to enjoy what we have to offer. And I would love to answer any questions you may have."

A man raised his hand, "Do the Fornacisians suffer from any STDs?"

"Oh, never," Klick said. "In fact, they will screen everyone for any STDs before entering their ship. It takes them just an instant to genetically remove any pathogens from your system. They don't want any beings tracking mud through their home!" A few laughs came from the crowd.

I spotted a box of something with the Provincetown Portuguese Bakery label sitting next to a row of liter Coke bottles. It reminded me to hit the place on the way back. The questions stopped and the guests started talking amongst themselves. I approached the bald man and said, "Hi, your name is Klick?

Klick put his arm around two of his male followers. "Yes," he said "I saw you come in with Jennifer. Are you a lesbian seeking euphoria?"

"Huh? No, I'm a reporter."

"How do you know Jennifer?"

"I'm a friend of Noodles."

"Oh wonderful!" Kick pulled his two male followers closer. "Jennifer speaks highly of Noodles. We enjoy his company."

"I'm doing a a story on last night's UFO sighting. Did you witness it?"

"No, but some of my followers might have. Where are you from?"

"The Cape Cod News. I did the story on the first sighting at the county fair. I was there."

Klick's eyes widened, "You saw its arrival?"

"I was so close, I almost could have touched it."

His jaw dropped open and smiled. "You were invited here!" He turned, the two men still under his arms, towards the crowd. "Attention everyone!" he called out. "Who here saw the spaceship last night?" A few people raised their hands. "This is a reporter from the Cape Cod News. She's doing a story." He leaned over to me and asked, "What is your name?"

"Mel."

"Mel?"

"It's short for Melissa."

"Are you sure you aren't a lesbian?"

"I'm sure."

Klick pointed at me and announced, "Mel here would like to

speak to you."

I spoke with several witnesses. At that point, all the reactions to the UFO were getting redundant. Everyone was freaked out by what they'd seen, couldn't believe it, etc. The only details I got were that it was V-shaped. It was probably the same thing Ken and I saw at the fair. After speaking with enough observers, I had enough information to triangulate its flight path. It roughly followed the causeway in from the ocean, crossed over the rotary at Pilgrims' First Landing Park, went up Commercial Street, then took a left and flew over the Pilgrim Monument. The last person to see it said it flew over route 6 and out past Clapps Pond, beyond where the sand dunes start. Apart from one guy who made the "I got probed" joke, it was a good set of interviews. It seemed everyone else was taking it seriously.

I spoke with Klick for a while. He insisted on telling me the location of all the places on the Cape he planned to give his presentation. He kept flattering me about my appearance, touching me occasionally, leaning in to listen carefully to everything I said. They were all good power-of-persuasion techniques; it was evident he was a pro at this. Of course, he was just sucking up to me to get as much publicity as possible out about his cause. I mentioned we had some standard advertising rates on our website and gave him the direct number of the ad department. I thought about of giving him Norm's office number instead, just to get back at him for giving me the tin foil hat.

19

"Dude, your entire package is showing!" I said to Noodles as he got into my car, "Seriously, what the fuck?" He had on the same tight bicycle shorts the male Fornacisians wore. I hadn't seen this much of my best friend's anatomy since gym class.

Noodles shrugged and said, "Jennifer likes it when I wear this."

The WCOD station manager had given Zeke his own show on Sunday night and we needed to get to the station before 10 o'clock. The whole Cape UFO thing had gone off the charts since the P-town sightings and everyone was looking for answers. Unfortunately, Zeke had become the defacto expert on the subject. His Twitter and Facebook following had grown substantially. He had a lot of pull. I would give him that at least. My eyes kept going down to Noodles' bulge. "Dude, go back inside and put some pants on."

Noodles wouldn't look at me. He just sat there, staring out the car window. "Everything is in the laundry," he said quietly.

"Seriously? You joined Klick's UFO cult? What is wrong with you?"

"I didn't really join it. I'm just trying to impress Jennifer."

"So you're doing this just to get laid?"

Noodles finally looked at me. "C'mon, she is pretty hot, right?"

He had a point there. Noodles normally wouldn't be able to get the time of day from a woman like Jennifer. This would probably be the best chance in his entire life to boink someone that far out of his league. As a guy with my own primitive urges, I understood this; but intellectually it was still messed up.

"You don't actually believe any of what Klick says, right?"

Noodles shrugged. "He can be pretty funny."

"Well, OK. Just don't drink any Kool-Aid."

He smiled and said, "You should feel what Jennifer can do with her tongue."

I started the car. "You know what they say? Don't stick your dick in crazy, right?"

"She's not crazy."

"OK fine—highly delusional then."

Noodles just looked out the window and didn't answer.

We got to the radio station with just ten minutes to spare. Noodles and I went to our usual spots behind our mics. Zeke was struggling with some knobs on a new professional console. Eddie was planted on the studio couch holding a microphone with one hand, and an open beer can in the other. He was relegated to the background because they had a famous guest tonight—Tom Frazier. He was in his early forties, wore glasses and a golf shirt and had a neatly trimmed haircut . He looked like he would hurt his arm if he tried to throw a football. He was well-known within the UFO community as that guy who saw alien bodies and who worked for some government agency. I considered him the king of wingnuts, but his notoriety did give him some presence in the room. Zeke's annoying music started.

"Tonight we have with us a special guest," Zeke announced. "He's known throughout the UFO community as one of the most significant people to reveal government secrets that have been covered up for decades. We welcome Tom Frazier."

"Thanks for having me," Tom said. "The Cape has recently become a hotbed for sightings and I know the reason why. The government doesn't want me revealing this and are out to stop me any way possible."

Zeke said, "You say the FBI has an arrest warrant out for you?"

"They'll probably be here in half an hour." Tom looked up at the studio clock. "I've got to leave in exactly twenty minutes."

"What can you tell us?" Zeke asked.

Tom was dead serious as he spoke. "I've seen the bodies." He paused and made eye contact with each of us. "I also have the classified documentation from hundreds of military radar UFO sightings."

"The bodies of aliens from crashed saucers?" Zeke asked.

"OK, hold on," I interrupted. "Did it ever bother you guys that the extraterrestrials never seemed to care that one of theirs died on our planet? They just went, *Eh, Zork crashed, the dummy. Let's just leave him there.*"

Tom nodded. "Of course," he said, "that's why they're showing up here right now."

"What the hell does a UFO over Cape Cod have to do with alien bodies at Area 51?" I said.

Tom glared at me. "I never said the bodies were at Area 51."

"Ken...listen," Zeke said, "he's got the goods."

Tom leaned forward in his chair and stressed with his pointed finger. "First off, Area 51 is a complete front at this point. There's no way you can keep anything under wraps with all those people working out there. Somebody is bound to speak up at some point.

They know that. The government wants to maintain a sense of mystery about this obscure spot in the desert, to keep us off track. Second, it would be better if they hid the bodies near where they perished. How would extraterrestrials even know they needed to go to Groom Lake or any other place to retrieve their companions?"

Zeke was wide-eyed as he continued. "So where are these bodies?"

Tom took a sip from a cup of coffee and paused. "I was an outside contractor working for the military at Beale Air Force Base in California. I worked as a computer maintenance technician on their PAVE PAWS radar installation. As a civilian, I had top secret clearance to enter their facility."

Zeke said, "PAVE PAWS were used to track incoming missiles during the cold war."

"Exactly," Tom said. "We're able to monitor the entire west coast from there. It's a phase array system designed to monitor anything up to 3000 nautical miles out into space. It's now mostly used to track satellite orbits and other space debris. I was able to look over everyone's shoulder on a day-to-day basis."

"You must've seen some pretty interesting things," Zeke said.

Tom's voice lowered, "Let me tell you, I've seen objects that go at right angles to the rest of the satellites up there."

I spoke up. "We have a bunch of military satellites that orbit from north to south. What about those?"

"Yes," Zeke said. "Typically everything is launched with the Earth's rotation. We were seeing stuff go in the opposite direction all the time. These craft would come in from space at all sorts of weird angles, then leave our atmosphere. Nobody on the ground can see this happening. They had a code name for them—runners."

"How many runners did you see?" Zeke said.

"We were supposed to log and record everything, even if it's not reported to the higher-ups at the ISR. They had data tapes

going back to the eighties—at least a thousand sightings, all classified. I managed to smuggle out copies of everything."

Zeke said, "What led you to the bodies?"

"Typically the PAVE PAWS transmit a narrow beam of 145
kilowatts within the 420-450 Mhz range. Once a week, the system
would spurt out this huge signal, four pulses, 20 milliseconds each
at over 5,000 kilowatts in all directions. It was like it was broadcasting something to outer space. I was told that when the system
does a hard reset, it relays these four pulses at full power through
all of its transmitting elements to recalibrate itself. I looked into
this; it was total bullshit. It was more like they were trying to contact something or someone."

I said, "Like it was a homing beacon?"

Tom nodded his head. "Exactly. I also noticed that a liquid
nitrogen tank truck would come by once a year to the site. Next to
the radar is a building with a huge generator inside. If power ever
went out on the base, they would be self-sufficient. There were a
pair of huge storage tanks full of diesel fuel for the generator. At
least that's what I thought at first. Come to find out the second
one was filled with liquid nitrogen."

"Why would they need liquid nitrogen at a radar facility?"
Zeke asked.

"That's what bothered me," Tom said. "I followed the lines
into the main building and it led me down some stairs to a room
below ground level. There was a green door that didn't have a door
knob or locks of any kind. Instead of a door knob, there was just a
black metal box next to a pull handle. I spent months studying this
door. What I discovered after much trial and error is that if you
key in the same four pulse, twenty millisecond sequence next to
the box, the door opens! It made sense. The aliens knew how to get
in because we were broadcasting the key!"

Zeke sat upright in his chair and eagerly asked, "What did you
find?"

"The lines led to three horizontal freezers. A window had been cut into them near the top; beneath it I could see a pale alien face. Whoever built those metal sarcophagi must've been inspired by the movie E.T. It looked pretty much like the one in the movie."

I rolled my eyes and said, "From when E.T. died and phoned home?"

"Right," Tom said, "but we've been doing the phoning for them. I couldn't really see much of their bodies through the window, but they looked much more human like than the typical greys we've come to expect."

I had heard enough of his story. These guys always have an excuse why they can't prove their extraordinary claims. "OK…so did you take any photos?" I asked. "Where's your proof?"

Tom continued as cool as before. "I did, I took pictures with my phone from every angle. About thirty minutes after I went back to work, a crew of MPs and high-ranking officers descended on the compound and immediately went for the room. There must've been an alarm system that contacted someone, telling them the aliens had come back for their man. When they saw that nothing was out of order, they did a lockdown and started interrogating everyone who worked there. I played dumb, but left my camera inside since they were doing full-body searches that day. I never went back to work."

"So how did they know it was you?" I said.

"I'm sure they found my phone, and my fingerprints were all over that room. From there they figured out I had stolen all of their records, going back decades."

"We have a PAVE PAWS installation right here on the base at Otis," I said. "Are you saying there are alien bodies in the town of Sandwich right now?"

Tom looked back up at the wall clock and said, "I'm saying I need to go." He stood up and walked straight out of the studio. There must've been a solid fifteen seconds of dead air as we watched him walk past us without saying a word.

Zeke made a lame joke about not wanting to be abducted by the authorities. The rest of the show was taken up by callers talking about the radar building and remarking on its odd, wedge-shaped pyramid design. The implication being that, if it's weird-looking, something weird must be happening inside of its walls. Somebody had called up its location on Google maps and confirmed the existence of a building with odd, protruding vents. Beside it stood a pair of liquid storage tanks. That was all very interesting, but it didn't prove anything. We finished the show with the last few callers giving their theories on the Roswell crash and Area 51.

We handed the studio over to the last DJ of the night and our entire crew went out into the parking lot. We all stood in a yellow pool of light, thrown off by the street lamp that illuminated that part of the parking lot. It was a clear night. Noodles had his head tilted back with his mouth open, looking straight up at the stars. "Do you think we'll ever get a chance to meet an alien?" he asked.

Eddie was walking towards a dumpster and yelled out, "Not while wearing those shorts, dude."

Zeke did a half-circle around Noodles, trying to get a better view of his attire in the poor light. "Why are you wearing those?"

"He's trying to get laid," I said.

Eddie snickered, his voice coming from the darkness. "By a guy?"

"No, I met this girl, Jennifer," Noodles said.

"She's part of that UFO cult that's been making the rounds," I said.

Zeke shook his head. "Those people are fucking nuts."

Noodles shrugged, "I really like her."

"Listen," I said, "do you guys want to get a drink somewhere?"

Zeke called out, "Eddie, you want to get a drink?"

Eddie was peeing on the dumpster; the sound of his urine resonated off the metal. "Do you even have to ask?"

I asked Zeke, "So how did you get a hold of Tom Frazier?"

"He called me. He said he was researching the recent UFO sightings and was staying down here."

"His story seems pretty far out there," I said.

"With his documentation," Zeke replied, "he's ready to blow the whole thing UFO conspiracy wide open."

I said, "It never bothered you guys that the aliens didn't come back for their dead associates?"

"Maybe they're few and far between," he said.

Two figures dressed in dark suits got out of a parked sedan and approached us. As they came into the light, it was apparent that one was male and the other female. They each pulled out a badge and showed them to us. They were from the FBI. The male agent spoke first, "Can we speak to you gentlemen for a moment?"

The female agent continued, "We're trying to locate a Tom Frazier. Have you seen him?"

Zeke asked, "What is this about?"

The male agent said, "There is an open investigation on Mr. Frazier. Have you been in contact with him?"

Zeke paused for a moment, sizing them up. I knew what he was thinking. These people were, in his little conspiracy-laden mind, the ones who were blocking the truth from getting out there. I was getting nervous. You don't screw with these people, they were the FBI for chrissakes. "Yeah…" Zeke sneered, "he was just on my show. He took off about an hour ago."

The female agent said, "How did you get in contact with him?"

"He called me. I told him he could come on my show, to just show up here at ten p.m."

"Do you know how we could get in touch with him?" the male agent asked.

Zeke crossed his arms. "Nope."

Both agents looked annoyed. The male agent exhaled slowly

and said, "Can we see some identification from all of you gentle-men?"

I went right for my wallet. Zeke fired back, "Why?"

I shouted at him, "Jesus Christ, Zeke, give them your ID!"

Everyone quickly handed their IDs to the agents except Zeke, who only reluctantly gave his after a delay. My heart was pound-ing. I couldn't believe I was associated with a nitwit who was antagonizing the Feds. These types of things don't end up well. Images of David Koresh flashed through my mind. I had no idea if Zeke was a gun nut or not. The agents checked our IDs with a little flashlight.

As we waited, I made tight fists with my hands and held in a chestful of air as I studied the people around me. Noodles looked petrified. Eddie was swaying back and forth slightly, having a hard time keeping vertical. Zeke continued to glare at them as if his precious rights have been violated. I closed my eyes and repeated to myself, *Zeke, just keep quite, just keep quiet, just keep quiet.* But no, Zeke just had to say it. "Hey look, it's Scully and Mulder!"

The agents looked at each other, then continued to study our driver's licenses. "Yeah. Agent Williams and I hear that one a lot," the male agent said.

The female agent grinned, "Ever see Men in Black? How would you like your memories erased?"

The male agent smiled, then regained his composure. He held up all four of our IDs like he was holding a poker hand and said, "We could have you boys come back to the office and do this. Right now. Or maybe we should have you stay overnight and we'll do this tomorrow morning."

I yelled at Zeke, "Shut the fuck up! Just tell them what you know!"

Zeke finally got the idea, he started babbling, "I don't have any other information on him. He called me, I told him to come down. That's all I know!"

The agent handed our IDs back, then passed out a card to each of us, "If you find any more information about him, give us a call," he said. His card read Agent Powell, Special Agent - Counter-terrorism Division.

Jesus Christ, I thought, *how did I end being associated with a terrorist?*

20

"It was right there," the man in the white visor said as he pointed his nine iron into the sky. "Then it flew right over the third fairway and out towards the ocean." He swung his club wildly in a big arc to illustrate its flight path. I took a step back.

Behind me, a man sitting in a golf cart said, "All the guys in the clubhouse saw it too."

I nodded and pretended to write something down. I could tell this sighting wasn't the real deal. Norm had sent me out to the Highlands Links golf course in Truro to follow up on another UFO sighting. Apparently the golfers had seen something, but it certainly didn't sound like what I witnessed.

For a nine-hole golf course, Highlands Links looked pretty desolate. There weren't many trees growing in the sandy soil beside the National Seashore. The biggest obstacle was the old lighthouse behind us. I looked in the direction the first man had pointed. On the horizon I could see a white dome sitting atop a tower. I was pretty sure it was the radar at Highlands Center.

"When did you see it?" I asked.

The one with the visor said, "About this same time yesterday."

"And what did it look like again?"

"It was silver and dish-shaped. It flew nice and steady out towards the ocean. I could't believe what I was seeing!"

The man in the golf cart said, "We heard about all the UFO reports that have been going on lately. I was kind of skeptical, but once I actually saw one, I became a believer. It was pretty amazing."

"Right," his friend said. "We figured we needed to report this immediately."

They looked at me for a moment in silence, as if I was going to supply some kind of answer to what they had seen. I'm a reporter, I only take down the information. How did I become the go-to person for supplying answers? I looked back to where he pointed and asked, "It wasn't V-shaped?"

"No," he answered, then walked over to his friend in the golf cart. "Donald, show her the video you took."

Donald pulled out his phone. His movie showed a circular white dot moving slowly across the horizon. His friend's voice could be heard saying, "Donald! Are you getting it? Are you getting it?" And Donald replying, "I'm getting it! I'm getting it!" The white dot slowly receded into the distance. The footage became shakier, then the video stopped.

He looked at me and asked, "Can you believe it?"

I scratched my forehead and said, "I think it kind of looks like a weather balloon."

"What the hell are you talking about?" he shot back. "It was a disk!"

"Yeah," Donald said, flinging out his arms. "And it just shot off into the distance!"

Carefully, I replied, "Well, I remember seeing a video online of somebody launching a weather balloon at Highlands Center. Some kids were on a field trip."

"Weather balloon, my ass!" he said. "I saw it myself."

Donald shook his phone at me. "And we have video!"

I put away my notepad. I needed to get the hell out of there; I wasn't going to convince those two of anything.

"The military isn't going to tell us what's happening, are they?"

"No," I said as I shook my head. "No-one at Otis is being forthcoming."

"Why don't they tell us the truth? Something clearly is going on!"

"I don't know" I replied, "but I'll be reporting on it the second I do."

I left them watching their video again. As I walked back to my car, the Channel 5 news van pulled into the parking lot. *Wow, that was fast!* I thought. I approached the vehicle and waved at the driver. He rolled down his window. I pointed to the two golfers and said, "You'll want to speak to them."

"Did they report the UFO sighting?"

"Yeah," I said and walked away. I got into my car and pulled out of the parking lot. I had a hunch. I drove the short distance past the North Truro campground, went down Old Dewline road and followed it into Highlands Center. The place is part of Cape Cod National Seashore. There's a performing arts center and the remains of North Truro Air Force Station. I followed the signs out towards the old radar installation.

I came upon a white van parked next to a rusted chainlink fence. A man was unrolling a long white tube of some sort onto the cracked pavement. Next to the van stood a large tank with a hose attached. He seemed surprised to see me. I rolled down my window and asked, "Is that a weather balloon?"

"No, it's a bouncy house," he said.

I looked around at the desolate parking lot. Why the hell was he setting it up way out here? There wasn't a kid in sight. Was I early for a birthday celebration? Was he some kind of homicidal maniac, luring children into his bouncy house, then dumping their bodies out in the sand?

"I'm kidding," he said. "Yeah, it's a weather balloon. I'm doing atmospheric monitoring for the Department of Energy." He went back to unrolling his balloon.

What an asshole, I thought. Good thing I hadn't told him where my mind had gone. "You didn't happen to launch one yesterday around this time?" I asked him.

"Yup."

"A couple of golfers over at the course think it was a UFO."

"We get that all the time," he replied

"Maybe you should warn people?"

He looked at me. "What? That a UFO is coming?"

"No, a weather…." I stopped myself and laughed. He probably went through this routine for everyone who fed him the same stupid questions. I waved and said, "Thanks!" He gave me a quick salute and went back to work.

Back in my car, I rolled up my window and headed back to the highway. I briefly though about going back to tell Donald and his buddies at the golf course what really happened. *Screw it.* They've got a story to tell for the rest of their lives.

At the office I found Norm with his feet up on his desk, reading a copy of Weekly World Gazette. The headline shouted ALIENS HAVE ARRIVED. He had a big grin on his face as I walked past him. I dumped my things onto my desk and collapsed into my chair.

"So what happened at the golf course?"

I slumped further into my chair and sighed, "It was a weather balloon."

He showed me the tabloid he was holding. "Hey, did you

know they've found a baby Bigfoot ?"

I glared at him. He was probably waiting all day to tease me about my Weekly World Gazette article. I just sat there and took my lumps.

"Have you seen this? You have a two page spread." With that stupid grin still on his face, he handed me the paper and said, "I see you left a lot of the details out of your local report."

Across two pages was the headline UFO ATTACKS CAPE COD! In addition to my photo near the bottom of the page, they showed an "artist's rendition" of a V-shaped craft flying over Nauset Lighthouse in Eastham and the Pilgrim Monument in Provincetown—obviously must-see tourist spots for intergalactic travelers. I had specifically used the word "allegedly" a few times when mentioning the abduction reports. It was gone. I never used the world "panic" and it was sprinkled throughout. All of my numbers were exaggerated. I had said a few hundred people probably saw it at the fairgrounds; now it was thousands. I said it flew down the length of Commercial Street, but they made it sound like War of the Worlds was happening. I read aloud, "'Beams of light shot down Commercial Street, searching for people to pull up into their spaceship.' I didn't fucking write that."

Norm laughed. "Maybe it was some form of advanced gay-dar."

On the page was a photo of Mantis Man on a dock, hiding behind some lobster pots. I shouted, "Mantis Man?! Where the fuck did Mantis Man come from?"

Norm's face was red from all the laughing.

I pointed at the caption. "It says a fisherman spotted Mantis Man sneaking around the docks at Woods Hole. Where the hell did that come from? I said there were *alleged* sightings as far down as Woods Hole. I didn't say Mantis Man was catching himself some lobsters."

Norm was practically hyperventilating.

"This isn't funny. They want me to write more. A lot more."

Norm wiped his eyes and sat up straight. "What did you get yourself into?"

"They want me to write a story every week."

"Why would you agree to that?"

I took a deep breath and exhaled. "The money," I said. I threw the paper back onto his desk. "I know it's complete bullshit. I know."

"Well what did you expect?"

I paced back and forth in front of Norm's desk. "The story is interesting by itself. There are some major news outlets following this. I didn't think they would turn it into complete science fiction."

Norm looked at me and shook his head.

"OK, look out," I said. "I'm calling him." I dialed David's number; he answered. "Is this David? Melissa here—your star reporter." I hoped he got the sarcasm.

"Oh hi Melissa! What you've been sending is wonderful! It's been extremely popular."

"Yeah, but that stuff is *not* what I've been sending you."

"We've seen a huge increase in sales. The entire country is dying to know what's going on down there."

I was ready to bite his head off. "Why are you changing everything I write?"

He condescendingly replied, "I did say we reserve the right to final edit. I just wanted to punch it up a bit."

"You just punched me in the face."

"We do what's necessary. We're a business."

I pulled the phone away from my face and gritted my teeth. I knew I shouldn't have written for such a shitty tabloid. What the hell I was thinking? "Alright, forget it!" I barked into the phone. "I'm not doing any more stories. Just make up your own copy."

There was a long silence. "Melissa, what you've been sending us is perfect." David had switched to his nurturing voice. "It's not often we have a legitimate journalist as a source of our information. Can I offer you some more money—let's say $1,500 a story?"

'Legitimate journalist'. I didn't reply; I was close to hanging up on him. I thought of the twelve hundred dollars that went into my bank account for what was pretty easy work. I thought, *fifteen hundred...for maybe two hours of work?* If he didn't care about the quality or accuracy, why should I?

After more silence, David pleaded, "Two thousand?"

"Twenty-five hundred!" I shouted. "I want two thousand, five hundred dollars—not a penny less."

"Wonderful! You'll have another story for us next week?"

"And take my name off the title. I don't want to be associated with any of this crap."

"Can we just change the spelling of your name?"

Gritting my teeth, I replied, "Just refer to me as Mel. Last name: Anoma. This whole thing is a cancer on my name."

"Mel Anoma it is."

21

Zeke had arranged a meeting with Tom Frazier at his house a few days after his radio show interview. Tom was supposed to show up around nine p.m. and fill us in on some big plan he had. The guy did offer up some compelling ideas, so I wanted to hear more from him. I would've remained firmly skeptical if it wasn't for the fact the FBI was actually after him. The Feds don't haul you away just because you're a wingnut.

I got to Zeke's garage studio ten minutes early and sat down on a lawn chair to wait. Eddie sat on a cooler, watching Zeke, who was pacing in front of him. For Zeke, the occasion was probably like meeting the Elvis of UFO sightings.

I asked him, "How did you set this meeting up?"

"He called me.....again."

"Do you think he'll show?"

Zeke continued pacing. "He said he had some extremely important information to get out. He'll show."

Eddie asked me, "So where's Noodles?"

"He's with his girlfriend. I haven't seen him in about a week."

Eddie thought for a moment. "Is that the chick from the cult?"

"Yes," I said. "I need to speak to Noodles about that. I think he's taking this getting-laid thing too far."

"Those people are fucking nuts," Zeke said. "Seriously—Fornacisians? I wouldn't…" His phone went off and he checked the caller ID, "It's Tom." He answered then listened intently as he nodded his head. "Sandy Neck Lighthouse," he repeated. He nodded a few more times, then hung up. "Tom's not coming here, we need to go to him."

"You gotta be kidding me," I said.

"He's concerned that my house is under surveillance. He doesn't want to come here. We have to meet him out at Beach Point on Sandy Neck."

"Way the hell out there?" I said.

"Yeah."

"Now?"

Zeke picked up his jacket. "C'mon, let's go."

"Do you know how far that is?" I said. "There's like six miles of beach you have to drive down before you get there."

"Look, he wants to make sure nobody is following us."

"Whose car we taking?"

"Mine."

"You don't have four-wheel drive," I said.

"It's fine. Let's go." Zeke bolted out the back door. Eddie picked up his cooler and I followed him out. We climbed into Zeke's piece of shit Toyota Corolla, I sat in the back next to Eddie's cooler.

Sandy Neck is a long spit of state owned land that shelters Barnstable Harbor. The cruel irony is the sand is mostly small rocks, so plenty of tourists have been disappointed when they've tried to throw a blanket down. At the far end is the Sandy Neck Lighthouse and a small community of cottages. There's an access road that takes you along a narrow stretch of beach. Zeke lived in Yarmouth so it only took us about twenty minutes to get to the Sandy Neck Gatehouse. It was empty so we drove right through. We kept going until we hit a little parking lot next to the ocean. The sun had already set and the sky was changing from twilight to darkness. Our headlights would have to guide us the entire way. Zeke had our location up on his phone. He pointed to our right and said, "OK, we need to go that way."

"Wait a minute, go back," I said. "I saw an access road that goes down to the beach."

He didn't listen. He put his car in gear, stomped on the gas and plowed directly over a sandy embankment. The tires spun like crazy and showered his car with sand. We fishtailed our way forward until we hit a section with more pebbles. The sound of hundreds of little missiles pelting the car's undercarriage didn't slow Zeke down.

Eddie let out a "WOO HOO!" as he stuck his beer can out the window. We eventually made it down to the flat part of the beach and got some forward momentum going.

Zeke laughed and said, "I told ya we'd make it!"

"Do you have any idea when high tide is? Can we even make it back?"

"We'll be back in no time, don't worry," he said.

We drove along the water for a while. The moon was throwing off a decent amount of light, so we could at least see the water line. The lighthouse grew brighter as we got closer. Occasionally a loud thump was heard as Zeke slammed into a rock. I was convinced the Coast Guard would be reporting a half-submerged Corolla in the morning, and some towing company would have to come rescue us. A dirt road branched off the beach as we got close to the lighthouse. Zeke drove off the path and continued down the beach for a few yards. He stopped his car, killed the engine and the lights.

"OK, now what?" I asked.

Zeke scanned the horizon. "He said he would meet us here."

We got out of his car and and fanned out. The top of the lighthouse rose above the dunes, its beacon blinking at us each time it rotated. The sound of waves could be heard off in the distance.

Eddie whispered, "I can't see a goddamn thing."

Zeke whispered back, "He said he'll meet us here."

I spun myself around and tried to orientate myself amidst all the desolation. Apart from the parking lot we'd left behind us, we were surrounded by nothing but sand and water. No one else was around for miles. I said, "Why are you guys whispering?"

"Security reasons," Zeke said.

"You gotta be kidding me."

Zeke quietly shushed me and peered into the darkness, listening intently.

I thought, *this is really stupid, how will Tom know we're here?* I yelled out, "HEY TOM! OVER HERE!"

Zeke frantically waved his arms at me and let out a huge, "SHUSH!"

"C'mon," I said, "he needs to know we're here."

Zeke threw his hands up in the air and walked away from me. We all stood still and listened. We could hear the waves and a distant lone sea gull. A voice called out from the dunes, "The mogul of New Mexico finds a distant bird."

Zeke responded, "Roswell that ends well."

I shook my head. *That's stupid. Do they really need to do secret agent shit?* Zeke walked towards a figure coming out of the darkness. When he returned with Tom, we all went back to Zeke's car.

Tom asked, "Were you followed?"

"No, no," Zeke assured Tom.

"OK, good. Wait here." Tom pulled out his phone, jogged halfway to the water and whipped his phone into the ocean. He came back and said, "I needed to burn that phone; it's no good anymore."

Zeke said, "The FBI is looking for you."

"They want to make me disappear," Tom said. "This information is too sensitive. If it got out... They've been following me ever since I walked off my job back in California."

"So what about this alien body at Otis?" I asked.

Tom leaned against the hood of Zeke's car. He spoke slowly as he revealed his secrets. "Otis was part of the Strategic Air Command back in its heyday. They had all sorts of nukes flying in and out of there during the fifties and sixties. Otis also hosted the 26th Tactical Missile squadron. They were ready to shoot down anything they saw as a threat."

Zeke nodded and said, "UFOs have been monitoring Air Force bases since day one."

"A Bomarc missile was launched on April 25, 1967 and brought down an unidentified target near the end of the runway," Tom said. "The wreckage was located in the town of Mashpee near what is known as the Makepeace Sanctuary area."

Zeke smirked and said, "How's that for ironic?"

Tom continued. "The report in the public archives mentions nothing about a missile launch. The Air Force claimed that a B-57 Canberra bomber fell short of the runway when it was coming back from a training mission. All personnel on the base were told not to go near the crash site and it was completely covered up. The few civilians who saw it go down were told to never speak about it or they'd be arrested."

"OK, hold on—we shot down a saucer?" I asked. "How hard can it be to avoid a missile from a civilization that's thousands of years less advanced than you are? C'mon, they're just not that dumb."

"I agree," Tom said. "But the beings responsible for sending the original spacecraft here weren't that advanced."

"Wait a minute; who is sending what, where?" I said.

"One of the pilots of that craft survived the crash, but was in rough shape. He and his dead crew were taken to Otis and treated the best way we knew how at the time. He lived for about two weeks and told them where he was from and why he was here. They were able to communicate with him because he wasn't that much more advanced than us. From what he observed of our planet, he said their civilization was only about a thousand years more advanced than our own. That's it. They were brought here by higher aliens."

I had to stop Tom right there. "Wait wait wait...*higher* aliens?" I said incredulously.

Tom's voice lowered. "Look, it's not just us versus them. There's an infinite amount of civilizations out in the universe, all at different levels of advancement. It's not in the interest of a higher intelligence to contact a lower form of intelligence. What do they get out of it? Anything we could offer would just be considered quaint to them."

"So why were they abducted and brought here?' I asked.

"The alien said they were a group of biologists on a mission to study the microorganisms on another planet orbiting their closest star. They were extremely surprised when they woke from stasis and found themselves in our solar system. Their data showed that they had been moved from one side of the galaxy to the other, by someone or something."

Zeke said, "Did they ever find out why?"

"This alien told us their civilization made it through their nuclear phase. They got close, but never blew themselves up. Their version of SETI had already discovered dozens of civilizations that had just ended before they even contacted them. Apparently intelligence destroys itself everywhere."

"That's not surprising," Zeke said.

Tom's voice climbed in intensity as he continued to speak. "Somebody, somewhere had put us on a galactic endangered species list and tried to do something about it. Apparently the alien species at Otis was the closest match to ours when the higher extraterrestrials paired us up. They figured that similar aliens had the best chance of communicating with us, to prevent us from going over the nuclear cliff. But guess what—we blasted them out of the sky before they could do anything about it! Their exobiologists weren't prepared to deal with a civilization that had nukes and missiles."

We stood there and looked at each other in silence for a moment. Zeke shook his head and said, "They actually came in peace and we blew them into pieces?"

"Take a guess why the government wants to cover this up?" Tom said. "Now they're coming back for their fallen comrades." He looked at me and said, "Did you notice how the UFO you saw at the fair eventually flew directly over the spot where the original one went down? Do you think that was just a coincidence? I need to get on that base, get to the evidence before the aliens retrieve their bodies. I know exactly where they are in the PAVE PAWS scanner building on Otis."

Zeke and I looked at each other. I was having a hard time processing all the information. Zeke asked Tom, "How can we contact you again?"

"I'll call you," he said.

The sound of a boat horn got our attention. About two hundred yards offshore, we could see what looked like a fishing boat. It flashed its searchlight across the water and the sound of its engine grew louder as it came towards us, following the shoreline. We watched in silence as it passed us.

I turned around. Tom was gone.

22

11100010 10000000 10011100 01010111 01101000 01111001
00100000 01101001 01110011 00100000 01101101 01111001
00100000 01100010 01110010 01101111 01110100 01101000
01100101 01110010 00100000 01101110 01100001 01101101
01100101 01100100 00100000 01010011 01101111 01100001
01110010 01101001 01101110 01100111 00100000 01000101
01100001 01100111 01101100 01100101 00111111 11100010
10000000 10011101 00100000 01010100 01101000 01100101
00100000 01111001 01101111 01110101 01101110 01100111
00100000 01101000 01110101 01101101 01100001 01101110
00100000 01100010 01100101 01101001 01101110 01100111
00100000 01100001 01110011 01101011 01100101 01100100
00100000 01101000 01101001 01110011 00100000 01100110
01100001 01110100 01101000 01100101 01110010 00101110
00001101 00001010 01001000 01101001 01110011 00100000
01100110 01100001 01110100 01101000 01100101 01110010
00100000 01110010 01100101 01110000 01101100 01101001

01100101 01100100 00101100 00100000 00100010 01010111
01101000 01100101 01101110 00100000 01111001 01101111
01110101 01110010 00100000 01100010 01110010 01101111
01110100 01101000 01100101 01110010 00100000 01110111
01100001 01110011 00100000 01100010 01101111 01110010
01101110 00100000 01110100 01101000 01100101 00100000
01100110 01101001 01110010 01110011 01110100 00100000
01110100 01101000 01101001 01101110 01100111 00100000
01001001 00100000 01100100 01101001 01100100 00100000
01110111 01100001 01110011 00100000 01110100 01100001
01101011 01100101 00100000 01101000 01101001 01101101
00100000 01101111 01110101 01110100 01110011 01101001
01100100 01100101 00101100 00100000 01100001 01101110
01100100 00100000 01110011 01100001 01110111 00100000
01100001 00100000 01100101 01100001 01100111 01101100
01100101 00100000 01110011 01101111 01100001 01110010
01101001 01101110 01100111 00100000 01110100 01101000
01110010 01101111 01110101 01100111 01101000 00100000
01110100 01101000 01100101 00100000 01100001 01101001
01110010 00101110 00100010 00001101 00001010 01010100
01101000 01100101 00100000 01111001 01101111 01110101
01101110 01100111 00100000 01101000 01110101 01101101
01100001 01101110 00100000 01100010 01100101 01101001
01101110 01100111 00100000 01110100 01101000 01100101
01101110 00100000 01100001 01110011 01101011 01100101
01100100 00101100 00100000 00100010 01010111 01101000
01111001 00100000 01101001 01110011 00100000 01101101
01111001 00100000 01110011 01101001 01110011 01110100
01100101 01110010 00100000 01101110 01100001 01101101
01100101 01100100 00100000 01010011 01101001 01110100
01110100 01101001 01101110 01100111 00100000 01000010
01110101 01101100 01101100 00111111 00100010 00001101
00001010 01010100 01101000 01100101 00100000 01100110
01100001 01110100 01101000 01100101 01110010 00100000
01110011 01100001 01101001 01100100 00101100 00100000

00100010 01010111 01101000 01100101 01101110 00100000
01111001 01101111 01110101 01110010 00100000 01110011
01101001 01110011 01110100 01100101 01110010 00100000
01110111 01100001 01110011 00100000 01100010 01101111
01110010 01101110 00100000 01001001 00100000 01100010
01110010 01101111 01110101 01100111 01101000 01110100
00100000 01101000 01100101 01110010 00100000 01101111
01110101 01110100 01110011 01101001 01100100 01100101
00100000 01100001 01101110 01100100 00100000 01110100
01101000 01100101 00100000 01100110 01101001 01110010
01110011 01110100 00100000 01110100 01101000 01101001
01101110 01100111 00100000 01001001 00100000 01110011
01100001 01110111 00100000 01110111 01100001 01110011
00100000 01100001 00100000 01100010 01110101 01101100
01101100 00100000 01110011 01101001 01110100 01110100
01101001 01101110 01100111 00100000 01100100 01101111
01110111 01101110 00100000 01101001 01101110 00100000
01110100 01101000 01100101 00100000 01100110 01101001
01100101 01101100 01100100 00101110 00100000 01010111
01101000 01111001 00100000 01100100 01101111 00100000
01111001 01101111 01110101 00100000 01100001 01110011
01101011 00100000 01010100 01110111 01101111 00100000
01000101 01100001 01110010 01110100 01101000 01101100
01101001 01101110 01100111 01110011 00100000 01000110
01110101 01100011 01101011 01101001 01101110 01100111
00111111 00100010

23

Sitting alone in my house all day, I came up with some inter-esting insights. It's strange how these thoughts never occurred to me before. There are times when Ken leaves me alone in the house for long stretches of time. I'm not sure if Ken is avoiding me or just has something important to do, like buying more tennis balls or frisbees. I've heard others use the word "Ken" when referring to him and he seems to respond. I knew I was associated with the word "Astro", but I had never assigned a word to him. It's frus-trating that I can't reproduce that sound "Ken" with my voice. Previously, if I wanted to get his attention, I used a crude bark that meant "Hey you!"

My greatest concern has always been the idea of him never re-turning. I would be very disappointed if he ran away from me, I've put an enormous amount of energy into him happy and occupied.

I've amassed a huge collection of bones out in the back yard that I don't have access to during the days when I'm alone inside.

I like to keep a few indoors to chew on and enjoy. The bones have such a nice savory flavor to them, which Ken doesn't seem to appreciate. He seems to have a rather crude sense of smell and taste, I'm not sure what can be done about that. I wish I could somehow get him to develop a palette for the finer things in life. It's inconvenient to hide my "indoor" bones before Ken returns home. If he spots any of them, they will get deposited in the back yard. Hiding them under the couch no longer suffices. I have to go through the trouble of carrying them all down to the basement every day before he comes back.

I recently discovered something that's of great convenience to me: I am now able to defecate indoors. Normally I would have to wait until Ken comes home so I could relieve myself in the back yard. He gets upset if I excrete on the carpeting. I learned this early: don't do it or there will be consequences. I've done some analysis about the situation but haven't come up with a good answer. What exactly is his concern? Am I competing with his own odor markings? He certainly seems to have a vast indifference to marking his territory with his own urine. And I've seen him react strongly when he steps in feces, immediately running for the garden hose and removing all traces of it from his shoes. Why he doesn't rub it all over his back is beyond me...

Ken has a favorite spot to defecate—a tiny room that we hardly ever play in. I've observed him doing this into a water-filled chair. It seems like such an odd behavior. Why would he deposit his feces there? My hypothesis is that he wants to keep them moist so he can consume them later. It occurred to me if that's what he prefers, I might as well mimic him. I gathered that if I could deposit my ejecta into the water-filled chair, Ken wouldn't have any concerns. On my first attempt I defecated onto the little rug surrounding the device, then carefully picked it up with my teeth and dropped it into the water.

I felt a great sense of satisfaction knowing there wouldn't be any hysteria from Ken when he arrived home later that day. I wondered if I should be placing other things into this storage receptacle as well. There's some kind of lever that triggers the sound of running water. Ken seems to have no problem activating this lever. I can get it to jiggle, but I'm not sure of its function. That will require some additional experimentation.

I have become rather blasé about the food choices Ken has been offering me. For years, I've been getting fed from the same bag of food that he keeps under the kitchen sink. Ken doesn't realize it, but, if I want to eat, I simply have to push the cabinet door open with my nose and stick my head into the bag. I am thus able to devour a mouthful of food whenever I wish. It seems strange that it never occurred to me to do this in the past. I've always been able to clearly smell the bag's contents behind that panel.

Recently, Ken came home holding a flat box that smelled wonderful. He put the box down on the kitchen table, patted me on the head and said something to the effect of "Astro, you're a positive individual, have you not seen me recently?" I had the sense that he was patronizing me, but still felt compelled to get excited. I had really missed him all day. He avoided me when I tried to lick his face. I was fascinated by the delicious smell emanating from the box. As usual, Ken filled my bowl with food from the bag under the kitchen sink, but I sniffed at it indifferently. I wasn't sure how I could explain to him that he no longer needed to go through the formality of pouring the food into my bowl. I had eaten plenty of it during the day, along with anything else on the floor that was edible.

He placed the wonderful-smelling box on the small table next to our couch and sat down. The thing that I call the "image device" somehow activated itself and started displaying moving pictures and sound. I think it sensed Ken had entered the room and decided to get his attention. It doesn't seem to have a preference for me when I'm in the room with it by myself. I know I've shown indifference to this device in the past unless an image of another dog appeared and even then it would hold my interest for only a few moments. Now that I understood it was symbolic in nature, the device had become much more fascinating to me.

A crowd of tall skinny humans, chasing a large ball, appeared on the image device that day. These humans obviously had the same obsession with chasing a moving ball as I did. Ken and I have played some fun games of keep-away, but these obsessed individuals took it to the next level. They kept trying to place the ball into a storage bag that had a hole in the bottom of it. Once the ball had fallen through, they would attempt to place the ball in a different storage bag a short distance away. These humans were pretty dim, as this bag too had a hole in it. They kept running back and forth, repeatedly trying both options to no avail. They were clearly getting frustrated with all the pointless activity. I'm continually fascinated by what humans will put themselves through. Occasionally the image device would show people eating and going for car rides, something both dogs and humans enjoy. I found myself staring at the image device and losing track of all sense of time. Only when I became distracted by the smell of the food Ken was eating did my focus waver.

I watched him pull a piece of flat triangular food from the box and bite into it. My mouth immediately watered. I put my paw on his leg, hoping for a sample. He continued eating until there was just a small piece remaining, then he handed it to me. Whatever was in my mouth was delicious. It wasn't the monotonous dry food he typically provided for me.

This is what I wanted.

I put my paw back on his leg. He ignored me and continued chewing. I had a repertoire of activities I could perform that would typically elicit a response from him. Remembering the "speak" command, I conjured up a little woof.

He kept chewing. Nothing.

I tried the "sit" command response and dropped my hindquarters to the floor.

Nothing.

I continued with the "down" command response and laid myself prone on the carpet.

Still no reaction.

I pulled out all the stops out and did the "beg" command response: I reared up on my hindquarters and hung my front paws limply out in front of me.

He mumbled something dismissively.

I needed to somehow communicate with him that I desired more variety in my diet. Specifically something like what he was eating. The occasional canned cuisine was all right, but I was desperate for something else.

I had an idea. What if I tried to communicate with Ken through symbols? He seemed to grasp the concept of symbols so I just had to figure out what represented my idea of food to him.

My bowl!

I ran to the kitchen and emptied out its contents onto the floor. I'd eat those later, I just needed the container. I brought it back to the living room and dropped it next to him. He glanced down and intoned something along the lines of "You've already been fed".

He wasn't getting it. I needed to convey the concept of "variety" to him. I need to show him a series of objects. I looked around the floor and spotted my squeaky toy. I placed that into my food bowl. I needed something else, but what?

Ken's smelly sock.

I ran upstairs and grabbed one from the bedroom floor. I placed that into the bowl and looked at him. He didn't notice and continued watching at the image device. I remembered a tennis ball had rolled under the coach a while ago. I crawled under there and retrieved it. That went into my bowl too.

I studied my creation. I now had a variety of objects in my bowl. I looked up at him in anticipation of some sort of response.

Nothing. He was still transfixed by the image device.

I barked at him then put my paw on the bowl. How could he not understand? I-want-food-variety.

Ken pushed the remaining triangular piece of food into his mouth. He chewed slowly as he looked down at my bowl then up at me. We stared at each other for a moment, but I wasn't sure if I was getting through to him. He got up and went into the kitchen. I heard the sound of his feet crushing the dried food I had abandoned on the floor, then an angry cry that I assumed was directed at me.

What is wrong with him that he can't comprehend a simple concept like "variety"? I thought humans were supposed to be intelligent.

24

I had to do an intervention for Noodles; he was taking this cult thing way too far. He exhibited all the classic signs of cult membership: lack of critical thinking, conformity to a weird dress code, avoidance of friends and family. I hadn't spoken with him in over a week. How much humping can one guy do?

Klick had rented a large old house in Marston Mills. It was listed on the National Register of Historic Places as the Ada Hollis House, built in 1793. The place was fairly substantial in size. I'm sure the original owners thought the only "aliens" entering their home would be British Redcoats.

I parked on the street in front of Klick's headquarters and waited for Mel to show up. She was interviewing Klick for a story and I wanted to come along and have her witness my intervention with Noodles. We both agreed there was safety in numbers. If one of us ending ended up wearing spandex, the other would have a bucket of cold water ready.

It looked as if Klick had increased his following substantially; his driveway was filled with cars. As I waited for Mel, I listened to three NPR stories and watched a bunch of strangely-dressed cult members enter the house. Mel pulled her car into a spot in front of me and we got out of our vehicles at the same time. I asked her, "So are we doing this?"

Mel hit the lock button on her car remote. "Does Klick even know you're coming?"

"He knows who I am, I wanted to surprise Noodles."

"Klick didn't blink when I told him I wanted to write a story about him for the Weekly World Gazette," Mel said.

"Seriously?"

"Yeah, I think he wanted the free publicity."

Incredulous, I looked right at Mel and said, "You're now writing for the Weekly World Gazette?"

She exhaled deeply and said, "The money they offered was too good to pass up. Yeah, yeah, I know—I'm a journalism whore for doing it. Never mind, let's get this over with."

We got to the front door and paused; inside we could hear a group of people doing some sort of bizarre chanting. I recognized the sounds as those I'd heard Klick making inside the college bathroom, but this time he had dozens of people following him.

"KKKkkkkkkkkkkkkkkkkkkkkkkkkkk"

It sounded like the furniture was being torn apart, slowly.

"SSSSsssssssssssssssssssssssssssssss"

I wondered if that was the sound of Klick systematically deflating their identities. We stood there and listened for a good minute. I whispered to Mel, "Are you gonna hit the doorbell, or should we just wait until they're finished?"

"I'm scheduled to speak to him in fifteen minutes. Let's just wait."

A car pulled into the driveway and wedged itself into the remaining parking spot. A male cult member got out and approached the entrance we were blocking. Mel met him at the bottom of the steps and said, "I'm here to interview Klick. Can we go inside?"

"Oh sure, come on in," he said. He casually threw the door open and led us in.

The front living room was filled with dozens of people sitting on a huge polka-dot carpet, all of them in the lotus position. There were posters of planets and stars incongruously tacked over the antique wallpaper. Klick was sitting near the fireplace, I noticed Noodles and Jennifer off to his side. No one reacted to our entrance. We made our way along the wall towards the dining room and stood behind a large oak table. With their eyes closed, the crowd raised their arms together and let out a series of sharp sounds.

"PIST! PIST! PIST! PIST!"

My heart jumped for a moment. *Did we just cause that?* There was a moment of silence after they all lowered their arms.

Klick announced, "Let the power of the consonant recede from your body!" The crowd exhaled and dropped their heads to their chest. He stood up and said, "OK everyone, let's prepare for the coil coalescence. Tammy, can you get the spinner?" Everyone stood up, laughing and chatting while stretching in various positions. I couldn't tell if they were getting ready to run a marathon or throw a party. Klick sounded like a cruise ship director coordinating his guests. "Whoever is going to pair off in the study, please don't disturb my papers on the table. Also, if anyone uses the tub, please leave the bathroom door unlocked so others can use the toilet."

Noodles spotted me and came over, "Hey dude! Surprising seeing you here!" In my peripheral vision I could see my best friend's bulge prominently outlined by his bicycle shorts. I tried like hell not to look down at him, but focused instead on Jennifer's body. Jesus, I could see why Noodles had gone to the dark side. Jennifer hung off his shoulder, smiling and gorgeous.

"Oh! Have you decided to start following the teaching of the Copacetic Coition Ambassador?" Jennifer asked.

"Ahhh…no," I said. "I'll be keeping my own sense of identity, thank you."

Klick and two male members approached our group, "Melissa!" he said warmly as he shook her hand, "I was expecting you!"

"Mel," she said. "I hope we didn't disturb you as we came in."

"No, not at all," he said. "The power of the consonant keeps your mind focused on the chakras. I didn't even know you had come in."

Klick turned to the two men behind him, "Bobby, Danny, this is Melissa…sorry! Mel. She is the reporter who wants to get our message out there. She's also one of the Chosen Ones. They all shook hands.

I leaned towards Noodles and whispered, "Hey, can we talk someplace?"

Jennifer said to Noodles, "I'm going to go help in the kitchen."

"OK," he said. They kissed and she skipped off towards another room. Noodles led me into the study and closed the door.

"Dude, what the fuck are you doing here?" I said.

Noodles gave me that same dopey look he wore whenever he didn't have an answer to something. He looked down at his feet and muttered, "Yeah, I know it looks kind of weird. But I haven't had this much sex ever."

"Well…OK. But a place like this can be dangerous."

Noodles looked up at me. "How is this dangerous?"

"I dunno, they want to fuck with your mind. They'll make you do things that you don't want to."

He stood there and with his mouth open for a second, then said, "I haven't done anything that I didn't want to do."

"Look at what you're wearing."

Noodles shrugged. "I dunno..it's pretty comfortable."

"You know what I'm saying. This is all classic cult behavior.

C'mon, let's get out of here."

"And do what?" he said.

I had to think for second, then replied, "And do what we normally have been doing. You know…"

Jennifer stuck her head in the room. "Hey you guys! Come on out…Klick is giving a toast!" We went into the living room and found Mel interviewing one of the male cult members. Klick approached us, holding a tray of Dixie cups filled with some kind of purple liquid.

"Hey everyone!" he said, "I would like to give a toast to our special guests Mel and Ken who are helping spread the teachings of the Fornacisians."

Smiling, Klick offered the tray first to Mel, then me. Everyone else grabbed a cup until the tray was empty. I was riveted by the purple liquid in my cup. Was I perhaps staring into my own oblivion? Now I knew what cold sweats felt like.

Klick raised the paper cup into the air and said "To that first step to euphoria!"

I looked over to Mel, who also had a deep look of concern on her face.

Everyone else was staring at us, waiting for us to drink first. I considered dropping to the floor and faking a full blown epilepsy attack. I held the cup up to my lips for a moment and waited. Klick tilted the cup up to his lips. Just as the liquid reached my lips he pulled his cup away…he was pretending to drink. I snapped the cup away from my face. He grinned at me and raised his cup again. The guy was just screwing with me. "Drink up everyone!" he said.

I saw Noodles bang back his cup. Everyone else drank theirs. "Come on Ken, you're not going to drink?" I closed my eyes and took a sip. I waited for a searing pain to shoot through my system. It was vodka. I opened my eyes and saw Mel was still holding her cup.

Klick said to her, "It's made with 100 proof Absolut. You don't want any?"

"No," she said slowly; "I can't drink while I'm working."

Klick asked me, "Ken, do you want any more?"

Screw it, I thought; *after that I need a drink.* I took her cup and downed it. "I'm not working," I said.

Everyone formed a circle around the polka-dot carpet in the middle of the living room. The dots formed a grid of colored circles; it certainly didn't match the early American decor. Klick was holding a board with some kind of pointer attached to it.. He flicked at it with his finger then announced, "Left foot, green."

Everyone scrambled onto the carpet and planted their left foot on a green circle. *Shit—it's an industrial-sized version of Twister!*

Klick continued calling out the commands, "Right hand, blue! Left hand, yellow!"

As the game progressed, I could hear moaning emanating from the entangled pile of human limbs. The sight reminded me of a carton of bait worms. Klick called out, "Left hand, left breast!" Everyone reached for their nearest female partner, male or female. They all went through the motion of groping each other, their moans increasing in volume.-

I looked over to Mel. She silently mouthed "What the fuck" to me.

Klick called out, "Right foot, any genital."

The event degenerated into a bizarre game of footsy. Everyone prodded their neighbors in the groin while attempting to keep their hands on the colored circles. People laughed as they lost their balance and rolled over on top of each other, groping and kissing. I definitely did not remember any of those commands in my childhood versions of Twister.

25

Ken told me about another one of his strange friends, Tom
Frazier. Apparently Tom claimed there were alien bodies on the
base at Otis and he wanted somebody to publicize his information.
The whole thing sounded exactly what David Brown at the Weekly
World Gazette wanted to hear. I was starting to get desperate for
stories to feed them. You can run only so many alien abduction
accounts. Ken and I were supposed to meet Tom at the Marconi
Wireless Station site on the National Seashore. We had driven out
there together in my car. From the front gate, we followed a long
narrow road that was the only way in or out. We passed through
clumps of scrub pines--the only trees that seem to flourish in the
salt air and constant wind.

Ken casually put his foot on my dash and rested his arms on
his knee. "What's going on with the Klick story?" he said.

I frowned and stared at his shoe, slowly grinding its pattern
into the vinyl. He was too busy staring out the window to notice. I

sighed and said, "They published the entire Klick story. They didn't change a thing."

"I could see Mantis Man joining Klick's cult," he said with a grin.

"I wasn't going there."

The access road eventually brought us to the Interactive Pavilion sitting next to the ocean. We parked at the end of the cul de sac, got out of the car and headed towards the building.

I said, "So Marconi more or less invented radio..."

"Right," Ken said as he scrolled though a Wikipedia page on his phone. "It says he figured out how to transmit over short distances around 1895."

"What was he doing here in Wellfleet?"

"By 1903 he wanted to communicate across the Atlantic ocean. This was one of the spots he built a huge antenna." Ken put away his phone. "As you can see, it's long gone."

We made it to the open air pavilion with its model of Marconi's antenna. From a patch of grass next to it, a sandy cliff dropped down to the beach. Ken leaned back on the railing and studied the rafters above us. "What I find amazing is the SETI guys are betting that Marconi found the best way to communicate through light years of space."

I slowly circled the inside of the pavilion, studying the model. "You don't think ETs would communicate though radio waves?"

"Well, they could. But who says there isn't a better way to communicate across those vast distances?"

"Like what?"

"I dunno. Maybe the aliens discovered something like 'Zeta' waves that can travel across dimensions. From their standpoint any intelligent beings out there would be using them, so thats what they'd be looking for."

"What's wrong with using radio waves?" I asked.

"It's like saying we should still be sending up smoke signals because there might be some Native Americans around. Just because we no longer see smoke signals doesn't mean there aren't any Native Americans; it just means they're using cell phones now."

"So the SETI guys shouldn't be looking?"

"No; it just seems odd that an Italian guy back in the 1890s might've figured out the best way to do it."

From the pavilion, you could look out at the horizon and see almost the entire length of beach that made up Cape Cod National Seashore. I took in a deep breath; the air was salty and clean and the only thing we could hear was the surf rolling onto the sand.

The tiny parking lot behind us was still completely empty. I asked Ken, "Do you know what kind of car he's driving?"

"Nope." Ken yawned and crossed his arms. "What are you doing Saturday?"

I scanned the road for any vehicles approaching. "Not much, why?"

"Do you want to have dinner at the Tiki Harbor?"

Tiki Harbor? That wouldn't be my first choice. I hadn't been there in years. "Ok. What time were you thinking?" I said.

"Around 5? I'll pick you up."

Five? That's a bit early. "How about 5:30 or so?" A faint, high-pitched sound was coming towards us from the direction of White Cedar Swamp. "Do you hear that?" I asked.

"Yeah."

We both scanned the horizon. An ultralight plane appeared just above the treetops, its engine growing louder as it approached us. The tiny triangular-shaped plane bobbed up and down as if it were trying to swim through ocean waves. It flew directly overhead then turned left over the water. It came back and did a complete circle around the pavilion. I could see the pilot leaning out, looking at the ground below him. "Who the hell is that?" I said.

Ken laughed. The pilot did a graceful figure eight as he descended over the water and lined the plane up with the beach. The craft rolled to a stop below us, at the bottom of the cliff. Silence returned when the pilot killed the engine. He took his helmet off and climbed out of his aircraft.

"Is that him?" I asked.

Ken smiled. "Yup."

We watched Tom struggle up the steep sandy embankment. He made it to the top, stood upright and brushed himself off.

Ken said, "Roswell that ends well?"

"No need to do that," Tom said dismissively as he dropped his gloves into his helmet. "I scanned the area before I landed. It's clear."

"Tom," Ken said, "this is Mel. She's the reporter."

With a stern look on his face, Tom shook my hand. "I've got some serious information I need released to the public. Your life might in danger if your name is associated with it. Are you up for this?"

Ken had already told me that Tom was a fruitcake of the highest order. I was sure the Gazette would snap his story up. I took out my note pad, made an effort to furrow my brow and nodded my head.

"Good," said Tom. "The government is hiding one or more extraterrestrial bodies in the PAVE PAWS radar building on Otis."

He stared at me for a moment, gauging my reaction. I fought back a smile and scribbled on my notepad "wingnut".

Ken said, "Tom worked at the installation on Beale Air Force Base. He knows the layout of these places."

I said, "The PAVE PAWS installation—thats the pyramid-shaped building surrounded by woods out on Otis?"

"Exactly," said Tom. "They've been using it since the cold war to transmit the location of the alien bodies."

"It's basically a giant homing beacon," said Ken.

Tom said, "You both saw the UFO that came by about a month ago?"

"Yes," I said.

Tom said, "You believe in UFOs, right?"

I said, "I believe what I saw was real."

"You were only six miles away from the installation at the time of your sighting. They're coming back."

"Wait a minute," I said. "How did these aliens get there?"

Tom pointed at my note pad. "Write this down: April 25, 1967. At exactly 22:31 hours they shot down a saucer that was hovering near the end of the runway, with a Bomarc missile. They cordoned off the entire area and retrieved the remnants of the saucer and its occupants and brought them back onto the base."

Ken said, "I've seen the newspaper reports. One news photographer said they had their camera taken away from them."

"The civilian witnesses were intimidated into silence. The Air Force reported that a B-57 Canberra bomber crashed in woods short of the runway in what's now the Makepeace Sanctuary area. That was all a cover story. They never reported who the pilot was. There was no pilot."

I said, "So what am I supposed to write?"

Tom frowned and started pacing. "I need to get on that base and get to the alien bodies before the UFO comes back to retrieve them. I need photographs, video and physical evidence. When I get it, it needs to be released to the public."

"OK, but how are you getting on the base?" I said.

"I was thinking of flying in under the radar on my ultralight."

Ken said, "But how are you getting back out? Once they hear you coming and see you land, they'll be all over you."

Tom thought for a moment. "The risk is worth the reward."

"What you need is a distraction of some sort," Ken said.

Tom leaned on the railing and looked out at the horizon. "It would have to be something huge."

"Really?" I said, "You guys are talking about breaking onto a military base?"

A police vehicle appeared on the access road, heading our way. We watched it pull into a parking spot. The officer got out and approached us. "Did you guys see anyone land an ultralight plane around here?" he said.

Ken and I said, "Yeah."

"Where is your friend going?" the officer said, looking toward the ocean.

Tom had disappeared. He was already on the beach, sprinting towards his airplane. The police officer stood next to us and we watched Tom scramble into his aircraft and start the engine.

"Why are you looking for him?" Ken asked the officer.

"He's been buzzing the airfield at Otis. A lot of people want him stopped."

The three of us stood on the edge of the cliff and watched Tom accelerate down the beach and get airborne. We watched the plane fly north along the coast until we could no longer see it.

I heard Ken whisper to himself, "He did it again."

26

From the moment I saw her, I found Mel attractive. I liked her attitude and sense of humor. We had a ton of things in common, and it felt right to ask her out on a date. After experiencing the UFO together, she practically felt like a war buddy. I was going to let our evening play out and see how she responded. I figured standard Chinese food would be a safe bet. On the Cape, the Tiki Harbor restaurant is epitome of a white person's idea of Polynesian-Chinese food. Plenty of deep-fried everything soaked in duck sauce with enough MSG to make your face explode with the sweats. The drinks are the main reason to go there. There's enough booze in every tropical concoction to make any Hawaiian shit faced.

I picked her up at her apartment and we headed over there fairly early. We were going through the Route 28 rotary when my playlist on the stereo hit "Do It With A Rockstar" by Amanda Palmer.

Mel said, "Did you ever see her in The Dresden Dolls?"

"I love those guys. Went to see them at the Paradise."

"Speaking of Boston, have you ever gone to Chinatown and had dim sum?

"I've heard about it. What is it?" I said.

"It's an endless parade of dumplings and other appetizers—usually brought round on food carts. You just pick and choose and eat till you hate yourself."

"Sounds interesting. Back when I lived near there, I used to make the trip into Chinatown when the bars closed and I still wanted a beer at 2 a.m."

We pulled into the Tiki Harbor parking lot and found a spot. As we got out of my car, a crushed McDonald's bag fell onto the pavement. I threw it into my back seat. "Don't you ever clean your car?" Mel said.

"I've been busy, I was gonna do that later."

Mel shook her head. "No, I meant the entire car. Seriously, I could've written 'wash me' in the dust that's on your dashboard."

"There's been a high pollen count this year."

Mel grinned. "Right."

We went inside and stood next to a five-foot-tall golden Buddha statue, waiting to be seated. The place had all the classic Asian-Hawaiian decor: a fountain with a penny-filled pool, red and black Chinese lanterns, a mural of pagodas on the wall and a pair of Asian warrior statues guarding the dining room entrance. Emperor Kublai Khan would've felt right at home there. A older Asian gentleman motioned us over to a booth. He dropped a pair of menus on our table and walked away. I opened it up and went right to the drink choices. "OK, whatta ya think? Do you want to share a scorpion bowl?"

Mel did one last scan of the drink menu and said, "Sure, why not."

Our waiter came back and placed a silver tea pot on our table.

"We'll have the scorpion bowl for two," I said. His expression didn't change; he just did an about-face and walked away.

While scanning her menu, Mel said, "So Game Of Thrones this week—I had to watch it twice to take it all in."

"You caught that bit with Gilly, right? What she read to Sam?"

"You know I didn't fully get that until the second watching. The thing that excited me the most was Jon and Drogon."

"That was pretty cool!"

The waiter placed the scorpion bowl between us and ignited the little bit of alcohol in the middle depression. I plunged my straw into the drink and drew in a mouthful, keeping an eye on the little flame six inches from my nose. The waiter patiently held his notepad and watched us in silence.

I asked Mel, "Should we start with an appetizer?"

"Ok." She flipped to the front of the menu. She looked at me and asked "Crab rangoon?"

"Sure!"

"Ok, we'll start with an order of crab rangoons."

I told the waiter, "I'll do Szechuan scallops. Can we have fried rice?" He didn't react and kept writing.

Mel said, "And I'll have General Tso's Chicken." The waiter finished writing and walked away.

I pulled the little paper umbrella out of the drink and twirled it between my fingers. "So what do you think of Klick?"

Mel finished taking a sip and swallowed. "I did some research. Klick's real name is Arthur Peachtree. His group is from Sacramento. He owned a chain of porno stores back in the eighties. He also published a series of magazines which such names as Butt Maids and Hefty Hooters. And he produced a series of videos, Xenohobic Nymphos 1, 2, 3 and 4."

"Oooh! those were good ones!"

Mel did a quick eye roll.

I smiled and said, "I'm kidding." I went back to my drink.

"He sold everything in the early nineties before porn went online. Apparently he did all right for himself. He'd been slowing gaining a following out in California. And then he came here."

The food came and we took turns peeking at what was under the silver domes. It all looked delicious. I went crazy spreading the scallops all over the fried rice on my plate. I motioned to Mel with my spoon, "You gotta try these scallops."

"Eh, they're not my thing. You want some chicken?"

I speared a piece with my fork and dipped it in some hot mustard. Mel shook her head. "What?" I asked.

"You ruined a perfectly good nugget of flavored unhealthy goodness."

"I like hot mustard!"

She shrugged. "I don't think that cop believed you when you said that Tom landed on the beach and asked where the restroom was."

I laughed. "Hey, I was trying to improvise under pressure." I poured a cup of tea, tore open three packets of sugar and dumped them in.

"Have a little tea with your sugar," she said.

"I don't know why I'm having tea; it was just taunting me over there."

"You don't have to drink it."

"I think I'm achieving a higher level of consciousness by combining alcohol, caffeine and MSG." I took a quick sip of tea and went back to my food. "A pair of FBI agents were also looking for Tom at the radio station."

"Really? He seems pretty far out there."

"He's got some interesting points," I said. "It's been proven that he did work for Raytheon and was assigned to the PAVE PAWS at Beale. He says that the PAVE PAWS installation has been sending out much stronger signals than they've told the public. They've been using the installation to communicate with something or someone outside our solar system for a while now."

Mel swirled her straw around in the ice and took one last sip of the remaining drink. "Interesting," she said. "I was going through some old articles. There were anti-radar station bumper stickers back in the late seventies protesting possible health concerns. Some people even moved out of Sandwich because of what they were experiencing. Everyone said the health studies were flawed because they were paid for by the military."

"I wouldn't put it past the military to do that."

"Now *you're* starting to sound like a conspiracy nut," she said.

I pointed my scallop impaled on the end of my fork at her and stressed, "You said yourself that people were being affected by it."

"I said *possible* health concerns. In 2007, a series of studies commissioned by the state Department of Health concluded that the high incidence of sarcomas and other cancers on the Cape weren't related to anything the military had."

"Of course not," I said. "Hey, do you want another scorpion bowl?"

"As long as you're drinking most of it."

I flagged the waiter down, gave him our empty bowl and ordered another one. We finished up eating the rest of the food and started on our second scorpion bowl. I felt pretty good about how our date was going up to that point. Mel seemed to be relaxed and enjoying herself. I was pleased that I could get her to smile at most of my jokes. The waiter cleared the table and brought us the check and a little bowl of pineapple chunks. With a bloated stomach, I put my back to the wall, slid my legs up on the seat and relaxed. I said, "Tom claims the extraterrestrials in the PAVE PAWS building were brought here by higher extraterrestrials."

"That sounds like Klick's story—higher beings coming here to have sex with him and his followers. You could almost put the two together."

I thought for a moment. "That would be interesting."

Mel looked at me and said, "What?"

"I wonder if Klick could be convinced that Tom's UFO is the same one he's waiting for."

"I thought that's why he was here."

"If Klick and his followers thought the UFO was going to land at Otis, it would make a hell of diversion."

"A diversion for what?" she said.

"So Tom could get inside the radar installation."

"Oh come on; you don't believe that guy?"

"Do you have a better explanation for why the UFO has been returning so often?"

Mel pierced a chunk of pineapple with a toothpick and popped it into her mouth. "No I don't, unfortunately."

I had a pretty good buzz rolling after two scorpion bowls. I was desperate to keep the connection with Mel going. I didn't know if it was from half a pot of tea or the MSG, but I felt the urge to do something besides just sitting there and talk. We had been doing that that for an hour; I was getting twitchy. It was a nice night out, why not have some more fun? I knew the perfect place: Pirate's Lagoon miniature golf.

27

What the hell was I thinking with that second scorpion bowl? I'm not twenty-two anymore. It was a decent enough meal, though I'd probably never go back to there on my own. And Ken's open mouth-chewing was starting to bug me. I felt like propping a chopstick under his chin to keep it closed. I don't know why I agreed to go miniature golfing, but Ken seemed adamant. I'd hit my alcohol limit for the night, so getting out in the fresh air was probably a good idea.

We got back into his car and headed for our destination. There's more than one mini-golf place along route 28. The moment we pulled into the parking lot, I recognized that particular one. For the longest time they featured a crashed airplane sticking out of a water fountain, but now it was a crashed UFO. I guess they wanted to capitalize on recent events.

The parking lot was full and the place was scattered with a mix of families and couples. We got in line. In front of us was a forty-something couple with their two kids, a boy in a striped shirt and a little girl who was twirling around in place. The boy locked eyes with me; I tried to ignore him.

I said to Ken, "I haven't played mini-golf since I was a kid."

He was standing fairly close to me and I had to resist the urge to put an arm out. "This is gonna be fun," he said.

I took a subtle half-step backwards and said, "Wasn't it Mark Twain who said, "Golf is a good walk spoiled?"

"He never did it on green outdoor carpeting."

"Do we have to keep score?" I said. "I really don't care if the ball goes into the hole."

"That's not the point. You do it to have fun."

A kid screaming by a fake shark momentarily got my attention. "I guess you're more easily amused than I."

Mini-golf places had changed since the last time I putted a ball through a windmill. Pirate's Lagoon was constructed on multiple levels, water flowed everywhere and there were hundreds of fake rocks as obstacles. Colorful pirate figures were posed randomly around the grounds. Walt Disney himself could not have designed it better. The family in front of us paid and moved ahead. We approached the payment counter. Ken said eagerly, "I'll pay."

I watched a guy take a selfie with his head inside a stock and said, "It was your idea!"

Ken finished paying, took a little pencil and scorecard and handed me a ball. I picked out a putter from the blue plywood rack and we approached the first tee. The family of four was now playing ahead of us. As we approached the dad was helping his daughter with the first shot. Her brother watched us as we approached. I locked eyes with him and gave him a subtle frown. He finally looked away. *Relentless little bastard*, I thought. *He'll probably grow up to be a sociopath.* Eventually they all took their first shots and moved on.

I held the putter out in front of me. "Bear with me—I haven't done this in years."

"Oh! Let me show you!" Ken got behind me and wrapped his arms my torso and held the little club like he was a golf pro. "Like this," he said as he wrapped his fingers around my hands. He was getting too touchy-feely for comfort. I hoped once his buzz wore off he'd come to his senses.

I gave my ball a smart tap and wriggled away from him. It rolled down the carpet and bounced off a fake rock that was blocking the hole. It almost rolled back to my starting position. "What do you call it when you want a do-over?" I said.

"A mulligan."

I looked down at my ball in dismay, it rested only three inches closer to the hole. "I don't like the color of my ball, let me get another one."

Ken laughed and shooed me away from the rubber mat and placed his ball down. He took his first shot and it easily went past the rock. "So my dog is acting weird," he said.

"How so?"

"He likes to watch TV."

"What's so weird about that?" I said. "Most dogs will look at a TV screen, especially if another animal comes on."

"No, no...he really likes to watch TV, like for hours at a time."

I finally got my ball into the hole, after four shots. "Maybe he's bored," I said.

"He once watched an entire basketball game. It was really cute, he kept tilting his head when players did anything different." Ken lined up his ball and tapped it into the hole. "It was like he was trying to make sense of it."

"So your dog likes to watch TV," I said.

"That's not everything. I think he's learned how to toilet train himself."

"Get out."

"Seriously. He hardly scratches at the back door anymore."

I grinned. "He's probably pissing on your carpet somewhere."

"Last night I heard the toilet flush. I got up to see what was going on, and I saw him coming out of the bathroom."

"OK?"

Ken thought for a moment. "He also keeps arranging his toys in front of me and pawing at them, like I need to do something with them."

"Then why don't you play with him?" I said.

Ken shook his head. "No, he doesn't want to play. It's like he's trying to show me something."

"Maybe he wants new toys."

"I dunno. I don't think that's it. It's weird."

A backup of players had formed at the fourth hole. The little bastard with the striped shirt was waiting for us. Ken and I got in line and leaned against a fake rock, waiting our turn. Ken also noticed the kid staring at us. We all locked eyes for a moment and the kid spoke up. "Are you guys married?"

"No, not to him," I said.

Ken said with a grin, "Do you know what an affair is, kid?" He pointed at me and said, "That's what she's doing to her husband right now."

I gave Ken a friendly jab. "Will you shut up!"

The kid didn't react; just turned away. Eventually the family in front of us finished. This was the hole that featured the crashed saucer. An alien body stretched across the putting green as an obstacle. I put my ball down and said to Ken, "So I have a question for you. If aliens are supposed to be secretly observing us, why do they leave their lights on?"

"I dunno."

I gave my ball a tap and watched it disappear behind the alien. "Why would they want to make their presence known? You'd think they'd want to remain hidden, to avoid influencing their subjects."

Ken put his ball down and lined up his shot. "Maybe it's their propulsion system."

"If, as you keep saying, if they're supposed to be really advanced, how hard could it be? If you're going to send spacecraft to study other beings, wouldn't being able to turn your lights off be up there on the design spec?"

Ken hit his ball and watched it roll past the alien body. "Never thought about that."

"Let's say you want to study lions from your jeep. Leaning on the horn on the whole time would not be the best idea."

"I got it." Ken stopped smiling and a strange look came over his face.

"What is it?"

"I feel kind of weird." Ken held up one finger and stood very still and with his hand on his chest.

"You OK?"

He nodded then burped. He coughed and seemed to recover himself.

We got to a hole where we had to hit our balls up a steep incline. We couldn't see where the ball would end up until we were on the other side. I smacked my ball hard and watched it clear the top. When I got on the other side I saw that little kid again. He was standing next to the hole, watching my ball roll towards him. He nudged his foot forward, letting the ball bounce off his sneaker, then he ran over to his family. Ken's ball came flying over the incline and he appeared behind me. I pointed at the family. "That little fucker just kicked my ball."

"Where?"

"He was standing right here next to the hole."

"I thought you didn't care what your score was."

"That's not the point. He touched my ball."

Ken laughed. "Just think of him as another obstacle on the course."

"Obstacle?" I repeated. "I'll be an obstacle to the kid reaching his next birthday. He better not try that again."

Ken laughed and said, "I thought you weren't going to take this seriously?"

"Yeah, I know…" Maybe it was the second scorpion bowl talking.

We tried to play another hole, but the expression on Ken's face slowly deteriorated. "I don't feel good," he said.

"Was it the booze?"

He leaned forward and propped himself up by his putter. He leaned forward like he was going to puke. "That's not it. Something else is going on."

"What do you want to do?"

He looked at me with a sad puppy-dog expression on his face. "Can we get out of here?"

We headed for the exit. "What do you want to do?"

Ken had a horrible expression on his face. "I gotta go home," he said. "I'm *really* not feeling well."

"Do you want me to drive?"

"No, I think I'm OK for that." We got on route 6 and drove for about a mile before we got caught in a line of traffic. Ken was slowly rocking back and forth in his seat. He rolled down his window and said, "Fuck."

"What?"

Ken's face went pale. "Ah fuck," he whispered. He pulled over, opened his door and puked. I could hear his stomach contents splashing against the pavement. This in turn started a gag reflex on my part. I knew if the smell hit me, it would be over for both of us. I tried to take my mind off what I was experiencing and focused on the sign in front of us. We were outside the Kwiky Klean Kar wash.

I couldn't help myself; the coincidence was too good. A car wash—clean out the contents of you car and your stomach at the same time. I felt like such a shithead. Poor Ken was barfing his lungs out and I found humor in the situation. I hoped he would feel better once this was all over.

Ken leaned back into the car and closed the door. He rummaged through his side door pocket, found a napkin and wiped his face. He gave me a sorry look. I put my hand on his shoulder and said, "Are you still sure you're fine?"

He nodded. "I don't know what the fuck is going on."

"Do you want me to drive?"

"No, I feel better."

"What do you think is going on?"

Ken stared at the dashboard. "I don't know. It might've been the scallops." He rested his forehead on the steering wheeled and exhaled deeply. He looked back at me with an uncomfortable grin.

I pointed up at the sign.

He looked up and read it. It took a moment to register. He smiled, put his head back down on the steering wheel and groaned.

28

It took me a entire day to feel normal again. I managed to drop Mel off and get home before another round of puking went off. She called me the next day and said Cape Cod Hospital had been treating people for apparent food poisoning. They tracked them all back to Tiki Harbor. Apparently they'd had previous health violations. I told myself I'd never go back there no matter how much booze they put in their Mai-Tais. So much for making my move on Melissa; I was sure she thought I was just a big bag of bile.

I had spoken to Klick earlier in the week and told him about Tom Frazier. I told Klick that he had important information about the UFO sightings on Cape Cod and that it was relevant to him. He said he knew who Tom was and would love to meet with him. Of course, Tom wouldn't meet Klick at his compound in Marston Mills and keep things simple; he was still convinced that everyone on Cape Cod was being watched by the authorities. He said he

would contact Zeke and we would all meet at a location of his
choosing. I prayed to God that he wasn't thinking of sending us
out to Nantucket on the ferry.

We waited in Zeke's garage for the initial contact from Tom.
It was a warm night out so his garage door was open. Zeke paced
nervously while Eddie sat on his cooler. Zeke said, "Satellite is
thinking of picking up my radio show."

Bored, I leaned back in my lawn chair and stretched my arms
out, "Really?"

"My audience has grown like crazy," he said.

"I noticed your Twitter account is up to 80,000 followers."

Zeke kept glancing at his phone. "There's a lot of people
around the country paying attention to what's happening here."

"If Tom is right," I said, "it's gonna be like The Day the Cape
Stood Still around here."

Eddie blurted out, "Klaatu barada nikto dude!"

I said, "We've got to somehow get Klick's entourage onto the
runway on Otis."

"Tom thinks if this diversion works, we can get into the PAVE
PAWS station through the woods on the Bourne side of the base,"
Zeke said. "We can cut a small hole though the chain link fence
where the power lines cross route 6."

An email alert went off on Zeke's phone. I looked over his
shoulder to see who it was. Tom had sent a message, but it was
just a series of scrambled letters. Zeke said, "He sent it with PGP
encryption. I have his public key."

"I thought people who are only into child porn use that," I
said.

Zeke frowned. "You can't be too careful." Zeke entered the
information and the letters descrambled revealing the message in
the email:

I'm here at Baxter's in Hyannis, outside on the pier.

I sent a text message to Klick:

We're meeting with Tom at Baxter Boathouse in Hyannis.

After a minute, Klick replied with:

On my way.

Baxter's Boathouse is a seafood joint that sits right over the water. You can pull your boat up to the side of their restaurant and get a meal. We drove out there and found Tom sitting at a table at the end of the pier. There were a dozen other tables that were mostly empty. The way he sat—back to the ocean, scanning the pier in front of him—he looked like a character from some gangster movie. The three of us headed towards his table. Behind Tom the lights of the houses surrounding the harbor shone off the water. He was eating a lobster and had a bottle of wine beside his plate.

We all sat down across from him. With a loud snap Tom crushed a claw with a nutcracker. "You guys weren't followed?"

"No," Zeke said.

"OK, good, good," Tom said. He scanned the tables behind us. There were only two other couples seated on the pier. Most of the noise came from the crowd inside the restaurant.

I said, "I messaged Klick when we got your message, he's on the way."

Tom smiled. "Fornacisians? He sounds like a piece of work."

Zeke said, "It sounds like he has a huge following. If you can convince him to get on the runway, we'll have a clear shot at the radar building."

Tom nodded and dipped a piece of lobster into a dish of butter. He held up the fork with the little chunk of meat and studied it. "This whole thing is going to blow your mind."

"I've got a high end DSLR." I said. "I'll be shooting 4k footage of everything."

Tom took a sip of his wine. "I've got samples bags. I want some hard evidence that our subject is real."

Eddie said, "Should we just take the whole body?"

Tom said impatiently, "What are we going to do with it? Have it melt in our hands? I don't think they would be too pleased. I want to make sure they retrieve their comrade fully intact. I'm sure their version of cryogenics is much more advanced than ours."

"So Tom," I said, "Klick claims his father was a Fornacisian."

"From one of the stars in the Fornax constellation?" he said.

"Alpha Fornacis precisely," I said. "His father's name was Tick. He also said he looked kind of like Elvis."

Tom wiped his hands on a napkin and repeated quizzically, "Elvis?"

I nodded. "Yeah."

He took a sip of wine then thought for a moment. "I can work with that; good." He put his glass down. With an odd look on his face, he stared over my shoulder. I turned around. Klick, wearing a green silky robe, was at the entrance, accompanied by several members of his silver-spandexed entourage. We motioned at him to come sit next to us. Noodles and Jennifer took a table next to me. I nodded at Noodles and he smiled back. The dozen or so other followers spread out to the other tables.

Klick came towards us. "So Klick," I said, "this is Tom Frazier."

They shook hands and Klick sat down. "I've heard a lot about you," he said.

Tom said, "I've got some amazing information to tell you." He waved the waitress over to us. "Can I get anyone a drink? Do you guys want some food?" Everyone promptly ordered beer and appetizers. "So Klick," Tom said, "I think we have similar objectives."

"I've heard about the alien bodies at the radar installation," Klick said.

Tom leaned towards Klick and said quietly, "The government doesn't want me telling anyone what I've learned. They're willing to do anything to silence me."

Zeke said, "We've all been interrogated by the FBI. They're looking for him right now."

Klick looked at me. "It's true," I said.

"There are some things I've never told the public," Tom said.

Klick smiled and said, "There are some who don't want to hear the truth."

"I worked at the PAVE PAWS radar installation at Beale," Tom said. "I've had access to some important documents. Do you know they brought down a saucer on the night of April 25, 1967?"

Klick shook his head. "No."

"It was hovering above the end of the runway at Otis. The bodies were recovered and brought back onto the base," Tom said.

"It's all classified;" Zeke said, "it's all been covered up."

Tom looked right at Klick. "One of the aliens lived for a short time. He said his name was Tock and he was from the constellation Fornax."

I had to correct Tom. "I thought you said his name was 'Tick'?"

Tom said dismissively, "Tick...Tock...the reports said they had a hard time understanding him. He was in a lot of pain."

Klick asked Tom, "What did he look like?"

Tom took a sip of his wine, put it down and ran his finger along the edge of the glass. He took his time speaking his next sentence, milking it for all it was worth. "Here's the thing, Klick," he paused dramatically. "The reports say he was a very attractive being."

"How so?" Klick asked,

Tom paused for a moment, then said, "He looked like a famous singer. Kind of like Elvis."

Klick was silent for a moment. "Are you sure?"

"Why would I make this up?"

Klick's expression sank; he was devastated. I didn't think he really believed all that stuff about his father being a Fornacisian. I thought he was just making it all up to get laid. Klick was starting to tear up.

"Yeah," Tom said wistfully, "they said his favorite song was Love Me Tender. It was the last thing he sang before he died."

I felt like kicking Tom under the table. I couldn't believe he was laying it on that thick. How the hell would an extraterrestrial know the song *Love Me Tender?*

Klick whispered, "My father loved that song."

"Does any of this make sense to you?" Tom said.

Klick stared at the table. "I've always wondered why my father abandoned me on this planet."

"When did you see him last?" Tom asked.

"The fall of 1966."

"As I said," Tom said, "the saucer was brought down on April 1967."

Klick slowly shook his head. "My father told me we shouldn't be using nuclear weapons."

Tom gave Klick a reassuring touch on his forearm. "He was trying to make a difference Klick. He told us himself."

"Where can I see him?" Klick asked.

"The same UFO has been coming back to Cape Cod because the Fornacisian are returning for their dead comrade. They'll be looking for him at the exact spot where he disappeared, at the end of the runway on Otis."

Klick was deep in thought. He said, "I've got to be there."

"The documents said they'll be returning on Saturday, August 26th, during the waxing crescent moon."

Klick slowly nodded. You could see the wheels spinning in his head, forming a plan. Klick formed two fists on the table and said, "It's my *birthright* to be there." He was silent for a moment, then announced, "I've got to tell my followers." He got up and said something to Noodles and Jennifer, then moved to the other tables where his followers were sitting.

Tom looked at me and smiled. "This guy is fucking nuts."

Noodles came over to our table and said, "So what is going on August 26th?"

Tom said, "Something wonderful!"

Noodles thought for a beat then said, "Jupiter will turn into a sun?"

I laughed. Tom referred to a line from Arthur C. Clark's 2010 and Noodles immediately got the reference. I pulled Noodles over to another table and told him, "The Fornacisians will be arriving at Otis on the night of August 26th"

"Really?" Noodles said, "I thought this was all bullshit."

"Sssshhh!" I said. "I know, I know; just go with it. Trust me."

Noodles went back to Jennifer and I sat back down with Tom and Zeke. Klick was very animated, explaining this new information to his followers.

Zeke said, "I think it worked."

"Hopefully he'll be such an annoyance we can get to our objective without any interference," Tom said.

"Do you think the military will have to foam the runway to get rid of them?" I asked with a grin.

Tom smiled and went back to eating his lobster. Four guys in Coast Guard uniforms appeared at the entrance. They had everyone's attention for a moment as they laughed loudly over a joke one of them had made. It looked like they were just waiting for a table.

I asked Zeke, "Do you think they patrol the outside perimeter of the base?"

"Not since the Cold War ended", he said.

I was going to ask Tom a question but he had vanished. Zeke did a double take at the empty spot in front of him. "Where did he go?" he asked.

We both spun around in our seats and scanned the pier. *How the hell could he vanish like that?* We heard the sound of a motor starting up below us on the water. Zeke and I stood up in time to see Tom in a motor boat pulling away from the dock. The outboard engine went up in pitch as he gunned it. "Really?" I said. "He thinks the Coast Guard is also looking for him?"

"I guess you can't be too careful in his position," Zeke said.

Klick came over to us. "Where's Tom?"

We pointed to the little boat heading out towards the middle of the harbor. "Where is he going?" he asked.

"We're not sure," Zeke said, "But he does this all the time." The rest of Klick's followers formed a crowd at the railing. We listened as the sound of his engine faded away into the darkness.

Behind us, we heard an annoyed voice say, "Excuse me. Excuse me."

We turned around in unison. It was our waitress. "Where does your friend think he's going?" she said. We all shrugged. The waitress impatiently tapped the bill on the edge of a table. "Well then, who is paying for all this food?"

29

Purina Dog Chow.

That's exactly what the bag read. I've been watching Ken empty that bag into my bowl for the longest time, but I never understood what the pattern on the side of the bag represented. They were *letters*, and when strung together, they convey meaning. Isn't that something? I never realized that. I've been surrounded all my life by these symbols and now they just pop out at me. I discovered reading by accident and it has become a passion of mine. The thing that led me to this discovery was a colorful puppet show on our PBS station. The puppets' fast motion caught my attention, and I eventually realized they were wielding letters of the alphabet. From there it was easy to learn sentence structure and syntax.

By now I had collected a substantial amount of femur-like bones and they were neatly tucked away in my back yard. I can chew on those until my jaws give out. It's child's play getting out of my yard. Ken has no idea that I can easily get through the gate and have my run of the neighborhood. It still puzzles me why Ken keeps me fenced in. Is he concerned I won't be available to placate him with a lick at a moment's notice? He does seem extremely needy for my attention at times; I need to come up with a method of breaking him of this behavior.

I thought I had collected every bone in my neighborhood; it was a case of diminishing returns each time I went out to hunt them. But, on a recent expedition, I noticed an intense odor that seemed to come from beyond my neighborhood. It appears I somehow missed a monster-sized bone. When I had let myself out through the gate, I trotted a good twenty minutes towards this new objective, taking mental note of the landmarks I passed.

I ended up tracking the smell to a large warehouse. The same white van I discovered earlier was parked in front of an open garage door. The man in the Hawaiian shirt was unloading bones from his vehicle and transferring them to a large pile of boxes. There were about two dozen open boxes overflowing with the things. The smell was incredible; I was salivating just looking at them. This discovery explained why I hadn't found many bones in my neighborhood—my nemesis in the flowered shirt was beating me to them. I hid behind a metal dumpster on the other side of the parking lot and watched him empty the precious cargo. I made sure he couldn't see me. I was sure he would recognize me from our previous encounter when I emptied his van of all the bones he had collected. It seemed odd that this human had the same obsession as I do. Ken always seemed repulsed any time I offered him a bone from my collection. I watched the man finish unloading his cargo, close the door, and drive off.

I sat there for a few minutes and waited. I didn't see any other activity so I ran into the building, grabbed a bone off the top of the first box and ran back to my spot behind the dumpster. I did this a second time then realized that it would take forever, I still needed to get everything back to my house.

I ran back inside the warehouse and surveyed the situation. There must've been a couple hundred of these bones, overflowing the dozen or so boxes that were siting there. It would take me weeks of shuttling back and forth to move all these. I didn't see any good place to hide so many. Outside of the warehouse, there was just an open parking lot surrounded by other buildings. If I made a pile of them behind the dumpster, anyone could easily spot them. I looked around: there were odd pieces of machinery scattered around the floor and rows of tall shelves circled the inside of the warehouse. I heard a door open behind me; somebody was coming my way.

I sprinted to the side of the warehouse and hid under some shelves. A pair of workmen came out and one of them closed the garage door. As I watched the opening to my freedom squeeze shut I was a little concerned that I might not be able to get out of there. One of them started to move boxes from one pile to another. He struggled for a bit, so the other one said something about using the 'electric pallet jack'. He went over to a device that looked like a u-shaped platform on wheels. Attached to it was an arm with a handle of some sort. By moving this handle, he was able to slide this device under a large stack of boxes and move them without any effort.

I ended up sitting there for hours, watching them open and close the garage door as other vehicles arrived. They would unload their cargo onto stacks of other boxes, or what one of them called 'pallets'. I never had the opportunity to run back outside as they quickly closed the door once they were done unloading of each vehicle. From my vantage point, I did get a good look at how the door operated.

The last truck left just as it was getting dark. Before the men left for the night, they wrapped all of the bones with some kind of plastic and parked the electric jack under their pallet. The lights turned off as they left through the back door. I heard the voices of the two workmen fade away as they went deeper inside the building. After some minutes, I heard two cars start up outside and drive away.

I was now alone inside the building. The glowing EXIT sign above the door threw off enough light so I could see. I remembered how Ken turned off the lights in our bedroom by flipping a switch next to the door. I hoped I could find something like that near the door where they left. I crawled out of my hiding space and stretched. It felt good after being wedged in there for so long. I went to the back door and found a familiar switch to the right of it. I flipped it up with my nose and the lights came back on.

My first order of business was: could I get out of there? I found the button on the wall which seemed to activate the door. I stood up on my hind legs, steadied myself with my front paws and gave the button a push with my nose. The door slowly opened.

That was easy.

I was ready to take off for home, but something got me thinking. It seemed the electric pallet jack could easily move the huge pile of bones that were now wrapped in plastic, sitting on a pallet.

Could I somehow move the entire thing?

I walked around the pyramid of boxes that were supported by the pallet jack and studied this puzzle.

If I climb up onto it and pushed the handle down with my front paws, can I twist it with my jaws to get it to move?

If it worked, I could take the entire load home with me! It was an exciting thought. If I could add this many bones to my collection, I could start my own canine theme park. It took a few jumps, but I managed to get myself up onto the jack with my front paws resting on the handle. The boxes were behind me and I was facing in the opposite direction a human would push it. I slowly leaned forward as I put my body weight on the handle, then gave the bar a twist with my teeth. The whole thing suddenly lurched backwards with me on it and I crashed into some shelves behind me.

Wrong way.

I steadied myself and gently bit down on the handle again. I could feel the pallet jack slowly inch forwards. I applied a little more pressure with my jaw and the entire unit accelerated. I locked my paw on the spot I had twisted and watched the garage door pass overhead as I rode straight out into the parking lot. I released the pressure on the handle and it rolled to a stop.

OK, this is going to work.

I jumped off and gave myself a shake, I would have to think this through. How was I going to get home without anyone seeing me do this? I didn't want the guy in the Hawaiian shirt coming after me, he'd definitely want to know where his pallet of bones went. I ran to the edge of the parking lot and scanned the street for anyone coming. There were a few street lights in the distance. I didn't hear any cars coming, only crickets. I got back on the pallet jack and got it moving a little easier this time. Steering was kind of tricky; it took a couple of tries of shifting my weight to get myself lined up in the right direction so I would be heading home. I discovered that if I lost my grip on the handle, I was able to reset my position and get a little more speed going. The pallet jack whirred as I passed the familiar landmarks that led me to the warehouse. Everything was dark except for the occasional pool of light under a street lamp. I didn't see anyone as I passed rows of houses with their lights off.

This is kind of fun.

I was trying to imagine all the places I could go on this thing. I understood why Ken likes to drive his car.

It took me a about thirty minutes to get the pallet jack and its cargo back to my house. I stopped in front of my driveway, hopped off and took a quick look around. I was all alone. I spent a good two hours shuttling all the bones, two at a time, to the back yard. I told myself I would bury them later; I was too exhausted at that point to start digging any holes.

The final thing I needed to do was to move the pallet jack away from the house; I knew those guys back at the warehouse would come looking for it. I was able to move the empty jack only a few driveways down the street before it just stopped. I don't know why I couldn't get it moving again.

I also needed to move all the empty boxes that were strewn around my driveway onto the porch of my neighbor's house. I figured it would give him a good place to store all the bags of my feces he'd been collecting. The sun was just starting to come up as I closed the gate behind me, went inside and collapsed onto my doggy bed. I fell asleep dreaming of the field of bones I had collected for myself.

30

The old man took a blue corner piece and placed it next to another blue puzzle piece. He picked up a mostly red piece and held it up to the box. "I've never been to the Nauset lighthouse, isn't that something?" he said. The box showed what his final puzzle would look like, the restored red and white light house that's out on Nauset Beach in Eastham.

Earlier in the week, I did some research on the Tom Frazier crashed saucer story of 1967. I found the incident mentioned in an article on some microfilm at the Mashpee library. The headline read: Mysterious Plane Goes Down. On April 25, 1967, an aircraft of some sort really did crash near the end of the runway on Otis Air Force Base. The Air Force never disclosed the type of aircraft that went down, nor did they mention anything about a Bomarc missle being fired that night. There were no photos associated with the story. It said all civilians were escorted out of the crash site by Mashpee police chief Charles Clipstone.

I had tracked down the ninety-four year old Charles Clipstone putting together his puzzle at Bayberry Hills Nursing Center. We sat next to a window framed by two ficus plants. An old woman sat motionless on a bench, watching a network morning show on the wall-mounted TV. I tried my best to ignore the screen, as the host, Pam Meagan blabbered on about the latest events.

I asked Charles, "Do you like doing puzzles?" I caught myself speaking in a slightly patronizing tone the way most people do, under the assumption that very old people and children don't have the same mental capacity as adults.

Charles stared at the pieces, let out a deep breath and said, "What else is there to do?"

"You were the police chief for Mashpee back in 1967?" I said.

Charles picked up a piece and hovered it over a nearly complete section. "I had a part-time department of three men: one sergeant, two patrolmen and one cruiser. That's all we had."

"I guess things were slower back then," I said.

"If you wanted waterfront property, you could afford it. You just had to drive a little further."

I showed him the printout of the article I found. "This says an aircraft of some sort crashed out in the woods of Mashpee on April 25, 1967. Do you recall anything about it?"

He studied the article for a moment. "Before I became chief of police I had retired from the Air Force as a lieutenant colonel in the 551st Airborne. We were stationed at Otis. We were flying F-94 Starfire aircraft out of there. We had responsibility for the air defense of Boston." It seemed his longterm memory was intact, thankfully.

"Did you see anything unusual that night? One story I read said a B-57 Canberra bomber crashed in the woods."

He shook his head and handed the printout back to me. "No, that was a cover story. They didn't want the public to know anything."

"A cover story?" I said, "Who else knew about it?"

"The entire base did. I knew the station commander; I actually recommended him for his promotion."

"So no one was supposed to know about the crash? Do you remember anything about a photographer having his camera taken away?"

Charles pushed his finger through a pile of pieces. "Yeah, that guy was a trouble maker. We told him not to take any pictures. We were dealing with very sensitive hardware out there."

I sat upright when he used the term 'sensitive hardware'. Maybe Tom was onto something after all. I pulled out my notepad and asked him, "Were there any bodies?"

"The pilot ejected ten seconds before he hit the ground," Charles tapped a piece in place. "We had to fish him out of Mashpee pond."

"What did this occupant look like?"

He studied his puzzle for a moment. "I don't know...Italian?"

I wrote down Italian with a question mark. "Where did they take the UFO?"

Charles stopped doing his puzzle and looked up at me. "A UFO? Who told you that?"

I had to pause for a moment. I wasn't going to say a "UFO conspiracy wingnut." I looked back down at my notepad and pretended to write something, "There was a rumor."

"It was an A-12 Oxcart," he said. "The program before the SR-71 Blackbird, a top secret spy plane. One was flying back from Europe, had a flameout over the Atlantic and had to land but it fell short. I got out to the crash site before any of the MPs showed up. I knew all of them by name. I saw exactly what I was dealing with and helped keep the public away."

I asked, "So this was classified information you had access to?"

"I got a debriefing about a week later," Charles said. "This was all off the record and I understood that."

"Did they tell you not to talk about it?"

He studied another piece of his puzzle. "They were glad that I was the only civilian who knew what was going on and could do anything about it." Charles dropped the piece he was holding into a section in front of him.

For a moment I wondered if this was a cover story for the cover story. Would he take the truth to his grave, or was I just being as paranoid as Tom? I felt kind of silly mentioning a UFO. It seems to take about thirty years with any kind of incident for folklore to develop. Memories get fuzzy, second-hand accounts are taken as facts. In the original newspaper reports out of Roswell, nothing was mentioned about alien bodies. It took an additional thirty years of retelling the same story to include them.

I was ready to thank Charles and leave him with his puzzle when I saw my UFO footage appear on the TV. Pam Meagan, the world's most insipid daytime talk show host spoke over my footage. "What is going on over Cape Cod? Are aliens here to invade us? A rash of UFO sightings has really shaken up a tourists and experts alike." They cut back to the studio with its audience of mostly women. Next to her was Russell Holt, sitting there with that smug look on his face. Considering his pathological need for attention, I wasn't that surprised he got himself on a show like that. "I'm here with Russell Holt," Pam said to the camera, "a reporter from the Cape Cod News and a local UFO expert. Welcome to the show Russell!"

UFO expert?

"Hi Pam! It's really great to be here!" Russell said, "I have to say those shoes look fabulous on you!"

Pam laughed. "I think I'm a little over-dressed for aliens! You've been covering this story since it started," she said. "Walk us through. Have aliens arrived? Do UFOs really exist?"

"Well," Russell said with a grin, "this one sure does! A

V-shaped UFO has been sighted numerous times over Cape Cod. We've had hundreds of witnesses and dozens of people have captured footage of it." My footage appeared on the screen again. "It's been spotted all the way from Falmouth to Provincetown."

Pam pretended to think, then said, "Why do you think it's here?"

"We're not sure. It's got everyone baffled."

We?

She leaned towards her audience and said, "Sort of like when Ciara wore that dress to the Grammys. Could you believe that?"

Russell and the audience laughed. "Well, this is much more intriguing," he said. "Only we don't know why they're here, like in the movie Arrival. Did you see that?"

Pam shook her head. "I don't watch scary films; they keep me up all night!"

"That one isn't too scary;" Russell said, "it's good."

"I heard the Air Force has offered up the usual 'don't know exactly'." She turned to her audience again. "So helpful, right?" They murmured in agreement.

"Yes; they should have spotted something on the radar at the nearby Joint Base, but haven't come forward with anything," he said. "We believe they might be covering something up. Critics are having a time dismissing this. We've all seen the UFO from different angles, from various perspectives."

"What do you think the aliens want?"

Russell shrugged. "We have no idea."

Pam grabbed Russell's arm as if she needed reassurance. "I can only hope they've come in peace!"

"It doesn't look like they mean us any harm."

Pam feigned concern. "Have they started abducting people?"

"We've had rumors, but nothing has been confirmed."

Pam's tone changed as if she were giving friendly travel advice. "What should someone do if they're being abducted?"

"You should not fight back," Russell said with a straight face. "They just want to check your vital signs and observe you."

Pam played to the audience and said, "I hope they don't abduct me on a bad hair day." Everyone in the studio laughed.

"Again," Russell said, "we can't prove that anyone has been abducted."

"No one has taken a selfie with an extraterrestrial?" Pam asked. "That would be the first thing I would do."

"Well if you get a selfie with an alien, Pam," Russell grinned, "I'm sure you'd both look fabulous."

"What kind of clothes do aliens wear?"

"Well, Pam, I'm not sure. Most reports make them out as naked."

"Oh my God!" Pam exclaimed in mock horror, "I can see why most people are traumatized by their encounters. Isn't it cold in outer space?"

Russell played along with his host and said, "I guess they set their thermostats inside the spaceships to a comfortable temperature."

"How many nude aliens were in Star Wars?"

"Not a lot Pam. And most of them wore clothes from the seventies."

Without looking up from his puzzle, Charles muttered, "Those people are idiots." Any concerns I had about Charles' mental faculties were swept away by that comment.

31

I finished my sip of Young's Double Chocolate stout then said, "The Voyager spacecraft will be smashed by vandals in the year 2200."

"What are you talking about?" Zeke said, "It'll be found by another civilization way in the future."

"No it won't," I said. "By tomorrow's standards, it's moving very slowly. For the longest time, we will be the closest civilization to it. We'll know exactly where it is."

Zeke bit into his burger and spoke with his mouth full, "What? Some redneck Luke Skywalker will go out there and fuck with it?"

"He'd probably be drunk and push one of the lunar rovers over before he heads out to there," I said.

Eddie raised his glass. "To drunk vandals of the future."

I was doing my *predictions for the future* rant. I always get like this on my third beer. "They'll have barriers up around the Apollo 11 landing site so people can't walk all over Neil Armstrong's footprints."

Zeke took another sip of his beer and said, "Like another national monument?"

"There'll be a snack bar right next to it," I said. "They'll probably have a hologram of Buzz and Neil recreating the entire mission, right where they did it."

Zeke laughed. "And kids with their parents will be bored with the whole thing?"

"It'd be like going to Plymouth Rock. Who the hell cares?" I said. We had ended up at Flynn's Irish Pub in Sagamore after a day of scouting the perimeter of the base, looking for a spot to get through the fence and give ourselves quick access to the PAVE PAWS building. It's mostly woods on that part of the base. Long ago the government did a land grab and took control hundreds of acres on the Cape. I guess they figured if the Russkies wanted to take out the radar, it would be practically a second target in addition to the runway and airplanes. I had Google maps up on my iPad and showed it to Zeke and Eddie. I zoomed in on the screen. "I showed Klick this spot on Google maps. Route 130 goes past a gate in the fence which leads directly onto the runway. A pair of bolt cutters will get his entire crew on the field in no time."

Zeke asked, "And where are we going to be?"

I slide the location of the map over. "There's another little gate we can hop over here by these power lines. That will lead us to a dirt road called Monument Swamp road. It goes right past the radar building."

Zeke zoomed in on the location. "There's a second fence around the building itself. We'll probably need some wire cutters. And what about the guys who are actually working at the radar?"

"Well, there should be some major chaos going on in the base. Tom says he knows exactly where he's going." Zeke's phone rang and he fished it out of this pocket and answered it. "I figure we have about thirty minutes before Klick figures out that he was sold a bullshit story," I said.

Eddie swallowed a mouthful of beer then said, "This is going to be epic."

Zeke sat transfixed, the phone up to his face. "Ah-uh....no fucking way." He looked like he was being told his mother had died. "Where?" he said. He stood up, breathing heavily while he listened. Eddie and I were wondering what the hell was going on. He said, "Ok...OK..," then hung up. "That was one of my fans from the Maritime Academy. They said they just saw the UFO going over the railroad bridge."

"No fucking way," I said. The Maritime Academy was located in the town of Bourne, on the western tip of the canal. There are only three ways to get to Cape Cod by land—the identical Bourne and Sagamore bridges and the railroad bridge at the entrance of the canal.

"He said it was following the canal," Zeke said.

I said, "It's coming right towards us then."

Zeke practically pulled us out of the chairs and shouted, "Let's go! Let's go!"

We threw money on the table and yelled at the bartender that it was an emergency and ran out of there. We sprinted over to Zeke's car. Eddie got in the back and I sat in the front next to Zeke. He floored it out of the parking lot, fishtailed in the middle of Sandwich Road and ended up going in the wrong direction. Flynn's was near the Sagamore end of the canal. We needed to head west and follow the canal about four miles towards the Buzzards Bay end. I yelled at Zeke as the car accelerated, "Where the hell are you going?"

Zeke's knuckles where white as he he gripped the steering wheel and leaned forward. "I know how to get to the access road that follows the canal," he said.

"It's not a road," I said, "it's a bike path!"

"So what," he said cooly. Zeke had turned into Dirty Harry. We skidded onto a side street that ended at a row of bushes. He straightened the car then gunned it. "Hold on," he said. A row of vines sailed across the hood of the car as we went over an embankment. My head hit the roof as we got a little air, then landed on a bed of gravel next the train tracks. With two loud smacks, his suspension absorbed two rails of steel, then surfed down another pile of loose gravel. Another row of bushes disappeared under the car as he finally hit the brakes when we landed on pavement. The canal was right in front of us, flanked by a row of lights on either side. He cut his wheel hard left and stomped on the gas. I fell back into my seat as the car accelerated. He growled, "I gotta see this thing."

The canal lights whizzed past his window. I thought, *God I hope nobody's taking a stroll at this time of night.*

Zeke shouted over his shoulder towards Eddie, "Where's your camera?"

Eddie looked ill. "I don't have it."

Zeke fumbled with his phone for a second, but it fell into his lap. He rummaged between his legs. "Shit, my battery is almost dead."

I grabbed the wheel. "Dude, you drive, I have mine!" He found his phone and finally focused on the road. We could see the headlights of cars moving across the Sagamore Bridge as we passed under it. As we went around the bend of the canal, the Bourne Bridge appeared in the distance.

There it was—the UFO was just over the bridge.

I shouted, "Stop here! Stop here! Let me get out."

Zeke said, "Just a little farther."

"No no, it's coming this way, stop!" I ended up on the dashboard as Zeke slammed on his brakes. We piled out of his car and started filming. The lights of the UFO grew larger as it headed towards us. Something was weird this time; the lights didn't outline a V-shape. As it got closer, it became apparent that what we were looking at was a cross.

Zeke said, "Jesus, look at the thing!"

"Jesus is right," I said, "A cross?"

The outline of the UFO formed a Christian style cross. The color of the lights and the speed were the same as what I'd seen at the fairground. "See if you notice any anomalous affects on your body," Zeke called out as he was filming. "Do you hear any sounds?"

"Zeke, that's not the V-shaped spaceship," I said. "I haven't seen this!"

"It's probably an alternative craft. I wouldn't be surprised if there was a whole fleet of them." He kept repeating, "Jesus…look at that thing!"

As the UFO passed our location, the Cape Cod Canal cruise boat went under it. It let out a long toot as the people on board shouted and pointed to the object directly above them. The two craft slowly moved away from each other as the UFO continued its journey up the canal. I saw another set of headlights coming towards us on the bike path. It looked like someone else had the same idea and was following the UFO up the canal.

"Zeke—" I said.

"Yeah, c'mon, get back in the car," Zeke said, "Let's keep after it."

We jumped back into his car and went back the same way we came. The UFO wasn't going very fast, we were doing maybe twenty miles an hour and could easily keep pace with it. Zeke was trying to hold his camera out the window and drive at the same time. "Will you watch the road!" I said, "I'm filming with mine."

Zeke dismissed me as he fiddled with his camera. "I got it, I got it," he said. We went for another minute and then he tossed his camera into his lap. "Shit, it's dead; you getting it?"

"I'm getting it," I said. The UFO rose up as we approached the Sagamore Bridge. Just as we went under it, I heard a car crash above us. The people up there had an even better view that we did. We could hear car horns going off as we passed beneath the bridge. The service road brought us to the parking lot of the Sandwich Marina, a little cubbyhole for boats on the Cape side of the canal. We had to drive on the grass to get around a small crowd of people that were gaping in awe of what they were watching. The canal ended at a rock jetty in the Sandcatcher recreation area. We jumped out of the car and ran out onto the rocks as far as we could go and watched the UFO glide away, towards Cape Cod Bay.

I continued filming the UFO with Zeke in the foreground. "God damn it. God damn it," he said. "Can you fucking believe that?"

"Zeke," I said impatiently, "I can believe it." The UFO slowly turned north about a half mile off the coast and headed towards Sagamore Beach. We all sat down on the rocks and watched the lights as they receded into the distance. After another minute we lost sight of it.

Zeke had his hands up to the sides of his head as if it were about to explode. "Ya know, you read about this shit, but when you actually see it."

I continued to scan the horizon on the off chance it might've turned around. "I know," I said.

Eddie pulled out a silver body flask, took a swig and waved it in my direction. I nodded and he tossed it over to me. It didn't feel cool to the touch; it must have been nestled against his stomach the whole time. I winced as I took a sip of warm Southern Comfort and threw the flask to Zeke. My phone went off; it was Tom Frazier. "Yeah?"

Tom was all torqued up. "There's been another UFO sighting!" he said.

"Yeah…yeah…we just saw it. I'm with Zeke and Eddie. We're here at the canal right now, we saw the whole thing."

"I couldn't get through to Zeke. Did you get any footage?"

"Zeke's phone died while filming it. I got plenty."

"So listen," Tom said, "the Sagamore Bridge is less than a mile from the PAVE PAWS station. The extraterrestrials are getting closer, we need to get on that base before they do."

"We've got the entry spot picked out," I said. "Klick should be on board for next Saturday."

Tom repeated, "We are so close, we're so close."

I started to say, "So what are we…?"

He quickly cut me off and said, "Listen, I gotta go!" then hung up.

I looked my phone for a moment. *Why is it I've never been able to finish a conversation with this guy?*

Zeke looked at me. "What did Tom say?"

"He said we're close."

Zeke stared off into the distance and shook his head, "The world is going to change in a few days."

I leaned back on a giant boulder and exhaled deeply. Eddie offered me another hit off his piss-warm flask but I waved it off. He took a swig and said, "So why was it in the shape of a cross? Were they angels?"

"No," Zeke said, "What we saw was hardware."

"Maybe they're trying to appeal to the religious," I said.

"You think they're trying to prep us for their arrival?" Zeke asked.

"They know that most of the planet is made up of people who believe in a god." I said. "These people can only deal with things in religious terms. They know that."

"The church leaders are going to go off the rails when they show themselves."

"I don't know," I said. "Those guys always change their tune when new data appears."

Eddie tossed the silver flask to Zeke, who took a big sip.

"Well," Zeke said as he swallowed, "there are going to be a lot of disappointed people if Jesus doesn't come out of that spacecraft."

32

I waited in line at the Wellfleet drive-in to get into what I called the 'flea market of the damned'. The cop on Route 6 was inching us forward into the parking lot. The marquee above him said COME IN AND BE SAVED. It seemed a cross-shaped set of lights in the sky was an obvious prophecy and now everyone was in need of some emergency salvation. The "Canal UFO", as it was being called, quickly made headlines earlier in the week. I and four million others had seen Zeke's footage on his YouTube channel. Was someone or something trying to make a point by hovering religious iconography above the heads of Cape Codders? They must've known it would get a strong reaction; maybe ET was just screwing with us. The entire event was hosted by Bob Liston, a well known televangelist from the midwest. I recognized his name from his YouTube videos of him speaking in tongues.

As my car inched forward, I spotted a person on a milk crate holding a sign saying "the end is nigh". I thought only people in cartoons wielded that sign. I think I would've gone with "We're all holy fucked!" With the hysteria of recent events, I guess the antiquated phrase on that sign was no longer seen as parody.

I finally found a parking space and joined the crowd of a few thousand lost souls. Vendor tents were off to one side and a stage with a giant PA was set up in front of the movie screen. The entire place had a somber vibe: no laughing, cotton candy or cheerful music like the Barnstable fair. I checked my phone to see if I had any messages. Ken was coming down later and we were supposed to meet up.

I started to explore the solemn festival on my own. The first thing I discovered was an impromptu choir of about a dozen people who were singing "Morning Has Broken" by Cat Stevens. *Interesting choice*, I thought. I would've chosen something more recent like REM's "End Of The World As We Know It," but I guess nobody was feeling fine.

The next thing I encountered was an above-ground pool with a line of people in front of it. Most of them wore bathing suits; some were holding towels. They were all waiting to get baptized by a clergyman who was standing up to his chest in the water. Each person who entered the water held his or her nose and got the classic backwards dunk with a few words sprinkled over them. A few people went through the process fully clothed. It was a pretty warm day, so those already baptized were not in a hurry to get out of the water. No sense in rushing to your oblivion if you've got a nice cool spot to hang out in.

On stage Pastor Bob Liston was doing his thing. If one believed the YouTube videos, he had the power to drop people to the floor with his touch. Two men in suits carefully escorted a woman up to the stage. A woman's voice came over the PA saying, "This woman was abducted recently and has an alien implant in her abdomen."

"Where are you from, darling?" Bob asked her.

"Cotuit," she said.

"When did these demons do this to you?"

"They came into my bedroom last week," she said quietly. "I was so frightened."

"Don't be afraid of the power of the Lord!" Bob shouted as he pointed skywards. "Show me where they did this to you?"

The woman carefully lifted up her shirt and pointed at her abdomen. "Right here," she said.

Bob extended his arms and braced himself in front of her stomach. "Woe to the inhabitants of the earth and of the sea!" he bellowed. "For the devil is come down unto you, having great wrath, because he knoweth that he hath but a short time!" He grabbed at the "implant" and shouted, "We expunge it! We expunge it! In the name of the Lord we expunge it!" On the words expunge, he flung the imperceptible foreign object behind him. I wasn't sure if he kept losing his grip on the implant or if there was more than one. He seemed fairly careless about where it ended up.

I continued moving through the crowd until I got to the vendor tents. A doomsday prepper tent offered everything a survivalist would need: bows and arrows, backpacks, freeze dried food, axes. . . I noticed a box of floss sitting next to some hand sanitizer. I pulled one out and asked the guy manning the booth. "Do we need to have proper oral hygiene at the end of days?"

He frowned and said, "Sutures."

I tried to imagine stitching myself up with this stuff; I had a hard enough time just flossing with it. I put it back and moved on.

The Bayberry Funeral Home had a shiny mahogany casket on display. On one side of it was a table with a diorama of cemetery plots. On the other side was a table covered in urns of assorted sizes. Who was supposed to guarantee delivery of all this in the event of an apocalypse? Were us sinners supposed to bury the saved? The sales rep—or whoever the guy in the black suit was—looked busy dealing with customers so I decided not to pester him with any of my questions.

One of Klick's followers, wearing the prerequisite silver unitard, appeared from the crowd and handed me a flyer. It had a photo of the V-shaped UFO and above it screamed the headline: TAKE YOUR FIRST STEP TO EUPHORIA—THIS SATURDAY! He continued past me, handing out more flyers. I folded the paper a couple of times, stuck it into a pocket, then headed towards a news truck with a satellite dish. From a distance, I saw a reporter on camera interviewing someone under some TV lights. As I got closer, I couldn't believe it—or maybe I really *could* believe it—Russell Holt was doing the interviewing. He was talking to Abigail Bishop from the Church of Holy Doctrinal Unity. I worked my way to the front of the crowd and listened.

"And then the sign of the Son of Man will appear in heaven," Abigail said in that plaintive voice of hers, "and all the tribes of the Earth will mourn. And they will see the Son of Man coming on the clouds of heaven, with power and great glory."

Russell asked, "Does that mean the canal UFO portends the second coming of Christ?"

Abigail looked right into the camera, "You must get right with the Lord or you will get left behind."

Russell stammered for a bit then said, "Did you ever see that Nicholas Cage movie 'Left Behind'?"

"That was not a Christian movie," she said as she crossed her arms.

"You are convinced it's now the end of days?"

"The divine beings will put an end to the failure of humanity." Abigail gestured with her fist as if she were a politician. "Homosexuality and sin will be repealed in the world to come of the New Earth!"

Russell looked very uncomfortable for a moment, forced a smile then said, "Back to you Pam in the studio!" A woman wearing a headset approached Russell and said something into her microphone. Under the lights, Russell seemed nervous as the woman nodded and listened to someone speaking to her remotely. Russell spotted me off to the side. He approached me and seemed relieved to see a familiar face. "Mel! What are you doing here?"

"I was going to ask you the same thing."

He led me over to the woman wearing the headset. "This is my producer Sandy."

Sandy seemed distracted as we shook hands.

"Hi," I said.

Russell said to her, "This is Melissa—Mel. She's a journalist I work with."

Sandy barely glanced at me and said, "Great to meet you." She said to Russell, "I've got to get back to the truck and send the promo spot to the network."

"OK," Russell said, as she walked away.

"So what are you doing here?" I said.

"I'm doing a remote feed for the network. They liked my onscreen presence when I went to New York for the Pam Meagan show. They wanted a local expert on the UFO phenomenon."

"Yeah, I saw that," I said. "But aren't you still working at the newspaper?"

"I had three weeks' vacation and unused sick time coming to me, so I decided to take it now and give this a shot. They're thinking of giving me a contract."

"And Laurie is OK with this?"

"They don't have to know what I do with my own time," Russell said defensively as he tapped his chest. "I'm looking out for number one."

I shrugged and said, "Whatever."

"I mean you're now writing for the Weekly World Gazette— how is that holding up?" he asked with a silly smile.

Here he goes again, I thought. Anything that could be taken as criticism was sure to get a rise out of him. "OK Russell," I said, "you do what you have to do."

He continued, with his stupid grin. "Hey, if you see Mantis Man again, tell him I said hi."

I resisted the impulse to throw something at him.

Sandy called out from the truck. "Russell, can you come here? We need to record some bumpers."

"OK. Back to work," he said as he back-peddled towards the truck. "You keep up the *reporting*," he said with heavy sarcasm.

I thought, *I hope he chokes on his microphone.*

I heard the text message alert go off on my phone and pulled it out of my bag. In my recent calls list I saw a number from St. Petersburg, Florida. It was probably another robo-call so I ignored it. The text message from Ken:

Ken: I'm by the trumpets tent.

I replied:

Mel: Be there in a sec.

I knew what he meant. There was a tent selling brass instruments. I guess they hoped somebody could play along with the angels when they cued the apocalypse. I walked towards the sound of a tuba; someone was blowing a long note. I saw Ken was standing next to a sign that said "Educator Discount".

"Where are you going to be this Saturday night?" he said. "Tom convinced Klick to wait for his UFO at Otis."

"I got the flyer; I saw that."

"There's probably going to be a huge ruckus on the airfield," Ken said. "You should be at the gate on Route 6. He's going to try to get in through there."

"I assume you and Noodles will be there?"

"Tom, Zeke and I are heading for the PAVE PAWS building."

I couldn't believe what I was hearing. It seemed Ken had completely swallowed Tom's story. "You do realize that could get you arrested?"

"It's now or never," he said. "The canal UFO passed right by there."

"I spoke to the police officer who was at the so-called crash site," I said. "There was no UFO that went down back in 1967. Where did Tom get his information from?"

"I dunno," Ken said dismissively. "There certainly is a UFO flying around now." He darted his finger at me. "You saw it yourself."

"I don't know what I saw," I said. "Everything is completely weird."

Ken exhaled as he took a text message on his phone. "It's my vet," he said. "You know what else is weird? My dog Astro."

"What's going on?"

Ken continued to type as he spoke. "He's gone completely catatonic. He stopped responding to anything I do for him. He doesn't eat, he doesn't want to go out, he even stopped watching TV. He just sits there on the floor whining."

"Is he sick?"

"I dunno. He's been chewing on a ton of those bones that are out in our backyard. Those things fucking reek big time. I think they made him sick, so I'm taking him to the vet tomorrow."

32

I will eventually die and my life will have been pointless. The thought had been tormenting me. I had become consumed with my own mortality and I couldn't escape it.

I was going to die someday.

I dropped my head to the kitchen floor and closed my eyes. The tiles felt cool under my neck, like they were trying to drain the last bit of vitality out of my body. I heard Ken waving my favorite squeaky toy in front of my face but I couldn't bother to look up. I knew today wasn't going to get any better than yesterday.

My descent into melancholy started with the concept of 'dog years'. I had discovered that humans typically live seven times longer than dogs. Golden Retrievers like myself only live for about ten years. I was pretty sure I was five years old at that point; five more and that would be it…oblivion.

I would no longer exist.

I've seen science do wonderful things to extend the life of

humans; why not dogs? Apparently parrots can live just as long as humans. Whose idea was this? Dogs are much more interesting than a stupid bird. Birds need to be kept in cages or they'll just fly away. I would never dream of leaving Ken.

I had also been suffering with some guilt from my youth. Back when I could just live in the moment as a puppy, chasing squirrels had been my obsession. I recalled the time I was able to catch one as it jumped off of a tree. I clamped down on its neck and shook it in celebration. At the time I thought it was only resting for another lap around our yard.

I had killed it.

How could I have been so callous toward another living being? I had become the destroyer of rodent worlds.

I heard Ken mention something about a 'car ride' as he connected the leash to my collar. In the past, this would have brought me such joy, but all I felt was complete emptiness. He tugged at the leash, coaxing me to stand up. He stroked my head and spoke to me in some soothing patronizing tones. Ken didn't get it. Didn't he know he was going to die too? I pulled myself up off the floor and with my head down, followed him out the door. We got into our car and I collapsed into my spot on the back seat. There was no point in watching the world go by, all those people would be dead eventually and they didn't even know it.

When we stopped at our destination, I immediately recognized we were at the vet's office. My tail wasn't wagging; nothing good ever happened there. I had learned that all dogs ultimately end up at the vet's office to get the final Big Shot. The owners want to end their animals' suffering, so they do the most humane thing possible—put them to sleep. I suddenly understood what was going on. Ken understood my hopelessness and wanted to put me out of my misery. I realized that I had to just accept my fate. I followed him into the office and onto the cold linoleum floor. I ignored the other dogs sitting across from us. I resented having to look at their joyful faces, panting away, adoring their masters sitting next to them.

They had no idea what was in store for them.

A pug with a fat little face and marble eyes kept staring at me. *What the hell is he so happy about?*

Didn't he realize that he would ultimately be eaten by earthworms in some landfill? An annoying white poodle was yapping away at nothing in particular. Each bark was a petulant demand for attention. Death would eventually silence the mutt, and…

Where the hell did he get that hair cut?

A German Shepard kept up a subtle whine. That's all that breed seems to constantly do, whine whine whine. Maybe if he knew his life will eventually end, he wouldn't be so high strung.

When it was my turn, I followed Ken into a little room. He hoisted me up onto a stainless steel table. The vet did a cursory exam of my mouth and ears, then proceeded to shove a glass tube into my anus.

Does he have to do that every time we come here? What does he think he's going to find back there?

I had just licked it clean a few hours ago. Ken and the vet had a discussion while I just lay there on the table with my eyes closed. I heard something mentioned about rabies. Did it look like I was rabid?

Where the hell did they get that idea?

I didn't want to attack anybody; I just wanted to disappear. From the corner of my eye, I saw the vet pull out a needle and insert it into a vial. I knew it, here it comes.

The big shot.

I felt the pinch of the needle as it pierced my fur.

Well that's that; it will all be over in a few moments.

I felt a sense of relief—my mental anguish would be over. What's the point of living another five years anyways?

I was going to the Big Kennel in the sky.

Ken picked me up and put me on the floor.

Oh the final humiliation.

I would be lifeless in three seconds and he wanted to drag my corpse through the vet's lobby past the other dogs. I closed my eyes and just stood there, waiting for a blanket of darkness to descend over me.

Ken kept tugging at my collar and calling my name. Where did he think we were going? I summoned all my remaining strength and took a few steps forward. We made it out to the waiting room. I didn't bother making eye contact with anyone. In fact, we made it all the way out to the car. I hopped in and wondered if I had not already died and my brain was creating some kind of metaphor in the shape of this car to help me travel to another plane of existence. All the way home I kept looking for any surreal images that would signify something had changed.

Is that guy in the Lumina next to us at the stop light some kind of otherworld demon? Is that traffic cop directing my soul to hell?

We got home. I collapsed onto the kitchen floor and closed my eyes, convinced it would be for the very last time. I didn't move and continued to wait for my impending death for the rest of the day.

Nothing happened.

I eventually got up and took a drink from my bowl. Ken let me out and I settled into my favorite spot in the backyard. As the sun warmed me up, I began to feel a little bit better. I enjoyed listening to the birds chirping around me. They didn't know they were going to die, but what the hell, they sounded nice anyway.

OK, I might've over reacted that day.

34

I was the first to arrive at the parking lot in Shawme Cromwell State Forest. Everyone was supposed to meet there, then enter the military base on the other side of Route 6. It was just starting to get dark; somebody had a fire going in one of the camping spots on the other side of some trees. I had been waiting for about ten minutes when I heard someone approach my car from the darkness. I heard Tom say in a monotone voice, "The Majestic 12 never held a grudge against a blue book."

"Tom," I said, "Zeke never told me the key phrase. I don't know the response."

There was a pause, then he repeated, "The Majestic 12 never held a grudge against a blue book."

I drummed my fingers on the steering wheel; I couldn't believe he was still doing that crap. "Tom, this is Ken. Zeke will be here in a minute. I know it's you."

There was a longer pause, then he said, "The Lubbock Lights

lingered on Gordo Cooper."

"Wait a minute, that's not even the same key phrase. How am I supposed to respond?"

"I did the wrong one," Tom said.

"Will you come out? I know it's you."

"Were you followed?"

"I wasn't followed. Zeke will be here any minute."

He came out of the darkness, carrying a gym bag and floating next to his head, was a mylar balloon. "You can never be too careful," he said.

I was going to say something about the balloon when Zeke's car pulled up behind me. He and Eddie got out and we all formed a huddle in front of my hood. Eddie had a t-shirt on but Zeke was in full camo and had his face painted green. He looked like Colonial Kurtz from Apocalypse Now. Tom and I were both dressed normally. "This is not the raid on Entebbe;" I said to Zeke, "We're trying to sneak around inside a building."

He pointed towards the woods, "We have to get to there first."

"But what if someone sees you like that?" I said. "You're gonna freak somebody out."

Tom interrupted, "Then they'll know we mean business."

"Listen," Zeke said, "I thought about this; we need to coordinate our attack. Eddie is not coming with us."

Eddie shook his head. "I'm not climbing any fences, no way."

Zeke said, "He's going to Klick's entrance and will call us when he's entering the airfield. That's when we'll do our final push to the radar building."

"This is good," Tom said. "It will give us time to scope out the situation." He rummaged through his gym bag for his iPad. He called up a satellite view of the base. "I've been looking at the Google images of the PAVE PAWS installation. It looks pretty much like the one at Beale. There's two fences we need to get through. The outer one is an exclusion zone to keep animals out of the radiation pattern and the other is an inner security fence." He showed us a spot on his iPad. "The guard is here, and the building we need to get to is to the left of the control center."

"Wait a minute," I said. "What guard?"

Tom continued to study his iPad. "There's a small security booth at the gate on the opposite side the compound from where we will be entering. The guard usually has a side arm."

"Wait..*an armed guard?*" I said. "You didn't mention that! I thought this was like a warehouse or something."

"Once the security alarm goes off and we're inside, this should buy us some time." He held out the balloon.

I said sarcastically, "What? We're gonna pop it in his face and run?"

"No," he said, "we're going to make it look like it got caught on one of the sensors. They'll think it just blew in over the fence and set off the alarm."

Zeke said, "I like it. Let's just hope Klick makes enough of a diversion to keep all eyes and ears focused on the runway."

"Once we're inside," Tom said, "I'll be getting tissue samples in these glass vials for physical evidence. If the alien is wearing any clothing, I'll take a sample of that too."

"I got my 4k camera," I said, "I'll be running super high-def footage during the whole thing."

Zeke held up his phone. "I'll be taking back up with my camera phone. In fact, once we're in the chamber, I'll go live on Facebook."

Tom looked at each of us and said, "You guys ready to do this?"

We nodded. Eddie headed towards Zeke's car. "OK, I'll call you guys when I see Klick actually entering the base." He got in and drove off.

Zeke asked Tom, "Which way?"

Tom oriented his iPad, looked up and said, "Follow me."

We followed some power lines that crossed over Route 6 and came to a small fence on the permitter of the base that we easily cleared. It seemed the military was completely indifferent to anyone wandering onto the base. I suppose there would've been much more security during the height of the Cold War. The night sky was overcast; through the trees, we could see the glow of the airfield off in the distance. The part of the base we were on was in a state forest. Acres and acres of pine trees formed a big undeveloped hole on Cape Cod. Sometimes they let hunters there to keep the deer and turkey population down. We followed the glow of Tom's iPad as he monitored his map.

We ended up on an access road that led to the outer fence that goes around the radar building. We huddled next to the rusty fence; thankfully there wasn't any barbed wire on top of it. Through the trees, you could see the lights of the radar installation. Tom whispered, "Who wants to go first?" Zeke immediately grabbed the fence and climbed over. Tom tossed over his gym bag and went next, then I followed him. We crept through an acre of trees towards the lights. We got to within sight of the pyramid shaped building that housed the radar and crouched behind a fallen tree.

The final fence was just a few yards in front of us.

It was quiet except for the hum of a transformer somewhere inside the perimeter. My heart was pounding like crazy. It felt like we were trying to pull off a Mission Impossible caper. I peeked over our log and scanned the compound. I didn't see anybody walking around. The place looked deserted.

Tom whispered. "One more fence stands between us and the world's greatest discovery."

Zeke whispered back, "Where is the alien body located?"

Tom carefully pointed over a log towards a grey building attached to the pyramid shaped radar, "It's in that one right there." He pointed to a tall storage tank, "You see that? That's the liquid nitrogen tank right there." Sure enough, there was a big vertical tank next to the main building. We studied the buildings some more. "There used to be a guard shack on this side of the compound; it's not there anymore."

Zeke whispered, "What if the aliens come back for their crashed comrade right now?"

Tom smiled. "Then we're really going to have some good footage."

We kept quiet and continued scanning the compound while we waited for Eddie's phone call.

35

I had to drive past a hot dog vendor, a guy selling inflatable aliens on a stick and quarter mile of cars just to find a parking spot along Route 130. I knew where Klick was going to make his entrance onto the airfield at Otis, but I didn't think this many people cared about it. Most of these people weren't his followers, just rubberneckers looking for something to do on a Saturday night. It was obvious that Klick had marketing skills because he had a couple hundred followers by this point. How far they were willing to go had yet to be seen. Although, failed predictions never seem to deter the true believers.

I parked near the Mashpee town line and followed the crowd back to where Klick was stationed. At that point, all traffic had come to a standstill. There must have been easily a thousand people spread out along Route 130. The road went through a cleared section of trees that extended out from the airfield. A chain link fence with a gate separated us from the end of the runway.

I spotted Klick's head above the crowd as he stood on top of a Jersey barrier in front of the gate. About a hundred of his followers were circled around him, each wearing their spandex uniforms and a fanny pack around their waist. "Does everyone have their final things in order?" he shouted to the crowd. "Please check them one last time so you are prepared. Does everyone have their IDs?"

Several of his followers raised them above their heads.

"Does everyone have their wet wipes?"

More hands went up.

"Guys; make sure you have your allotted condoms with you. Girls; you each should have one year's worth of birth control. Please check. It's very hard to find a drug store past the Crab Nebula."

I was only mildly surprised to see Abigail Bishop heading in my direction. She was muttering something to herself and seemed out of it. "Abigail," I said, "I never thought you'd be the one to amalgamate with a Fornacisian."

She didn't made eye contact. "Woe to the inhabiters of the earth and of the sea for the devil is come down unto you, having great wrath, because he knoweth that he hath but a short time!"

Does she only speak in biblical verse? How does she order a happy meal at a drive through? Abigail shuffled past me and disappeared in the crowd. If a UFO was coming to end humanity, I suppose she couldn't resist being the first pious moth to be consumed by the flames.

Behind me I heard Russell Holt say, "Fancy meeting you here." He had with him a camera man with a professional-looking rig and a sound guy holding a fuzzy microphone on a pole.

"I could say the same to you," I replied.

Russel put his hands on his hips. "Hey, when the greatest story in human history is about to happen right in your back yard, you're obligated to cover it."

The cameraman leaned over to Russell and said, "I'm going to get some shots of this crowd while were waiting." Russell gave his a quick nod.

I asked him, "You're working for the network now?"

"Not yet, but I quit my job at the newspaper yesterday," he said. "I'm going to New York to sign a contract next week."

"What did Laurie have to say?"

"I told her I wasn't coming back from my hiatus. I think she took it fairly well."

I thought, *Wow, the little shit just walked out on his boss. I guess the Cape isn't big enough for his ego.* I might look forward to our company meetings after all. I asked him, "So who is your crew?"

"I hired them with my own money. Chuck is one of the best cinematographers from LA. I flew him and his sound guy out here first class."

"So are you a nightcrawler now?" I asked.

"I'm a freelance producer," he replied, carefully enunciating the words. "Man's first encounter with an extraterrestrial being will be the greatest footage since the Hindenburg disaster. This will be shown and remembered for hundreds of years. That's why I paid for the best."

Remembering what Ken said about Tom Frazier's plan, I felt the subtle joy of pre-schadenfreude well up inside me. I smiled and waved my iPhone at him. "I have this ready just in case."

He snorted and said, "Good luck with that. So where can I find this Klick guy?"

I pointed towards the gate.

Russell whistled to his cameraman and waved him towards the gate. The cameraman spotted him and headed in that direction. "I'll see you around Melissa. Tell Laurie to call my agent if she wants the rights to my footage." Russell pushed through the crowd and followed his cameraman.

Trying to coordinate everything around him, Klick looked like a frantic football coach. He pointed and said something to one of his followers, who sprinted away, then he did the same to someone else. He frantically patted his pockets and said, "Did anyone see my Afrin? I think I left it back at the house."

A follower asked, "Do you want me to go back and get it?"

"No, we don't have time."

An obese woman wearing a similar silver unitard as the others approach Klick. "I would like to join your organization. Can I go with you?" she asked. She was easily twice the size of the other followers and looked very much out of place. I knew what Klick's answer would be.

Klick gave her a quick glance and frowned. "Sorry, The Fornacisians have a strict weight and balance limit for their craft. They don't want anyone throwing off their center of gravity."

The woman looked crushed, but I lost track of her as the crowd pushed closer. A young man with short hair threw himself at Klick and shouted, "TAKE ME! TAKE ME!" He latched onto Klick's shoulders and they both fell over.

Klick shouted from under him, "Get this wacko off me!"

A pair of his muscular followers pulled the guy off and tossed him back into the crowd. Klick got back to his feet, straightened himself out and said, "We need to go now." He picked up a pair of bolt cutters that were leaning against the fence and announced, "Can I have everyone's attention?" The crowd quieted down and focused on him. He held up the bolt cutters and said, "We will not let anything stand between us and our destiny with the Fornacisians!" Klick snipped the chain holding the gate closed and flung it open. He thrust the bolt cutter above his head and shouted, "Follow me on our first steps to euphoria!"

36

We huddled over Zeke's iPhone and heard Eddie say, "Holy crap, there's a crazy amount of people here. Klick is going through the gate now."

"Thanks Eddie," Zeke said, "we'll meet you at the campground when this is all over." Zeke hung up and we all looked at Tom. He took a deep breath and said, "OK, let's do this."

I was having second thoughts about breaking into an Air Force radar installation. *Why am I doing this? Oh yeah, to get to the truth.* Even if I got arrested and they threatened to shut me up, I would always know the truth. I could live with that.

We all hopped over the log at the same time and sprinted across the open ground to the first fence. Zeke made a beeline towards the main building with its octagonal wall, I followed Tom as he veered left. "Zeke…what are you doing?" Tom called out in a loud whisper, "You want to get fried by the transmissions? See the hazard fence? We need to enter on *this* side." All of us regrouped along the edge of the outer fence. We froze as sirens went off in the distance towards the airfield. I looked at Tom and he smiled. Klick was giving us the diversion we needed.

One at a time we climbed over the fence, then sprinted across the clearing to the inner security fence. Tom held up his fist to signal that we needed to hold. He pointed to a small, round device on top of the fence and whispered, "Intrusion sensors." He wrapped the balloon with its thin ribbon around the sensor and then scrambled over the fence. Zeke went over next and I followed. I thought for sure an alarm would go off. Nothing.

We darted across some gravel to a group of buildings. One had a little dome on it which housed some kind of radar. The huge pyramid structure was the object of our quest—the PAVE PAWS building. We ran up to the dome-shaped building and threw ourselves behind it. Tom peered around the corner; the PAVE PAWS pyramid was just a few yards away. I tried to catch my breath and felt my heart pounding like crazy. *This is nuts*, I thought. I couldn't believe I was actually going through with it. Nervously, I started humming the Mission Impossible theme to myself. Tom put his index finger to his lips to quiet me and peeked around the corner. He motioned for us to take a look. Stacked on top of each other, like the Three Stooges, we peeked around the edge of the building.

Two guys in uniform were standing on top of the pyramid. It looked like they were trying to figure out what the hell was going on over by the airfield. This was good—while they were focused on the airfield, we could scramble up to the side door below them. Tom took off first again, then Zeke and I followed.

The sign on the door said "Auxiliary Power Plant". We let ourselves in and gently closed the door behind us. Facing us were six giant turbines. We looked around for any personnel, but it appeared to be clear.

Tom said, "This is the backup power plant for the radar. If the power goes out, they can be self-sustained for an entire month in here." He pointed to a door at the top of a flight of metal stairs. It was enclosed by a railed-off landing. "The control center is through that door. Let me know if you see anyone come out." We looked at him and he said, "Follow me."

We went past the turbines. Zeke asked, "What are these things?"

"Diesel generators," Tom said. "They don't want the alien body to melt if the power goes out. This is why they put the sarcophagus down here." He grinned, "Of course they also help in keeping this radar station up and running." We followed Tom as he led us on a tour of the building, exploring most of the pathways. "The layout looks like the opposite of Beale's floor plan."

We came to a plain grey door set in a cinderblock wall. "OK, here it is," he said.

I remembered what he told us at the radio station. "I thought you said it was a green door." I said.

"The color is not important," he said. "What you are about to see is going to blow your minds."

I turned on my 4k camera while Zeke tapped at the screen on his iPhone. "Shit, I'm only getting one bar in here. I don't think we can stream live," he said.

"That's OK," said Tom, "The world will learn the truth soon enough." He put his hand on the doorknob and announced to Zeke and me, "Let me tell you, my friends, what you are about to witness will shock you. Ready?" We both nodded our heads like a couple of kids about to enter Disneyland.

He flung open the door; the room was in total darkness. I felt a bead of sweat form on my forehead and I tried like hell to keep the camera steady as I peered into the dark viewfinder. In my mind I could clearly visualize an alien body housed in a sarcophagus. Tom felt around the wall and flicked on a light switch.

The room housed a bunch of mops and buckets.

I don't know what could have been worse, finding out that a

hot chick you were dating was a transvestite or being led to this broom closet. I heard some cruelly ironic waa-waa horns playing in my head.

Tom shouted, "SHIT…they moved it!"

I said, "I thought you said you knew where it is."

"This place is a mirror to the Beale site." Tom pushed himself past us and said, "Its over here, follow me." We followed him over to the other side of the building and found another grey door set into another wall. "OK, here we go!" Tom opened the door and we found ourselves staring outside into the darkness. He looked behind the door and quietly said, "Oh, shit!"

I took a look. A guard stood at the spot we had climbed over, staring at the mylar balloon. I backed up, carefully closed the door and said to Zeke, "They know someone's inside."

Tom yelled, "SHIT!" and walked away from us. "They moved the aliens," he said over his shoulder, "They're probably unfrozen and being debriefed. They know their comrades will be here soon." Tom headed towards the metal stairs.

Zeke and I looked at each other, confused. He shrugged at me and I said, "Where the hell is he going?" We followed Tom to the bottom of the stairs that went up to the control center. "Wait a minute," I said to Tom, "you said that's the control room. There has to be people in there."

Tom started climbing. "We didn't come this far to be denied." He pushed open the door and went in. We found ourselves in a room filled with computer monitors and telephones. A couple of larger color monitors hung on the far wall.

A lone female sergeant in an Air Force uniform sat at a U-shaped desk surrounded by black and green screens. She looked very surprised to see us there. "How did you guys get in here?" she said.

Tom shouted, "THE ALIEN. WHERE IS IT?"

The sergeant looked perplexed. "What are you talking about?"

Tom strode around the perimeter of the room trying all the doors and disappeared down a hallway. He let out a yelp of frustration that sounded like a wounded animal. Like a faithful canine sidekick, Zeke followed him down the hallway. The sergeant said to me, "I have to call the MPs on you. You can't be in here!"

"Look," I said, "we just want to witness the retrieval of the alien body."

The sergeant looked at me as if I were a mental patient. She slowly asked, "What alien body?"

"You guys have been tracking things from outer space, right?"

"Well yeah, we're an air defense system. We scramble jets in response to ADIZ intrusions." She glanced towards the hallway where we could hear Tom banging on some doors, then back at me. "But seriously, you can't be in here."

"OK," I said, "but you guys have been tracking UFOs too, right? Runners."

The sergeant leaned back in her chair and said, "If it's not orbital or ballistic it won't show up on our screens. That's how the system was set up. What the hell is a 'runner'?"

"I thought you guys can track meteorite—everything from space."

"Meteorites have a ballistic trajectory, but their origin is so obviously non-planetary that they're ignored by the computers. We track very specific objects."

We both heard another high-pitched yelp from Tom down the hall as he tugged at another door.

"C'mon," I said, "you must of tracked the V-shaped UFO over Cape Cod."

"No," the sergeant said as she shook her head. "Even the guys in the tower haven't seen anything. Nobody on the base knows what the hell that is."

"Seriously? I've seen it myself."

The sergeant sat up. "Yeah? What was it like?

"I was hoping you could tell me."

She looked again towards the hallway. "I don't know. But you will get in trouble if you stay here."

Tom burst back into the control room. His expression was that of a complete lunatic. He yelped again and left through the door which lead back to the metal stairs. Zeke scrambled to keep up with him. We could hear Tom letting out short, intense screams as he crossed the generator room below us.

I knew what I was listening to. It was the sound of cognitive dissonance. There were no frozen aliens here and Tom refused to let himself believe it.

The sergeant asked me, "What the hell is wrong with him?"

"A lot," I replied.

Zeke shouted up from the base of the metal stairway. "Tom thinks they moved the body to a different part of the base. You coming?"

Before I could say anything, a shout came from the side door. "STOP! DON'T MOVE!" It was the armed guard from outside. Zeke immediately bolted towards the opposite side of the facility and went out another side door. The guard sprinted across the floor below me and went out the same way. I heard his footsteps sprint away on the gravel.

The sergeant said to me, "You have to leave."

I said, "Thanks…see ya around."

She shrugged, turned back to her console and picked up a phone. As I went down the metal stairs, I heard other voices enter the control room. It must have been the two guys from the roof. I was sure the sergeant had some interesting things to tell them about our visit. I quietly made my way back to the inner fence and climbed over. I heard some commotion on the other side of the compound by the front gate. I didn't care what the hell Tom and Zeke were doing; they were on their own. I felt relieved that I was finally getting out of there.

37

Klick strode onto the end of the runway, accompanied by his spandex-clad acolytes. The rest of the us—a substantial mob—followed behind them. I put myself in the middle of the pack; I knew it was completely illegal to just wander onto a military base. It didn't look like anyone else cared about such technicalities. I guess extraterrestrial visitation trumped the U.S. military.

About a hundred yards out on the runway, Klick stopped. "They are going to be here shortly," he announced. "We need to form three groups, boys, girls and gender neutrals. The Fornacisians will decide who goes where once we get inside the spaceship." He pointed to a spot in front of him. "Can we have the boys form a group over here for now?"

A few of his followers were pointing in the opposite direction, trying to get Klick's attention. Someone near me said "Uh-oh.."

At the other end of the runway, a row of cars with flashing lights was accelerating towards us. A round of sirens went off as they approached us. Klick held his arm up and calmly said, "OK everyone, let me deal with this."

The first SUV skidded to a halt a few feet in front of him. Over their PA system a voice said, "You people need to leave the area immediately. You are trespassing on government property."

Klick approached the vehicle with his arms open, "We've come in peace. There's no need to panic."

An MP sergeant got out and scanned the crowd as he approached Klick. "Are you in charge of this group? Who are you?"

"No, no…who are *you*?" Klick answered. "We have a right to be here!"

He fired back, "I'm Staff Sergeant James Barrett. You and your people need to leave this area immediately. You are trespassing on government property." It looked like the sergeant wasn't going to take shit from anyone, especially from someone in a satin Kung Fu robe.

"We're taxpayers; we pay your salary!" Klick argued. "We have a right to be here."

Sergeant Barrett pointed his finger directly at Klick's face, "Listen, get your people off of this runway or we'll arrest all of you."

Klick tried the heartfelt approach. He gestured dramatically, pausing after each phrase. "We are needed here…humanity needs us here…we are the chosen few. We are the copacetic coition ambassadors of a new generation!" A few of his followers applauded.

Another SUV pulled up and an officer got out. I recognized him as Lt. Colonel Daniel Patterson. He approached Sgt. Barrett and said, "Sergeant, what is going on here?"

The sergeant pointed at Klick. "Apparently this man is the leader of this group. He refuses to leave the airfield, Colonel."

The colonel shouted, "What the hell are you people doing here?"

Klick seemed indifferent to the hostility launched at him. "We are about to embark on the journey of a lifetime. We are waiting our turn on the spaceship of life."

"A SPACESHIP?" the colonel yelled. "We don't launch space-ships from this base. You and your people need to leave the airfield IMMEDIATELY!"

"We are awaiting the return of the Fornacisians!" Klick said. "They've been searching for us for the past few months! If you just wait a few minutes, we'll all be gone."

The crowd had grown even bigger during the conversation with Klick. People were wandering around behind the line of MPs. Colonel Patterson noticed some people putting blankets down on the grass at the edge of the runway. He pointed at them and shouted to the sergeant, "Get those people off the grass. This is not a fucking air show!" He moved in front of Klick's face. "You need to get these people off the fucking runway. This is your last warning. Move or get arrested!"

Klick pleaded with him. "Colonel, if we don't get on that UFO, humanity may not survive for much longer. Once it arrives, we'll be gone in a jiffy."

"UFO! What UFO?"

"The V-shaped UFO that has been searching for us," Klick said.

"You gotta be shitting me." The colonel addressed the crowd directly. "I've told you people a million times there's nothing up there. Has the whole world turned into a bunch of mental defectives? I can't get through to anyone!" Klick stood there with a smile on his face. The sergeant, who had been listening to his walkie talkie, asked the colonel. "Command wants to know what's going on."

"I want every MP on the base out here now," the colonel replied. "Call the motor pool and have them send every vehicle that can form a barrier to prevent these people from getting further onto the base. Then call the CO at Camp Edwards and tell them we need to deploy the National Guard out here."

A small section of the crowd was pointing off into the distance. On the horizon, a row of lights were coming towards us. The crowd noise lowered to a murmur as everyone watched the approaching lights. We could make out the familiar V-shape pattern. Klick said, "Mental defective, colonel? Who's the crazy one now?"

The colonel stood there, transfixed by the eerie shape. Everyone, including the MPs, stopped what they were doing and stared up at the sky as the V-shaped lights flew over our heads in a wide arc. Klick shouted out to his followers, "OK everyone, line up! This is your last chance to prepare for boarding. Form up in lines and don't move. Keep still—you don't want to fall out of their tractor beam."

His followers scrambled to form a grid, an arm-length apart. They stood at attention with their arms stiffly down by their sides like a company of soldiers. The UFO approached again and stopped directly over our heads and hovered. Everyone gasped and a few people bolted back towards the gate.

Sergeant Barrett lowered his walkie talkie and said to Colonel Patterson, "I just spoke with the tower. They've got nothing on radar, just an irregular signature."

The colonel stood there with his mouth open, shaking his head. "We need to scramble some jets," he said.

Klick closed his eyes, raised his arms above his head and went, "BBBBBBZZZZZZZZZZZZZZZZZ"

His followers raised their arms and joined in. "BBBBBBZZZZZZZZZZZZZZZZZ"

Some of the people near me were crying. I saw Abigail Bishop was on her knees, murmuring, "Though I walk through the valley of the shadow of death I will fear no evil…"

A low-flying helicopter approached us, its spotlight pointed down towards the ground. As it grew closer, it rose higher into the sky and hovered above the UFO. I felt the breeze from the rotor blades push down on us while the spotlight illuminated Klick and his followers. Klick was so enraptured he didn't even notice the copter was there.

He shouted to the sky, "TAKE US UP...UP! BEYOND OUR ATMOSPHERE AND INTO A EUPHORIC EMBRACE!"

The UFO lights began to stagger and move out of formation. No longer V-shaped, the lights were now a series of random dots. In a sequential cascade, they dropped from the sky and crashed onto the airfield all around us. They made a high-pitched sound as they plummeted to the ground, then went silent. One fell near me; it jittered and twitched on the tarmac like a swatted hornet. A few people cautiously approached the trembling spot of light. There seemed to be something growing out of it.

A woman behind me shouted, "Kill it! It tried to attack us!"

One brave individual was inching closer to it and said, "No; I think it's dying."

Someone shouted, "Dude, if a death ray comes out, you're fucked! Don't go near it!"

He waved the comment off, knelt down, gingerly picked it up and held it out at arm's length. The light was attached by a bunch of wires to a metallic box topped by a couple of mangled propellors. "It's a drone!" he shouted.

My mouth fell open. It all made sense! The lights were attached to drones that were flying in formation, so from the ground they looked like one solid object. Because it was an overcast night, there were no stars behind them to ruin the illusion. Someone had gone to great lengths to set up this stunt. I felt like an idiot for falling for it.

I squinted as the helicopter dropped lower and focused its searchlight on us. The downdraft was kicking sand in our faces; I could feel some crunching between my teeth. It felt like the helicopter was trying to blow us off the airfield. If so, it worked; it was time to get out of there. I followed a crowd of people heading towards the gate. As I walked back to my car, I wondered how I

was going to frame this story. Would anyone believe this whole
thing was someone's prank? I smiled to myself as I came up with
the headline: "Drones and Groans on Cape Cod!"

I heard a familiar voice next to me say, "I can't b'lieve it was
fuckin' drones!"

Another familiar voice replied, "That was pissah when they
came down!"

It couldn't be—it was Ralph and Lenny, the two idiots who
found the sunfish on Crosby Landing Beach. I listened to their
conversation as we continued walking. Ralph said "I knew that
UFO was fuckin' fake the whole time we been down heah."

Lenny shook his head, "No-suh"

"Yes-suh;" Ralph retorted, "it didn't move like no real UFO. I
know a real UFO when I see one."

"When did you see a real UFO?" Lenny asked.

"In Dickie's back yahd last yeah," said Ralph, "We was havin' a
pahty and I sawr it fly ovah the Charles Rivah."

"You sure those weren't planes goin' to Logan?"

"I'm shuah," said Ralph, "And I wasn't even high neither."

38

I stumbled back through the woods, came out by the power lines and checked my bearings. I could see a bunch of lights and a helicopter flying around in the direction of the runway. It looked like a hell of a commotion; Klick must have gotten a pretty good reaction. I followed something that looked like a trail as I headed off back towards the campground. I had no idea if Zeke or Tom were coming, and at that point I didn't care. I couldn't believe I fell for Tom's bullshit story. I knew Zeke would remain a true believer even if Tom pulled a dingleberry off his butt and called it an extraterrestrial. I replayed Tom's cockamamie story in my mind as I pushed through some bushes on the my way back to my car. *Bomark missle? Higher aliens abducting lower aliens?* He never worked at the PAVE PAWS installation at Beale and he had no idea where he was going. I should've noticed it right away and stopped following the lunatic. How the hell are you supposed to get at the truth when even the crazies sounded credible? I swore that I would stick to my guns and keep hammering on anything that looked like bullshit—fake videos or fabricated sightings.

I was almost to the road when I heard what sounded like high-pitched motors approaching me from behind. A pair of lights in the sky descended in my direction. I took a couple of steps back as they locked in formation, zipped past me and landed in front of two guys over by a power line pole. I hadn't noticed them standing there, I was so deep in thought. "GOD FUCKING DAMN IT!" one of them—the taller one—shouted. I headed over in their direction to investigate. The taller guy had blonde hair and was wearing a control panel of some sort around his neck. It was covered with switches and had a joystick. A large antennae was hanging off the back of it. "Motherfucker!" he shouted again, "Can you believe that, Stanley? MOTHERFUCKER!" His friend just stood there looking at the drones.

Wait a minute, I thought, *I recognize these guys.*

The tall blonde saw me approach as he hit a switch on his control panel. The lights simultaneously flicked out on both drones. He removed the device from around his neck, dropped it to the ground and shouted, "FUCK!"

I said, "Haven't I seen you guys before?"

The blonde guy surveyed the mess on the ground. He looked up at me and said, "Yeah—weren't you the one who fucked up our crop circle?"

"What do you mean *your* crop circle?" I said.

"Whatever," he said, dismissing me with a flick of his arm. "I just lost twenty grand worth of drones to a fucking National Guard helicopter. Can you believe that? MOTHERFUCKER!"

His friend pleaded, "We can do it again. We'll get the money."

"No we can't Stanley. Everyone knows they're fucking drones now. The gag is over."

"Wait a minute," I said, "You were the one responsible for all the UFOs?"

The blonde guy picked up one of his drones and clicked a switch, "You put enough bright LEDs lights up in the sky you can form anything. V-shapes...crosses...anything. The hard part is syncing and controlling them as one."

I studied the other drone sitting on the ground. I couldn't believe something so simple caused such a commotion. I said, "Ya know, you've freaked out a lot of people."

The blonde guy put his drone down and said, "Yeah? I've seen your website. I thought you'd be the one guy who would appreciate what I've done."

I had to admit he was right; it was a pretty damn good hoax. I certainly could not have done it myself; I wasn't a hardware guy. But I wasn't going to admit to him that I fell for it completely. I tried to act nonchalant about it, even though I was totally impressed. "So how were you going to reveal it to everyone?" I asked.

"The plan was to have the UFO come back during the Scallop Festival at the fairgrounds," he said. "I was going to have them land right in front of me. It would have been known as the world's greatest hoax, but no! Fucking helicopters!"

"So what are you doing here out at Otis?" I said.

"When I saw that—what's his name? Clock?"

"Klick."

"When I saw that Klick and his gang were going to be here, I couldn't resist one last time." He picked up the other drone, fiddled with a switch and looked at me. "How did you get Klick and his gang to form up on the runway? That was perfect. I'm sure the military were shitting their pants."

"I convinced Tom Frazier to get Klick to do it," I said.

The blonde guy laughed while he studied his drone. "Beautiful! Tom Fucking Frazier. That guy is so full of shit."

I forced a laugh and said, "Yeah...Tom Frazier."

"So what is your name?"

"Ken," I said, "And you guys are?"

The blonde guy put his drone down and said, "I'm Jason and this is Stanley."

I nodded back.

Jason asked me, "So what were you doing way out here tonight?"

"Huh? Oh I was watching Tom try to break into the PAVE PAWS station. It was the funniest thing."

Jason laughed. "Yeah? Did he find his frozen alien?"

I forced another uncomfortable grin. "Yeah," I said, "it was pretty funny watching him and Zeke climb the fence."

Jason shook his head and smiled. "Zeke. I love calling that guy's show and fucking with him." He picked up the control panel and turned off another switch. "Did you hear the call I made about the alien landing on a cranberry bog with a bottle of Stoli 100 and making cosmos?"

"That was you?"

Jason grinned. "That guy is such a fucking idiot."

I said, "Hey! Can you believe the farmer is now charging admission to our crop circles?"

Jason laughed and said, "That guys owes *us* money!"

39

"So c'mon Noodles," I said, "what were you thinking when the UFO was hovering over you guys?" He was leaning against my refrigerator holding a Corona. Mel was sitting at my kitchen table with hers. It was three days after the events at Otis and we were having a powwow at my house to catch up on all the details from the infamous night. Noodles stood there for a moment with his mouth slightly open then said, "I wasn't sure what was going to happen."

Mel laughed. "You mean you weren't anticipating the ultimate euphoria?"

Noodles took a sip from his beer and shrugged. "All I knew was that I was gonna get boinked by something that night."

"What happened to Klick once he discovered the drones?" I said.

"There was a huge argument back at his place later that night. Klick insisted that the real UFO would be there any day and they

should all hold on. I think the people who were there hoping to
have sex left."

"How many true believers stayed?"

"I would say about a dozen," he said. "After another night
Klick decided that the UFO wasn't coming and they should start
packing up for California. I wasn't going to go *that* far to get laid."

"Oh," said Mel with a grin, "you'd let yourself get sucked into
a Fornacisian spaceship but you won't go to the west coast for a
girl?" Mel and I both laughed.

Noodles looked down and rubbed the side of the bottle. "I
don't like L.A."

"Well," I grinned, "now you have some bitchin' cycle shorts to
tool around in."

Mel asked me, "How far did you guys get with Tom Frazier?"

I frowned and said, "There was nothing; he led us to a broom
closet."

She laughed. "You broke all the way into a military installation
to steal a mop?"

"I know, I know," I said as I shook my head, "He walked the
walk and talked the talk."

"I was trying to tell you that his story smelled fishy," she said,
"So what happened?"

"A guard started chasing us. He and Zeke went in one direction, I went the other. On the way back, I found the guys who
were controlling the drones."

"Really?"

"Yeah. Noodles and I had met them in a field of phragmites."

Mel thought for a moment, then slowly asked, "What were
you guys doing in a field of phragmites?

"Long story," I deadpanned.

Astro started barking in the back yard. I peeked out the
kitchen window, but didn't see anything. I continued my story. "I
got a phone call from Zeke later that night. He said they sprinted

out the front gate of the radar station, right past the other guard. They were chased through the woods for a while but managed to escape. Tom insisted he knew where the alien body was, so they explored the rest of the base, trying all sorts of doors. Somebody else noticed what they were doing and started chasing them; they eventually split up. Zeke managed to get out with the rest of the crowd by the gate; he had no idea what happened to Tom."

Astro was still barking like crazy. I yelled out the back door. "Astro! Will you shut up!" I took another look around; there was nobody out there. Astro looked at me and whined. I finished my beer and closed the door. I went to the fridge and got another Corona.

Mel said, "You didn't see the news story this morning?"

I opened my bottle, threw the cap into the trash and said, "No."

"They found Tom sleeping in the food pantry at the mess hall."

I almost spit my beer out. "No fucking way," I said.

"Apparently he kept yelling "Roswell is a fraud" as they dragged him away," she grinned.

"The military police have him?"

"No no, the feds are holding him under the terrorism act. Apparently he's been trying to break into government facilities all around the country."

I leaned against my refrigerator and grinned. "I guess aliens are everywhere."

Mel gave me a look. "The feds say they are looking for two more people in connection with the break in."

"SHIT!" I jumped up and started pacing, "Did he say anything?"

"It sounds like he pulled a Timothy McVey. He refused to tell them anything and kept ranting about a cover up. Something about not helping the New World Order."

"I'm sure he knows Zeke is a true believer and will continue on with the fight without him," I said. Astro was barking constantly. I grabbed my flashlight and barged out the back door. I went right up to my dog and yelled, "ASTRO! SHUT THE FUCK UP!" He stopped barking, looked at me sideways then started whining and pacing.

Noodles and Mel stood at the top of the back steps. The sun was just starting to set and the clouds were streaked with orange highlights. It was the beginning of a nice, warm, end-of-the-season summer night. It would probably be the last one we would have like this. I said, "It's probably the fox again. He goes nuts every time he sees the thing." The grass out in the middle of my yard looked like it was bubbling and moving, like something was crawling around under the surface. Astro started barking again.

Noodles said, "What the hell is going on?"

"It's probably groundhogs," I said. I grabbed Astro by his collar and yelled at him one last time. "ASTRO. SHUT-THE-FUCK-UP!"

A man in a Hawaiian shirt appeared at the gate. He had short dark hair and looked to be in his late forties. "Is that your dog?" he asked.

"Yeah, sorry that he's going nuts," I said. "Something weird is happening in my yard."

"I've been looking for your dog for weeks, I knew he was around here somewhere," he said. "I work for the government."

I said, "Look, I'll pay the dog license when I send in my excise tax. I've just been busy lately."

He shook his head and smiled. "No," he said, "I work for the Pentagon." He pointed to the middle of my yard and said, "Look." A few of Astro's bones lifted off the ground and were hovering about twenty feet in the air. It was the weirdest fucking thing I had ever seen—like a magician's trick, but without the magician. My first thought was, am I having some kind of LSD flashback, or did Noodles stick something in my beer? More started to work their way to the surface and rose into the air like dark bubbles. We stood there with ours mouths open as more of them came out of the ground and joined the others. "I've been looking for these," the man said. "I do advanced aerospace threat identification through the Defense Intelligence Agency."

"What are they?" I said. "My dog has been obsessed with these bones and won't leave them alone."

"They aren't bones," he said.

"What do you mean? They stink like crazy."

"We call them MAEBs; Multiple Autonomous Extraterrestrial Beings." Bits of dirt and grass fell away as new ones fitted themselves into the growing collection. The whole thing began to take on the shape of a slowly rotating disc.

I said, "What the hell are MAEBs?"

"Each one is its own entity, but they behave like a swarm," he said. "You could call them solid state extraterrestrials. They can either function separately, or group together like this and move as one."

"Move? Where?" Mel said.

"Anywhere. Upper atmosphere, outer space," he said. "They're pretty indestructible."

I took a couple of steps closer, ready to jump back if anything sudden happened. My curiosity was starting to override my fear, I had thrown enough of them out my back door. "Are they probes?"

"From what we've learned, they are their own creatures but can communicate with each other."

"Sort of like the Borg?" Noodles asked.

He laughed. "Sort of—they're much more benign."

They now formed a dark disc probably twenty-five feet across. I shined my flashlight on it and got even closer. I could see the individual shapes locked together like a giant jigsaw puzzle. The man in the Hawaiian shirt walked right up and placed his hand on it. The disc slowly rotated under his hand. "From what we can tell, they're trying to communicate with us."

"How?"

"We're not sure," he said, "Somehow they do it through touch, taste and smell." The disc slowly rose up and silently headed towards the west. I could clearly see its shape outlined by the sun glancing off the clouds. We watched it slowly shrink into a dark spot and disappear over the trees on the horizon. "Isn't that amazing?" he said, "I never get over that."

I finally pulled my eyes away from the sky and asked him. "So you're a Man in Black with a Hawaiian shirt?"

He laughed. "Hey, we don't have a dress code."

Mel asked, "You've seen them do this before?"

"Oh yeah, they seem to stick around one area for a few months, then change locations. Good thing they weren't inside—they've ruined a couple of warehouse roofs floating up like that."

I said, "How did you find us?"

"I knew they were in this area, but your dog here…what's his name?"

"Astro."

"Astro here stole our entire collection." He knelt down in front of him and scratched behind his neck. "That's one clever dog you got there."

I said, "So you're telling me I've been standing on top of aliens the entire summer?"

"How do you feel?" he said, "Do you have a deeper awareness of things? Insights? Panic attacks?"

I shook my head. "No. I chucked them out of the house every time he brought one in. Astro has been chewing on them the whole time."

He smiled and petted Astro as he spoke. "The last shipment was supposed to go to our lab. We've been doing research on them. Handling them imparts a higher wisdom to the recipient. They don't express themselves with words or symbols; you just get a deeper understanding of nature by being around them. We've had some breakthroughs, but our scientists are still working on it." He looked into Astro's eyes. "What are you thinking fella?"

Astro sat there and stared at the guy like he completely understood. Like an idiot, I called out to Astro in a patronizing voice, "Astro! Are you a good boy?" Astro let out a big sigh. He looked off into the distance as if hoping his collection of alien bones would come back to him. "He hasn't been feeling that well recently," I said.

The man stood back up. "That seems to be a common side effect of interacting with the aliens. It seems once they leave, the benefits of the proximity effect fade away pretty quickly. It's been my job to keep retrieving them so we can keep studying them." Astro took one last look at the horizon, hung his head down and slowly walked back into the house.

40

01010100 01101000 01110010 01100101 01100101 00100000
01101000 01110101 01101101 01100001 01101110 00100000
01100010 01100101 01101001 01101110 01100111 01110011
00100000 01100011 01101111 01101101 01110000 01100001
01110010 01100101 00100000 01110100 01101000 01100101
01101001 01110010 00100000 01101100 01100101 01110110
01100101 01101100 01110011 00100000 01101111 01100110
00100000 01101001 01101110 01110100 01101111 01111000
01101001 01100011 01100001 01110100 01101001 01101111
01101110 00100000 01100110 01110010 01101111 01101101
00100000 01100001 00100000 01110000 01100001 01110010
01110100 01111001 00100000 01110100 01101000 01100101
00100000 01110000 01110010 01100101 01110110 01101001
01101111 01110101 01110011 00100000 01101110 01101001
01100111 01101000 01110100 00101110 00001101 00001010
01010100 01101000 01100101 00100000 01100110 01101001
01110010 01110011 01110100 00100000 01101000 01110101

```
01101101 01100001 01101110 00100000 01100010 01100101
01101001 01101110 01100111 00100000 01110011 01100001
01111001 01110011 00101100 00100000 00100010 01001101
01100001 01101110 00101100 00100000 01001001 00100000
01110111 01100001 01110011 00100000 01110011 01101111
01101110 01101001 01100111 01101000 01110100 00100000
00100000 01000100 01101001 01100100 00100000 01111001
01101111 01110101 00100000 01110011 01100101 01100101
00100000 01110100 01101000 01100001 01110100 00101111
01101001 01101110 01100111 00100000 01101111 01110110
01100101 01110010 00100000 01110100 01101000 01100101
00100000 01101001 01101101 01100001 01100111 01100101
00100010 00100000 01110011 01100001 01101001 01100100
00100000 01101101 01111001 00100000 01100110 01100001
01110100 01101000 01100101 01110010 00101100 00100000
00100010 01000111 01101111 01100100 00100000 01110111
01101000 01100001 01110100 00100000 01101001 01110011
00100000 01110100 01101000 01100001 01110100 00111111
00100010 00100000 01001001 00100000 01101100 01101111
01101111 01101011 01100101 01100100 00100000 01110101
01110000 00100000 01100001 01110100 00100000 01101000
01101001 01101101 00100000 01100001 01101110 01100100
00100000 01110011 01100001 01101001 01100100 00101100
00100000 00100010 01001001 00100000 01100100 01101111
01101110 00100111 01110100 00100000 01101011 01101110
01101111 01110111 00101100 00100000 01100010 01110101
01110100 00100000 01001001 00100000 01110100 01101000
01101001 01101110 01101011 00100000 01101001 01110100
00100111 01110011 00100000 01100001 01101100 01101001
01100101 01101110 00101100 00100000 01100100 01100001
01100100 00101110 00100010 00100000 01001000 01100101
00100000 01101100 01101111 01101111 01101011 01100101
01100100 00100000 01100001 01110100 00100000 01101101
01100101 00101100 00100000 01110011 01101101 01101001
01101100 01100101 01100100 00101110 00100000 00100010
01001001 00100111 01101100 01101100 00100000 01110100
01100101 01101100 01101100 00100000 01111001 01101111
01110101 00100000 01110111 01101000 01100001 01110100
00100000 01110100 01101000 01101001 01110011 00100000
01101001 01110011 00101100 00100000 01110011 01101111
01101110 00101110 00100000 01010111 01100101 00100111
01110010 01100101 00100000 01101110 01101111 01110100
00100000 01100001 01101100 01101111 01101110 01100101
00100010 00101100 00100000 01101000 01100101 00100000
01100001 01101110 01110011 00101100 00100000 00100010
```

01001001 00100000 01110111 01100001 01110011 00100000
01110011 01101111 00100000 01100100 01110010 01110101
01101110 01101011 00100000 01101100 01100001 01110011
01110100 00100000 01101110 01101001 01100111 01101000
01110100 00101100 00100000 01001001 00100000 01110100
01101111 01101111 01101011 00100000 01100001 00100000
01110000 01110010 01101111 01110011 01110100 01101001
01110100 01110101 01110100 01100101 00100000 01101000
01101111 01101101 01100101 00100000 01110100 01101111
00100000 01101101 01111001 00100000 01110111 01101001
01100110 01100101 00101110 00100010 00001101 00001010
01010100 01101000 01100101 00100000 01100110 01101001
01110010 01110011 01110100 00100000 01101000 01110101
01101101 01100001 01101110 00100000 01100010 01100101
01101001 01101110 01100111 00100000 01100101 01111000
01100011 01101100 01100001 01101001 01101101 01110011
00101100 00100000 00100010 01011001 01101111 01110101
00100000 01100111 01110101 01111001 01110011 00100000
01100100 01101111 01101110 00100111 01110100 00100000
01110101 01101110 01100100 01100101 01110010 01110011
01110100 01100001 01101110 01100100 00100001 00100000
01000011 01101000 01110101 01101110 01101011 01110011
00100000 01101001 01110011 00100000 01101101 01111001
00100000 01000101 01100001 01110010 01110100 01101000
01101100 01101001 01101110 01100111 00100001 11100010
10000000 10011101

41

I pawed through the dirt where I had buried all of my bones and took a big sniff. I was hoping a couple were still there.

Nothing.

Just thinking about them got me panting. I felt a drop of saliva fall from my tongue as I licked my nose. I looked up in the direction where I had last seen them, just above some trees in our neighbor's yard. I stared up at the sky for a while.

I hope they come back.

I snapped out of it when a bird flew past, distracting me.

I shook myself and wandered over towards our gate. I thought I knew where I could find some more. I dragged my paw across the chain and hoped that it would open.

It rattled it a few times but it didn't budge.

I used to be able to do this, but it had me stumped. I dragged my paw across it a second time and hoped something would happen.

Nope.

I whined as I looked at the metal thing clamped around the pole. There's something about it that would allow me to leave, but I just couldn't think of it. I knew I had gone through this gate a bunch of times before, but I couldn't remember how.

I returned to my favorite spot in the middle of the yard, spun around twice, scratched a couple of times and settled in. A breeze kicked up and shook the trees in our yard. I watched a couple of leaves gently glide to the ground. They weren't big enough to chase so I lay back down and put my head on my front paws. The sun felt nice and warm on my fur. It was nice just lying there.

I tried to remember why I was getting so upset a couple of days ago. Something was really bothering me, but now it's gone. As my eyelids grew heavier, I wondered when Ken was coming home. Maybe be would bring me a new squeaky toy; one of those would be really nice. As I closed my eyes and drifted off to sleep, I imagined my bones coming back to me. My glorious yummy bones, falling from the sky! I could see myself trying to catch them as they fell all around me.

I was warm, I was full, I was safe in my yard and Ken would be home soon. With that comforting thought, I fell asleep.

42

I was filming Noodles and myself while were were camping in the Myles Standish State Forest outside of Plymouth. In the view-finder of my camera I framed the image of our campfire. Noodles pulled a marshmallow out of the bag in his lap, impaled it onto a stick and held it over the fire. Flames filled the background of the image as I zoomed in on the bubbling white nugget and watched it turn black. I followed the crispy fireball up to Noodles' face and watched him blow it out. He gave the camera a goofy grin. The whole scene looked pretty damn idyllic.

From behind Noodles, a loud snapping sound exploded, like something had stepped on a large branch. Noodles froze, his expression changing from placid to panicked. Wide-eyed, he said, "What's that?"

We both sat listening for a second. "I dunno," I whispered.

I quickly zoomed back and panned around into the darkness. I couldn't see much beyond the light of the campfire. Suddenly, a

Bigfoot strode out from the darkness, illuminated by the orange glow of the fire. It looked directly at us as it took three long strides, swinging its arms rhythmically. Its face looked like an evil mask. Noodles screamed, "OH MY GOD! OH MY GOD!"

I hollered "SHIT!" as I desperately tried to steady the camera and follow the creature as it moved across our campsite. The Bigfoot took a few more steps then stumbled on something, falling flat on its chest. As it hit the ground, I could feel the vibration through my butt.

It lay still for a moment then yelled "SHIT!" I stopped the camera. The creature did a pushup, rested on its knees and shouted, "GOD FUCKING DAMMIT!" Stanley came out of the darkness and helped the Bigfoot to its feet as it struggled to pull its head off. Inside the suit was Jason, his blonde hair soaked with sweat.

"That was take three," I said.

Jason took a deep breath then said, "I can't see where the fuck I'm going through this head."

"It's gonna look like shit," I said. "I think we should just go with a 3D model and render the whole thing."

Jason shook his head. "3D always looks fake as shit."

"Not if we use a motion capture system," I said.

"Look, I'm fine. I just need a little more practice."

Stanley had an iPad with the famous Roger Patterson bigfoot footage. He showed it to Jason. "You need to swing your arms counter to your step."

"I know, I know," he said. "This costume is incredibly uncomfortable; I'm sweating my balls off here. Just give me a minute." Stanley handed him a bottle of water and he took a deep swig, then sat down in front of the fire.

"Do you think we're gonna get this?" I asked.

"I might want to practice a couple of times without the head." Jason wiped sweat off his face with his furry arm.

"Knock yourself out," I said.

He sat back and studied the footage on Stanley's iPad. I grabbed a marshmallow and jabbed it onto Noodles stick. I held it over the fire and watched it turn brown.

We never did reveal who created the drone UFO. We figured it would blow our cover for other things we wanted to try. What's weird is there were still reports of a UFO being seen around the Cape even after what happened on the base. I guess you can't keep good mythos down.

Since then we've been working other hoaxes. Jason is a hardware guy who wants to do everything physically. I want to keep it simple and do everything inside the computer. Together, I think we have a nice combination of talents to pull one over on anybody. I tried to explain what happened at my house with the MAEBs. I told him real extraterrestrials don't look anything like the typical Hollywood aliens. Forever the skeptic, he thought I just saw a colony of bats taking off for the night. It's not my problem if he doesn't want to accept the truth.

Jason took another drink from his bottle and said, "You know, I was thinking about doing something with the Loch Ness mythology. I had the idea of an inflatable Nessie that I could pilot around remotely."

"What? You think you could fool everyone with a giant inflatable pool toy?" I said.

"No, no! From a distance, with the right lighting, I think it could work."

"How come you haven't done it?"

Jason zoned out while he stared into the fire. "My test rig didn't work out," he quietly said.

Stanley laughed. "Somebody is going to find a deflated lake monster on the bottom of Long Pond someday."

"I have another idea for a gag," I said. "Fake Virgin Mary apparitions. We have her outline appearing on all sorts of places."

Noodle said, "Sort of like when Jesus' face was showing up on people's toast?"

"Right," I said. "The hard part would be lugging a compressor and the spray gun out to different locations. Load it up with some fine powdered dirt and away you go!"

Jason thought for a moment then smiled. "The religious would go nuts when they found them."

"We'd have the footage to prove that they're fake," I said.

Jason thought about it for a moment. "That could actually work."

"What about creating fake tears?" Stanley said. "With a little hose?"

"I don't think we have to take it that far," I said.

Jason stood up and straightened out his costume. "People are so stupid, I'm sure it would work."

"I think Cape Cod is going to have a wave of Virgin apparitions shortly!" I grinned.

"OK, you ready to do this?" asked Jason, pulling the Bigfoot head over his own.

I turned my camera back on pointed it at him. "Take four? Let's go!"

43

My brother Brian waved at the Chevy van that tooted at us as it went under the Quaker Meeting House Road overpass. He waved back and shouted, "See ya!" It was the last overpass on Route 6 before you hit the Sagamore bridge. In big fat letters, he had a banner hung facing the outbound traffic that stated "Sayonara!" It used to be a Labor Day tradition for locals to taunt (or thank) the tourists as they leave the Cape for the season. The town had put an end to this a while ago, but I guess my brother didn't get the memo.

Now that Brian knew the UFO scare was fake, he felt safe going out in public. He no longer worried that aliens were after him. In fact, I suspect he's entering into a manic phase. He had called me earlier and asked if I could bring him a sub from D'Angelo's for lunch. I figured this was my chance to literally talk him off the ledge of this bridge and get him to go home. Another car honked as I handed him his food, but he ignored it. I guess his stomach overruled everything else.

"Did you get an Italian? No onions?" Brian asked as he tore open his sandwich.

"Yes," I said. "How did you get here?"

Brian took a bite and said, "Rick drove me."

He pointed the end of his sub towards a skinny guy in sagging jeans and backwards Red Sox cap. I suspected he was my brother's weed connection—and that he was under the delusion that the nineties never ended. He stared at us as Brian took another bite, then slowly headed in our direction. There was no way I was going to get that guy a sub. I told Brian, "You're not supposed to be doing this."

"Having lunch this early?" he said with his mouthful.

"No, taunting the tourists as they leave."

He shrugged and said, "Everyone's done this."

Rick came up to us and gave me the once over. Up close, he looked older--late forties, early fifties. If someone that age had nothing better to do on a weekday than ferry my brother around, chances are he was as bad off or worse than Brian.

I said to Brian, "No, everyone *used* to do this. You're not supposed to do it anymore. The cops might come out here—you know that?"

Brian continued chewing, "So?"

Rick gave me a vacant stare and looked out onto the row of cars passing beneath us. "These people should never have come here."

"It's called tourism economy," I replied. "We collect their money during the summer so we can survive the winter; that's how it's done."

I said to Brian, "If you come with me right now, I can drive you home. Let's go."

Rick frowned and said, "We need to show these people our lack of support."

Brian excitedly said, "OOH! You wanna drop trow?" Rick froze and gave him a nervous look.

"Brian," I said, "don't do that. Please."

If I needed further proof that my brother was escalating into mania, I just had it. This Brian is the polar opposite of the one hiding under the table with foil on his head.

I turned to Rick and asked, "Can you make sure he doesn't do that?" Just after that question left my mouth I thought, *I can't believe I'm relying on this person to keep my brother sane.*

He looked surprised; it was probably the first time anyone had asked him to do anything responsible. "Brian does some wild stuff," he said with a grin.

I ignored him and asked Brian, "How are you getting home?"

"Rick's gonna drive me."

"OK fine," I said. "I'm not picking you up at the police station. You got that?"

Brian shrugged and took another bite. I left them to their entertainment; I had to get back to work. The drive back to the Orleans office was glorious. I passed an endless line of cars slowly moving in the opposite direction. I understood the impulse to thumb one's nose. It was kind of like getting rid of annoying in-laws who've hung around way too long.

I thought about what happened at Ken's house. It kind of made sense that extraterrestrials needed to be indestructible to visit our planet. Anyone studying Earth would quickly see that we're all about violence. Yes, it's a big-fish-eats-small-fish world, but we humans take it to the next level. Just look at what we call entertainment: from low-budget slasher pics to Shakespeare, violence sells. No wonder they didn't want to land on the planet and ask to meet our leaders.

The UFO story played out as expected. Once it was revealed to be a hoax, no one wanted to be associated with it. Russell Holt never got hired by the network. Once the hoax was revealed, they tried to distance themselves from him and anything associated with it. He tried crawling back to Laurie Rudd to ask for his job back, but she couldn't be bothered with him.

The Weekly World Gazette never published the story I had sent them about what happened at Otis—a proven hoax wasn't exactly tabloid gold. At least I got paid for the last installment, even though they didn't run it.

I got to the Orleans bureau office and climbed up the rickety stairs. Norm was sitting at his desk; I went to mine and dumped my bag onto a pile of papers. It felt comfortable getting back in my spot, now that the craziness of summer was fading. I was looking forward going back to the mundane.

Norm approached my desk. "Eastham center has been evacuated after a gas leak," he said.

I rummaged through my bag for my phone. "Yeah? What's going on?"

"National Grid is kind of skeptical; they think people are just reporting swamp gas." He snickered. "Can you go out there and make sure it's not a hoax?"

"Yeah, sure" I said, rolling my eyes. "I'll grab my dowsing rod and get to the bottom of it."

"I got word back from Laurie that they are thinking of offering you Russell's job at the Hyannis office," he said.

"Really? I'm supposed to go there tomorrow and pick up some papers."

He zipped his fingers across his lips. "Mum's the word. I didn't say anything."

"I didn't hear anything."

Norm headed back towards his desk, spun around and threw his arms out wide. "You wouldn't leave me and all this, would you?"

"You know I'd always think of you, Norm."

"Who could ever replace you?" he asked, hand over his heart.

"Well, you did have an intern..."

He winced and said, "If I ever see anything that says 'whole grain' or 'non-GMO' it goes back on the shelf."

My phone rang. The caller ID read: St. Petersburg, FL. I had ignored the previous call from there. I reluctantly hit the answer button. "Yes?"

A carefully-modulated voice said, "Hello, I'm looking for Melissa. This is Thomas Hill from New World Media."

"This is me."

"I run the parent company of Weekly World Gazette," he said. "I've been reading the work you submitted to us. It sounds like everyone really had the wool pulled over their eyes about that UFO scare."

I sighed and said, "Yes. Now that it's all over, nobody wants to be associated with it. So you never ran my last submission."

He laughed. "I know, I know; David Brown is like that. He's been publishing what we call the deformed baby of the family. But, as long as it makes money we leave him alone. You received our check?"

"Yes, I did." *So much for journalistic principles...*

"Here's my offer," he said, "We have many different publications across many different platforms. We're starting up a new magazine for professional women—lifestyle, career challenges, etc.—and we would like to add you to our staff. You would work from our St. Petersburg office. You'd have a company car, full medical and a competitive salary. Sounds interesting?"

Is this guy for real? "This is kind of sudden," I said. Do I have time to think about it?"

"Of course. David has your email; I'll send you the details. I look forward to hearing from you."

He talked up his company for a little bit more and we eventually hung up. I sat there, trying to get my head around the fact that, in the last ten minutes, my world might have changed. I went over to Norm's desk and sat down. "So what were you saying about Russell's job?"

"It's probably yours," he said. "They just need to go through the formality of doing in interview."

"I just got a call from New World Media. They offered me a job in Florida."

"Where in Florida?"

"St. Petersburg."

He grinned, "Hey, that's right near Gibsonton. You could live with the carnies and commute to work. Maybe they'd teach you how to walk a tightrope."

"Haha, very funny. They're offering a car, stock options and full health—the works."

"You'd actually leave the Cape, in all it's rustic charm, for the tacky sands of Florida?"

Is that what I really wanted? I'd moved off this sandbar once already and ended up coming back. I'd been to Florida before. Yes, they had more white sandy beaches than the Cape, but the coastal housing situation was worse—and there's Disney and all that other Florida weirdness. Not that it wasn't interesting from a sociological perspective…

But the Cape? For three months out of the year, it's an introvert's nightmare of cars and sunburned tourists stuffing their faces with fried clams. And the other nine month a good percentage of the year-rounders collect unemployment, park their butts in front of NESN and drink.

But, there's quiet beach walks in October, route 6A at Christmas and. . .Wait, that's all I can come up with? Maybe it is time for a change. But what about Brian—could I just abandon him to the loving care of townies like Rick? (I love Brian, but there's no way I'd bring him with me!)

"Well?" Norm demanded, interrupting my reverie.

I sat there for a moment and ran through all the options in my mind. I looked at him. I really didn't want to decide anything just then. The image of Scarlett O'Hara flashed into my head. In my best southern accent I said, "I'll think about that tomorrow. After all tomorrow is another day!"

Your Writing Team:

Eric, a native New Englander, now resides on the other side of the bridge in Buzzards Bay. Upon arrival, he was disappointed to learn that there are no buzzards in Buzzards Bay, merely Crows and Ospreys.

Jan, who spent most of her life on the Cape, thought she had escaped until Eric dragged her back.

Widget, a Brussels Griffon, aka "stumpy butt/monkey-face" has been known to cosplay as an Ewok.

Author Website:

adeadguy.com

WARNING: Contains baby photos and cute dogs!

Book Website:

adeadguy.com/high-strangeness/

Other Websites:

facebook.com/adeadguy.bickernicks/
twitter.com/bickernicks
goodreads.com/author/Eric_Bickernicks

Widget's Website:

instagram.com/squidgeyface

Would you like a couch with that painting?

Obscurity is a way of life for Gavin Vonn Getch, a painter who works at a frame shop in a small New England town. His life changes when billionaire Gary Eastman enters his shop and becomes the ultimate patron: a lifetime commission for all his work in exchange for a crap-load of money.

Some of his artist buddies envy him and others think he's sold out. Curious as to where his paintings are being displayed, he makes a trip to the DLC headquarters, where a shocking discovery forces him to reevaluate his deal with Eastman and his identity as an artist.

Why does an artist create? What alternatives are there to completely selling out? Is there no genius—only marketing? The book is a satirical, and sometimes surreal look at the art world.